Some Kind of Truth

Westley Smith

Wicked House Publishing

Some Kind of Truth
By Westley Smith

Wicked House Publishing

Cover design by Christian Bentulan
Interior Formatting by Duncan Ralston

To Laurie
For always believing in me.

Chapter One

The package was marked...

ATT: STEVE JAMES

of the

PITTSBURGH TRIBUNE

...and wrapped in brown butcher's paper as if it were a poor-man's version of a Christmas present.

Steve had received anonymous packages before, some with leads to run down, others with incriminating evidence from a source he was working with. However, this package had not been delivered to the *Pittsburgh Tribune* like it should have been. It was left outside his apartment door.

Perplexed, Steve lifted the package, gingerly, from the floor. It was light and about six inches long by four inches wide. He shook it, but nothing moved inside.

He had not been expecting a delivery, certainly not one to his home by an anonymous person. His guts tightened into an uncomfortable, disconcerting knot. Turning, he looked down the hallway, to where the back stairwell led out to the rear entrance of the apartment building. Sunlight shone through the single window at the end of the hall and cut a sharp blade-like angle of light onto the floor. Dust particles floated in the air as if recently disturbed – maybe by the deliverer of the package.

Someone could have gotten into the building by the rear entrance, made their way up to Steve's apartment, dropped the package by his door, and slipped back out before anyone noticed. He did not live in one of the new high-rises being built around Pittsburgh – apartments that came with all the security bells and whistles – but rather an old turn of the century building on the lower east side of Pittsburgh. The rent was cheap, and the landlord damn-near nonexistent, especially when it came to the safety and upkeep of the building. It was what Steve could afford on a reporter's salary.

He looked back at the parcel in his hands. The sense of unease continued to coil his stomach. Was he being targeted like reporters after 9/11, with anthrax-sealed packages delivered to their homes and offices? Possibly.

The fact that his article "MOB IN PITTSBURGH" had helped put Anthony Palazzo, a local money launderer affiliated with the New York-based DeLuca Crime Organization, behind bars could have something to do with the mysterious package outside his door that afternoon. Again, he wondered what was inside and cautiously shook it, like a kid trying to figure out the present under the wrapping on their birthday.

Nothing moved, nothing rattled inside.

Steve knew he should leave the package alone; place it back on the floor where he found it, call the police, and have them look at it first. That was the smart thing to do. The right thing to do. There could be anything inside meant to bring him harm, especially nowadays, when reporters were being unfairly besieged for spreading false information to the public.

Against his better judgment, Steve forced the apprehension away like a fly at a picnic, tucked the bundle under his left arm, fished his keys from his jacket pocket, and opened the apartment door.

Once inside, he closed the door and peered through the peephole to the hallway. Still, the hall was empty, and no one passed by. Again, he felt the skin on the back of his neck prickle, and the hairs stand on end with nervousness.

Why was the package left and what was inside? Steve wondered.

Turning away from the door, he moved into the kitchen. He placed his laptop bag on the counter beside his keys, then removed a Zippo lighter and a pack of cigarettes and placed them beside the laptop bag. He put the brown package beside his things. It looked odd on the countertop, as if it were some evil present that had been left at his home – a gift from Satan himself.

There was nothing out of the ordinary with its appearance. Other than the handwritten address, there were no other identifiable words or labels on the outside. Gooseflesh rose across Steve's body. Whoever delivered the package knew who he was, where he worked, and where he lived.

Normally, Steve had all large packages sent to the Tribune's mailroom. He didn't trust his landlord, Horace Baker. The slimeball charged an extra ten dollars a month to hold deliveries larger than what could fit into the small gold mailboxes in the lobby. He called it a 'holding charge.' Steve was sure it was illegal, a scheme to get more money from the tenants.

Steve was not about to pay the extra money. He had heard stories from others in the building that when they received their packages some were opened, searched, and sometimes things were missing. Of course, Baker claimed it was how the parcels arrived.

This particular package, sitting ominously on his countertop, should never have made it to his floor.

Or maybe it IS from Palazzo, Steve thought. It could have been a scare tactic to get Steve to retract his story, setting Palazzo free from prison, while simultaneously clearing the DeLuca Family of any wrongdoing. For all Steve knew, there could be a small explosive inside the box, just big enough to rattle his cage but not kill him. Or, if they wanted to get the job over with, they could have laced it with anthrax, just like reporters received after 9/11.

Yet, he wasn't so sure Palazzo or the DeLuca Family were ready to make that kind of move against him. At the moment, Palazzo and the DeLuca Family were letting their mob lawyers handle the process through the courts with a defamation and source exposure lawsuit on Steve and the Pittsburgh Tribune.

No, Steve was confident it was delivered by someone else. But who? And more importantly, why?

He pulled a bottle of Jameson Irish Whiskey from the cupboard along with a small glass and poured himself a healthy snort.

Just to quiet the demons, Steve thought bitterly, taking a swig. *Just to quiet the demons.*

He studied the package while swirling the brown liquor around in the glass, knowing he should leave it alone and call the police. But intrigue was sinking its fangs into his mind, poisoning his thoughts with fantasies of what dwelled inside its dark recesses.

Someone knew Steve well enough to know he could never leave a mystery alone. He thumbed one of the cigarettes out of the box, popped it into his mouth and lit it with the Zippo lighter. He inhaled deeply. Smoke filled his lungs. Calmed his nerves. Helped him think straight – so he thought.

What's inside? a shadowy voice spoke from the alcoves of Steve's mind, pulling him from his reverie. He could not argue with this strange, archaic voice. He desperately wanted to know what was inside the package. Taking a long drag on the cigarette, he let the smoke out slowly between his teeth with a low *sssss*.

What to do? What to do?

There was only one thing *to* do.

Setting the cigarette in the ashtray, Steve picked the package up. He felt that familiar chill of disquiet crawl over him, like cold skeleton fingers walking up his spine, vertebra by vertebra.

"Enough of this guessing-game shit," Steve said and tore the heavy brown paper away, exposing a white box underneath which resembled something a pastry would come in. The lid was sealed shut with a single piece of Scotch Tape.

Steve knew no one would send him sweets – maybe anthrax, maybe a bomb, but certainly not sweets. In a career that spanned more than twenty years as a crime reporter for the Tribune, Steve had made more enemies, like Anthony Palazzo, than friends. Such was the life, he supposed.

He peeled the Scotch Tape from the box and then lifted the lid slowly, as if a venomous snake were about to spring out and bury its sharp fangs into his face. With the box lid cracked, he peered inside.

Instead of finding something harmful, the box contained a USB Flash Drive secured in white tissue paper.

Two words were handwritten on the front of the flash drive in black magic marker:

PLAY ME!

Steve frowned. Why would someone send him a flash drive anonymously? Did it have something to do with the Palazzo story he'd spent the better part of two years working on? Some missing information that would, without a shadow of a doubt, ensure that Palazzo stayed behind bars for the rest of his life?

Or was it something unrelated?

Steve didn't know.

Then he noticed the USB was not the only item inside the box.

Tucked beside the flash drive was a small piece of white plastic. Removing the plastic from the box, Steve found it was about the size of a credit card and coated with a reddish-brown dirt. He rubbed his fingertips together feeling a gritty dust, like a fine sand. Turning the card over revealed it was a Pennsylvania Junior Driver's License issued to a Rebecca Ann Turner of 428 Water Street, Abbottstown Pennsylvania. Her birthdate was 10/02/1982. The issue date on the card was 11/23/1998 — twenty-six years ago. The top right-hand corner, where the expiration date should have been, was broken, the plastic chipped away, forever lost to time, leaving a jagged edge that looked sharp enough to slice through flesh.

The driver's license photo of Rebecca Turner showed an attractive sixteen-year-old girl with blonde hair and bright blue eyes that sparkled with life. Her face was long, narrow, and innocent, holding the optimism of youth. Her beaming smile radiated from the picture, enhancing her natural beauty and charm. According to the driver's license, Rebecca was born in 1982, which would make her forty-two years old now. But Steve got the sickening feeling that Rebecca did not live to see her forty-second birthday.

He looked back to the flash drive resting inside the box. He was unsure how the driver's license and the USB were connected, but he was certain they were, or they would not have been delivered together.

What's on the flash drive? Steve wondered anxiously. His heart began to race, and his palms grew moist with sweat. A horrible notion rushed through his mind that something awful had happened to Rebecca Turner, something the USB would ultimately reveal.

"H-holy shit," he said aloud; the shudder in his voice surprised him. *Someone wants you to find out what happened to this young lady, Steve ol' Boy, and expose the truth.*

Reaching for the cigarette in the ashtray, he brought it to his lips and inhaled. The smoke settled on his lungs with a comfortable bite that he relished.

He looked back to the box; his eyes lingered on its contents. Possible scenarios played across his mind as to why someone would want him involved. But none of these thoughts made much sense at the moment.

Steve took another drag and stubbed the cigarette out in the ashtray. He had smoked it down to the filter as he often did; a haze of heavy, thick smoke hovered around the ceiling. He picked up the glass of whiskey and finished it in one swallow, and then poured himself another – three fingers worth this time. His mouth had gone bone dry, but he wasn't sure another shot – even three fingers worth – would wet his whistle.

The demons inside were growing, and Steve needed to

calm them. Or, at least, he continued to tell himself that on a nightly basis.

Warily, he lifted the USB from the box. Dare he view whatever was on it, or call the police and let them handle the situation?

He shook the thought off. His reporter instinct had taken over. He needed to know what was on the USB, how it connected with the girl on the junior driver's license, and why he was chosen to unravel this mystery before going to the police.

Chapter Two

By nine the next morning, Steve stood alone in his editor's office, flipping the Zippo lighter around in his palm nervously while staring out the window. He was tired, and his head throbbed from a restless night's sleep and too much alcohol to quell those pesky demons riddling around inside. The gruesome images he had witnessed on the video replayed in his mind while he gazed over Pittsburgh that morning. Would there ever be a reprieve from what he had seen last night, or would he be burdened with the images of a young girl being tortured by three sadist pigs for the rest of his life?

Charlie Bowers, owner and editor of the Pittsburgh Tribune, was on the third floor with Ricky Welsh from the social media/AV department, examining the video found on the USB flash drive that mysteriously showed up on Steve's doorstep the day before.

From the fifth-floor window of Charlie's office, Steve watched the congested morning traffic across the Fort Pitt Tunnel Bridge. As usual, traffic moved at a snail's pace on the upper and lower decks of the bridge. Below, the Monongahela River flowed lazily, cold and gray. The sun shone over the city that morning, but the day seemed a shade darker than it should have, matching Steve's somber mood.

He looked at the lighter in his palm and read the inscription now facing him for the millionth time.

To STEVE
For returning home
CHARLIE

The lighter was a memento from Charlie upon his joyous return home from Afghanistan as a war correspondent for the Tribune. Steve had volunteered for the assignment following the 9/11 attacks, a decision he would ultimately regret. The connotation was not lost on Steve, and he appreciated the sentiment from Charlie, but he viewed the lighter now with both fondness and disdain.

The door opened, pulling him from his troubled thoughts.

Steve turned as Charlie Bowers entered. Charlie's thick, pudgy face was pale, and a thin sheen of sweat glistened his forehead under a mop of curly blond hair. He looked ill, like he might hurl into the nearest wastepaper can, a feeling Steve was all too familiar with. Charlie closed the door and then rested his back on it.

"You watch it?" Steve asked, already knowing the answer.

Charlie nodded. "W-where..." he swallowed the bile back down into the pit of his bulging gut.

"I don't know where it came from. It was outside my apartment when I got home yesterday." He studied Charlie close, looking for a reaction, but didn't get one. "Did you watch the whole thing?"

Charlie shook his head and glanced at the picture above his desk, the one with his three smiling teenage daughters, oblivious to the unspeakable atrocities of the world outside the safety of their home.

"I-I couldn't." Charlie's eyes met Steve's, dancing with disgust from what he'd witnessed on the video. "Is it too early for a drink?"

"Never too early for a drink, Charlie," Steve replied, already feeling the itch – the need – to quench the thirst.

Charlie crossed the room to his desk on legs that looked unstable, rubbery. Pulling out the bottom drawer, he lifted a half-empty bottle of Jameson and two plastic cups from inside.

"Now you're speaking my language," Steve said, almost able to taste the fine whiskey on his tongue. A little hair of the dog never hurt anyone. And, besides, the booze would help the headache.

After pouring them each a generous shot into the plastic cups, Charlie passed one to Steve, which he nearly finished in a swallow. The strong liquor churned Steve's stomach like a cement mixer. For a moment, he thought the booze was going to come back up like it had last night after he finished the video, but thankfully, the liquor stayed where it belonged. He would stop at one drink, so not to upset his stomach further.

Charlie, on the other hand, took small sips from the cup and grimaced at the whiskey's sharp bite. His editor was not a drinker, but Steve figured Charlie was hoping the liquor would alleviate the inside turmoil picking away at him and help regain his usual stoic composure. They were silent as they drank, lost in unpleasant thoughts of the girl in the video.

Steve finished off the drink and set the cup on the desk. Charlie continued to nurse his drink while engrossed with the photograph of his three daughters above his desk, his face dim, filled with enraged thoughts. The video had hit home for Charlie – it could have easily been one of his children on there.

"Do you think what's on the video is real?" Charlie asked; his voice sounded thick, heavy with emotion like he was talking through syrup.

"I don't know. It looks real. What did Ricky think?"

Charlie lifted his shoulders. "He didn't say. He seemed as shocked as I was while watching it." His heavy eyes met Steve's. "Jesus, Steve." He ran a hand across the top of his head, fluffing the mop of curly blond hair. "That video is the single worst thing I've seen in my life. It should be burnt!"

Steve agreed. He found his eyes drifting to the Jameson bottle - *another drink wouldn't hurt, would it?* If nothing else, the booze would help simmer the residual unease the video had left him with. But he would hold off for now.

"I'd like to look into this one further," Steve said.

Charlie stopped mid-sip; his eyes shot over the rim of the cup, filled with dread. "No way."

"There's a story here," Steve said grimly.

"I don't disagree with you. But what we have in our possession is evidence of a crime, possibly a murder. You know as well as I do, we have to turn the flash drive over to the police."

"They won't know when I received it. Give me a few days to work on this, run some leads–"

"Do you have any leads?"

"Of course not! I just received the goddamn thing last night."

"Then, no. It goes to the cops."

"Someone left it for me, Charlie. Why do you think that is?"

"Because you have a hard-on for macabre stories."

"True. I don't deny that. But this is even a touch much for me, don't you agree?"

Steve had never shied away from the viciousness of human nature; in fact, he seemed drawn to it, or was it drawn to him? He could never decide which. He dove head-first into stories of murder, death, and debauchery, exposing the bleak, ugly parts of the human race that no one wanted to fall victim to.

Charlie swirled the whiskey around. He set the cup down and pushed it away with his fingertips, as if it suddenly disgusted him.

"I agree this is bizarre, even for your normal fare of twisted stories. But this... this is truly awful. I can't, in all good conscience – both as your friend and your boss – let you get involved. It *needs* to go to the police."

"Oh, that's bullshit!" Steve waved a dismissive hand and turned back to the window.

"Sorry, pal."

"Three days," Steve said, facing his boss again. "That's all I'm asking for – three days."

Charlie shook his head. "No. Not going to happen."

"Give me one good reason why you'd fuck us on this?"

Charlie's eyes grew into thin, angry slits and his face turned a dark red; he met Steve's intensity with his own. "Watch yourself, Steve. You talk to me like that again, and you can clean out your desk."

The threat was meaningless. Both of them knew it.

Charlie wouldn't fire him because he was the best reporter the Tribune had on their payroll at the moment. Still, the threat irritated Steve. It was being used to keep him in line.

Steve didn't walk lines, he crossed them to expose the truth.

"But you want a reason," Charlie continued. "Here are several. One: you still have heat from the Palazzo story you broke last year. Two: Palazzo's lawyers are suing you and *my* paper for defamation, which we're fighting to keep you, your sources, and the Tribune's reputation safe. Three: – and this is the big one, Steve, so listen up – let us not forget about Afghanistan and what happened over there twenty-three years ago. For fuck's sake, when is enough *enough* for you? Take a break. Take some time off. I'm saying this as your friend, not your boss. Go back to working on your memoir." Charlie paused a moment, observing Steve's haggard appearance. "Jesus, you look like shit."

"A very nasty thing to say to Jesus," Steve replied.

"Fuck you! Get out of my office. I'm calling the police." Charlie picked up the phone on his desk.

"I made a copy of the video."

"How did I know you were going to say that?" Charlie said, his face emotionless while slowly replacing the phone in its cradle.

"Because you know I'm a good reporter."

"You're a pain in the ass is what you are."

"Be that as it may, I'm still the best reporter you got."

"That's debatable," Charlie said curtly.

What does that mean? Steve wondered. He pushed the thought away and took a step closer to his boss. "Look, if we sit on this, we risk losing it to another paper or a TV outlet."

Charlie chewed on his lower lip, knowing the truth of Steve's statement.

In the last fifteen to twenty years, the newspaper industry had been suffering financially. The majority of the public was no longer buying newspapers. Papers, and the people who wrote for them, were a dying breed. Newspaper companies had to do everything they could to stay ahead of the twenty-four-hour news programs on cable and the internet.

The Tribune was no exception, and Charlie had to fight tooth and nail to keep the paper afloat with strong reporting and well-written, fact-based stories that attracted readers. But neither were enough to keep the Tribune functioning alone. To help offset some production costs, Charlie had turned to private donations from people who felt quality journalism still mattered in today's world of Fake News.

"Or worse, we lose it to some dipshit blogger," Steve added for good measure, knowing the statement would strike a nerve with his boss.

To Steve and Charlie, internet news bloggers were not only hurting the newspaper industry but also the fact-based reporting that, up until a few years ago, was considered sacred. Wannabe reporters, and in some cases foreign instigators with political motives, had enough writing skills to cause public outrage, gaslighted further by a complacent population too lazy to read – in some cases beyond clickbait headlines.

In the era of Fake News, bloggers were fueled by people who would rather believe wild conspiracy theories than the national news organizations that had been trusted for years. For these types of bloggers, there were no reins to draw them in. It was the Wild West in internet land, and anything and everything could be written without repercussions to the author.

Charlie stared at him with heavy eyes, filled with uncertainty, and the culpability of a man who knew what the right decision was. Steve knew he did not want to give him the go-ahead but, at the same time, understood the opportunity that had presented itself for the Tribune, especially in a time when the paper needed a huge story.

"Why us?" Charlie asked. "Why you? Whoever dropped the package off could have had more exposure had they gone with a bigger paper like *The New York Times* or *The Washington Post*."

"I don't have those answers. Not yet, at least." Steve paused, thinking, then said, "Maybe it's not about exposure."

Charlie's face took on a quizzical look. "If this isn't about exposure, then what's the purpose of sending the license and the USB to you?"

"I believe someone wanted me to know that Rebecca Turner was the girl in the video. But, before we go making assumptions, let me dig into it, see what I can rummage on why I was contacted."

Charlie looked away, still uncertain. Steve needed to persuade his boss to see this from his point of view. Luckily, he had an ace up his sleeve that would work to change Charlie's opinion.

"Charlie, if it was one of your daughters in that video, wouldn't you want to know who did that to her, and that their crimes were exposed?"

Charlie's eyes snapped back at him; anger touched his face in an unexplainable way. "You don't get to use my love for my daughters against me on this. And besides, it's the police's job to find those responsible. Not yours. You report the news, you don't make it happen."

"How many cold cases are still waiting to be solved? How many families are still waiting for the police to get past the bureaucratical bullshit, loopholes, the dead-end leads that hold them back from finding those responsible, bringing closure for those same families? Put yourself in their shoes, Charlie. You'd want to know." Steve pushed. "I can do that. I can work around all that shit and find out what happened to this young lady. I've done it before, and you know it."

"Goddamn you," Charlie said, shaking his head and lowering his eyes.

Steve knew he was right and so did Charlie; sometimes a fresh set of eyes could help propel a cold investigation into new territory, resulting in law enforcement action.

Charlie's eyes rose, heavy and guilted, and met Steve's intense gaze. "Where are you going to start? You don't know where the video was made or who left it."

"There's *one* clue." Steve crossed the room to Charlie's desk and pointed to the photo of Rebecca Turner on the junior driver's license. "I'll start by looking for her."

Chapter Three

Steve walked out of Charlie's office with his boss's reluctant consent to start an investigation. If he did not have anything in seventy-two hours, then Charlie would hand everything over to law enforcement. Seventy-two hours. Would that give Steve enough time to put a dent in this mystery?

It would have to.

Back at his desk, Steve pulled up the internet and typed: National Center for Missing and Exploited Children. On the home page, he clicked the SEARCH FOR A CHILD button along the right-hand side. When the page loaded, there was a box of fillable slots. There, he typed Rebecca Turner's full name, followed by the city, state, and county she was from. At the bottom were two start and stop date boxes. The issue date of Rebecca's driver's license was November 23, 1998; it was a good indication of where to begin. The crime had to have occurred after November of '98, but before December of '02 – when the license would have expired. He entered 11/23/1998 – 2/15/2024 into the system. He hit ENTER again, and the page loaded.

One name and face appeared on the screen.

Rebecca Ann Turner.

Bingo!

Steve clicked the link on Rebecca's name. Two pictures filled the screen when the page loaded. The first photo was one that had obviously been given to the police by her family. The photo was old, slightly faded, taken before digital cameras were the norm. The second photo was age-progressed to what Rebecca might look like at age forty-two. The age advancement likeness was uncanny to the real photograph of Rebecca beside it. Sandwiched in between the two pictures was more information to help identify Rebecca if spotted:

MISSING SINCE: 1/5/1999
MISSING FROM: Abbottstown, PA
DOB: 10/2/1982
SEX: Female
RACE: Caucasian
HAIR COLOR: Blonde
Eye Color: Blue
Height: 5'7"
WEIGHT: 110 lbs.

Below the identifiable markers was a phone number to the Hanover Police Department, instructing anyone who may have information regarding Rebecca to call. There was also a small blurb of information that read:

Rebecca Ann Turner was last seen on January 5, 1999, after attending a party. She was wearing a black Nirvana t-shirt, red windbreaker, and khaki pants. She was driving her mother's 1993 Blue Ford Tempo.

Steve exited the site and went to Google. Typing

Rebecca Ann Turner into the search engine, he hit ENTER. The usual stuff came up first: FIND REBECCA ANN TURNER WITH PEOPLE LOCATOR! REBECCA ANN TURNER – PHONE, ADDRESS, BACKGROUND INFO/WHITEPAGES. REBECCA ANN TURNER/FACEBOOK.

Rebecca went missing long before the internet became the principal place to locate someone, but Steve was not searching for Rebecca, rather for articles about her disappearance. Twenty-five years ago, a missing sixteen-year-old girl wouldn't have made a blip on the national news radar, but her disappearance would've been a topic of discussion for the local news and papers for sure.

Steve looked back at the photo of Rebecca on the junior driver's license. Anger coursed through his veins, warming him uncomfortably. After seeing what those three men did to her in the video, he was certain she was most likely dead. A sobering reality sunk in that no matter how deep Steve dove into this investigation, no matter what he uncovered, he would never be able to change that horrible fact.

I need a fucking drink.

Fighting the urge to dip into his emergency flask, kept hidden in his laptop bag for a much-needed snort, he began scrolling through Google pages. He found nothing useful until he clicked onto the fifth page. An article had been written a year ago by an Amy Richards for a local newspaper called the *Hanover Daily Record*.

Now we're getting somewhere, Steve thought.

He clicked the link, and the article opened on the *Hanover Daily Record's* website.

Some Kind of Truth

Twenty-Four-Year-Old Cold Case Still An Ongoing Investigation
by Amy Richards

The memory of Rebecca Turner looms ominously over Hanover, Pennsylvania, in the twenty-four years since the sixteen-year-old's disappearance. Last seen on the night of January 5, 1999, Rebecca was reported to have left a party around midnight in her mother's 1993 blue Ford Tempo. The car was later found abandoned along Maple Grove Road.

Since Rebecca's disappearance, two separate police departments have taken on the task of finding the missing teenager. But, so far, all efforts to locate her have led to dead ends, and to this day, Rebecca has not been found.

Some, like former Abbottstown sheriff, Dean Winslow, dedicated the rest of his career to finding out what happened to Rebecca Turner.

"I worked on that case for fifteen years," said Winslow. "I still have sleepless nights thinking about her, wondering if she's out there – she'd be a grown woman now. It's like I'm living in one of those *Unsolved Mystery* episodes. You want answers, you *need* answers, but they never come. It leaves an empty hole inside, one that can never be filled."

Sheriff Winslow is not the only person who wants answers. Rebecca's father, Dennis Turner of Abbottstown, spoke about his daughter and her disappearance.

"I think about her every day. I pray the phone rings and it's her – my Rebecca on the other end. I'm hopeful that she finds her way home…one way or another."

Twenty-four years is a long time. A lot has changed since Rebecca's disappearance, including the closing of the Abbottstown Police Department where Rebecca's case was investigated up until the day the department shut its doors.

"I worked on that case harder than I've ever worked a case before," Winslow said. "And I'd still be working it, had the township not voted to drop the police force and go with Hanover PD." Winslow shrugged at the thought. "What are you going to do, it's out of my hands now, and I'm retired."

Back in 2010, Abbottstown voted to disband their police force, in a cost-cutting measure, and decided to use Hanover PD instead. This meant that all open cases were transferred to the Hanover Police Department, including cold cases, such as Rebecca's.

Now, the fate of finding Rebecca lies in the hands of Sheriff Ben Meeker, of the Hanover Police Department. Though Meeker is not one to make statements to the press about ongoing cases, he did share a small detail.

"We're making headway," Sheriff Meeker commented.

"I'm glad to hear that Meeker is having better luck than I was," said Winslow. "And I hope my part in the investigation can help Meeker, and his team, close this case once and for all and give the Turner family some peace of mind."

When asked if he would ever stop thinking about Rebecca, Winslow replied, "No. Rebecca's a part of me now. She'll always be on my mind until she is either found or I die."

Dennis Turner had a similar view.

"I'll never give up hope of bringing our baby home,"
said Turner. "One way or another."

The article ended there.

There's only one way Rebecca's coming home, Steve
thought dourly. His mind flashed back to the video, as
Rebecca was yanked across a red table by one of the three
men, and her wrists cuffed to its legs.

Steve tossed the image from his foremost thoughts. He
could not think about the video now, nor what they had
done to Rebecca. He needed to keep his head clear,
focused; there would be time later to go back over the video
with a fine-tooth comb and look for clues. But for now, those
horrifying images needed to stay locked away.

On a legal notepad, Steve scribbled down the names in
the article for later interviews – though he was unsure how
credible their recount would be after twenty-five years.

He still had to try.

The phone number for the *Hanover Daily Record* was
at the bottom of the newspaper's webpage. Steve dialed it.
The line was answered by a young-sounding receptionist.
He told her who he was, and that he was trying to reach
Amy Richards, but withheld the real reason for his call. He
did not want anyone catching wind that he was looking into
Rebecca Turner, not yet anyway.

He was informed that Amy was on assignment and that
the receptionist would not give Steve her personal cell
number, but offered to have Amy call him back when she
returned. Steve recited his number and hung up.

Sitting back in his chair, he ran his hands over his face;
frustration washed over him like a tidal wave. He craved a
cigarette and a drink, as he always did when he seemed to

hit an impasse. A remaining twinge of the headache pinched the center of his forehead.

Standing, he made his way to the elevator and hit the number three button on the panel and rode down to the third floor.

The third floor of the Tribune building had been dedicated to a team of video journalists, writers, tech, and social-media-savvy people that had been assembled over the past fifteen years to catch stories on the internet, TV, or social media. Their job was to write quick articles and get them on the Tribune's website as soon as possible, hoping to reach readers faster than with print. Ricky Welsh led this team of unique journalists and had been the head of the department since its inception back in the early two-thousands.

When the elevator doors opened, the room was abuzz with activity, as if someone had died. These reporters – and Steve used the term loosely – were prone to leisurely searching the internet for stories while sitting on their asses, rather than beating their feet to gather facts. Whatever was going on now had them scrambling to find more information.

Ricky was in his office, seated at his desk with the door open. He was typing something into the computer. The letters clicked with the efficiency of a man who knew his way around a keyboard. Steve knocked. Ricky looked up from the monitor and waved him in.

"I suppose you're here about the video?" Ricky said, standing.

Ricky resembled a hipster who frequented microbreweries, with long red hair pulled back into a ponytail, a matching beard, and black-rimmed glasses. He wore an untucked green button-down shirt, and a pair of black skinny jeans clung to his legs so tight they appeared painted on. The Vans sneakers matched the outfit perfectly, like he had picked the entire ensemble straight off a mannequin at a department store.

"Yeah." Steve turned to close the door so they would not be interrupted. Again, he noticed reporters circling around the room like agitated bees trying to protect a disturbed hive. "What's got them agitated?" he asked, facing Ricky.

Ricky smiled and said, "Taylor Swift just announced, via Twitter, that she's coming to Pittsburgh for a concert. They're scrambling to get further details."

"Good thing our priorities are covered when it comes to reporting quality news stories." Steve crossed the room and took a seat. For a moment, they stared at one another without saying a word; the unspoken atrocity of the video hanging in the air. Finally, he asked, "What's your take on the video?"

Ricky's face grew grim, bearing the weight of what he had seen that morning. His eyes then drifted back to his desk, where the USB rested beside the keyboard; the words **PLAY ME** stood out on the front like some evil incantation that would summon an unclean spirit if spoken aloud.

"To be honest... I don't know. It's awful. I mean, what those three men did to her... my God..." Ricky trailed off. He gulped, and his Adam's apple bobbed deep in his throat, as if he were trying to dry swallow a pill.

"I know." Steve tried not to think of the video, but those vile images materialized behind his eyes. But the images were only half of the video; he could hear Rebecca's helpless screams too, echoing through the dark caverns of his mind, causing the pain in the center of his forehead to worsen. "Is there anything on the video that stood out to you, a specific scene where you questioned the authenticity or found something odd that stuck out?"

Ricky pondered the question for a moment before speaking. "There were no scenes where I questioned its authenticity. It looked real enough, sadly. However, I did notice one questionable thing."

"Oh? What's that?"

"The video's been digitized."

"Digitized? What do you mean?"

"I mean, the video wasn't shot with a modern-day camera or even a cellphone. The footage is old, grainy. Most likely it was shot on VHS."

"How can you tell?"

"Let me show you," Ricky said, waving Steve around to his side of the desk.

Ricky picked up the USB and inserted it into the computer. Once the flash drive loaded, he opened the video file and hit PLAY. He let the first few frames of the video roll, which consisted of two shirtless men wearing S&M masks dragging Rebecca, nude and bound, into a dingy room lit with a single overhead bulb that somehow made the room appear even more grimy, before hitting PAUSE. Ricky then pointed to the screen.

"As you can see, the video isn't in today's standard sixteen-by-nine format, like modern-day cameras use. Instead, this video's been recorded in the four-by-three format – which was common before everything went digital. The recording is also in standard definition."

"How do you know it's in standard def?"

"You see how fuzzy the picture is, soft, almost unfocused?" Steve nodded. "And these wavy lines at the top and bottom of the screen?" Ricky pointed to the top of the picture box and then to the bottom.

"I do."

"That's what leads me to believe the video was made

with an old VHS camcorder, one of those big clunky ones from the eighties and nineties. The video was copied from a tape before being put on the flash drive."

"How was the copying done?"

"Through a computer. There are programs that copy tapes and film to whatever you like – DVD, Blu-ray, hard drive... flash drive." Ricky met Steve's inquisitive gaze.

"Would the copying of the tape have to be done professionally?"

"Not at all. You can find converters on Amazon for around fifty dollars – higher-end ones cost more, but they all do the same thing. All someone would need is a way to play the tape – in this case a VCR. Hook the VCR to the computer and copy the video."

"Anything else?"

Ricky shook his head. "Not that I saw. Then again, the video was hard to watch closely without looking away a few times."

Steve understood. He had to look away from the screen himself last night, unable to watch the events unfold.

"Think you could go over it again, look for anything that doesn't add up, or could have been faked?" Steve asked.

Ricky expelled a whoosh of air, and placed his hands on his hips, like a kid about to protest eating his vegetables.

"I guess I could." He sighed, clearly disheartened at the idea.

"We're running with this one, Ricky, at least for the time being," Steve said solemnly. "I need your eyes, man."

Ricky met Steve's gaze with apprehension. They both knew the dangers of looking into the brutal video, and what holes Steve might have to venture down to expose its ghastly origins.

"You sure it's a good idea for you to be looking into this

one?" Ricky asked. "You were once on that side of the camera. You, more than anyone, know what it's like to have your life almost taken while being filmed."

"Yeah," Steve replied, trying not to recall those horrific days following the convoy attack in Afghanistan. "Look, would you mind giving it another go-over for me? I'd like to hear your thoughts."

Grudgingly, Ricky nodded. He would do what had to be done, even if he did not like it.

"Thanks. Let me know if you find anything out of the ordinary."

"Will do."

Steve had just gotten back to his desk when the phone rang.

"Steve James," he said, answering.

"Mr. James," the female voice on the other end spoke. "I was just informed that you tried to contact me."

For a moment, Steve was at a loss. His mind was clouded with troubled thoughts of Rebecca Turner and the video that somehow found its way to him. His silence must have given away that he did not know who he was speaking with.

"This is Amy Richards," the voice continued.

"Oh..." he laughed, feeling stupid. "Hello. I was told you were out of the office today, so I didn't expect you to return my call so soon."

"I was on an assignment. I just got back a few moments ago. How can I help you, Mr. James?"

Steve hesitated to gather his thoughts, then said, "Ms. Richards, the reason I called was because I found a story you wrote on Rebecca Turner a year ago. I was wondering if there's any new information on her disappearance since the publication of the article?"

Silence on the other end of the line.

"Ms. Richards?"

"Yes, I'm still here. Sorry, you just caught me off guard is all." She spoke cautiously. "Who did you say you worked for again?"

"The Pittsburgh Tribune."

"And how exactly did you come across this information, Mr. James? Hanover - and our paper - is four hours away from Pittsburgh, so I don't see how Rebecca Turner came across your radar."

Steve contemplated whether to tell her about the mysterious package or fudge the details and keep what he knew close to the vest for the moment.

"Her ID was discovered out here," Steve said. That would do for the time being.

"Are you sure it's the same Rebecca Turner from my article? It's been twenty-five years since she disappeared," Amy said. "Like I said before, Pittsburgh—"

"It's her," Steve replied in a matter-of-fact tone. "I've already confirmed through the National Center for Missing and Exploited Children."

"Oh! I see."

Amy grew quiet. Steve suspected she didn't know how to respond – how could she? – it was all so strange. He continued with his questions.

"Like I mentioned earlier, I was wondering if there was any new information about Rebecca?"

"Unfortunately, no. I was hoping my story would bring Rebecca's case back into the public eye. Then maybe, just maybe, someone would come forward with information after all these years. But the case remains cold."

"I believe someone *did* come forward with information," Steve said. "Just not to you."

"What does that mean?" Amy asked, as if Steve had insulted her skills as a reporter.

Steve decided to hold off telling her anything further.

"I'd rather not talk about it over the phone, Ms. Richards. Tell you what, why don't I come see you and we can discuss the case in person."

"I really don't know that much, other than what the police have released."

"Which was squat," Steve said.

"That's correct."

Pulling the white legal pad closer, he did not want his thoughts to slip away, as they often did when he had too much to drink. He jotted down how Amy's article had not helped progress the investigation, nor had it garnered any public interest into a twenty-five-year-old case; the police were not helpful and seemed to be keeping tight-lipped about everything; and that Hanover was about four hours from Pittsburgh – which again made him question his involvement. How had the flash drive and the driver's license found their way to him, and who could have delivered them?

If he wanted to get to the bottom of this mystery, he knew he would not get the answers to his questions over the phone. He needed to see where the crime happened, talk to the people involved. Amy was a good place to start. She had more knowledge about Rebecca than anyone else, outside of the police, and he couldn't just barge into a local station demanding answers to a twenty-five-year-old cold case. He'd be thrown out of the building and possibly run out of town for sticking his nose where it did not belong.

"I'm coming to Hanover this afternoon. I'd like to meet with you this evening if that's alright."

"Okay." She sounded nervous, as if the thought of

Steve's involvement in Rebecca's case would somehow taint it. "What time are you expecting to be here?"

Steve looked at his watch. It was twenty past eleven. He still had to make his way across town to his apartment, pack a bag, and then make it back through Pittsburgh's noon-hour traffic. That would put him on the Pennsylvania turnpike by one, at the earliest.

"I should be in Hanover around five."

"Okay, Mr. James. I'll see you in a few hours."

———

Twenty minutes later, Steve pulled into a parking space in front of his apartment building. Stepping from the car, the cold crisp air rushed over the mountains, and felt like a thousand tiny daggers driving into his flesh all at once, chilling him to the bone. The bright morning sun had done little to warm the earth, and the snow and ice crunched underfoot as he made his way toward the apartment building.

I need to move somewhere warm, Steve thought. Of course, he had been thinking about moving for the last ten years, even though he had lived and worked in Pittsburgh his entire forty-five years on earth. He supposed he was restless with life, maybe burnt out, and needed a change. He had heard Florida was beautiful; muggy, but beautiful. And then he'd think of all the old people down there, clinging to the last quarter of their lives, withering away until death came to collect them. *No thanks, not going to Florida to write the obituary column. Maybe New Mexico or Nevada? And what the fuck was in New Mexico or Nevada to write about, Steve ol' boy? Aliens? Roswell? Area 51?*

Like always, Steve pushed the thought of moving from

Pittsburgh to the back of his mind. Maybe someday he would leave, but he wondered if he would ever pull the trigger on the idea. Pittsburgh was what he knew. Pittsburgh was in his blood. Why would he want to leave the city he both loved and loathed?

Coming to the door of his apartment building, Steve noticed a tall, muscular Italian man across the street, smoking a cigarette. His black hair was glued to his scalp, keeping it in place even through the wind gusts. He was impeccably dressed: expensive black jacket, dark slacks, and a grey button-down shirt – all of it tailor-made to fit his muscular physique and intimidating presence. His shoes were leather – of course, probably Italian, just like himself.

The man leaned nonchalantly against an abandoned warehouse, as if he were waiting for the bus. But the bus did not stop there, and the warehouse had shut its doors three years ago; it now sat vacant and was up for sale. He was obviously not a realtor or a potential buyer of the property. And the way he kept glancing in Steve's direction told Steve all he needed to know about this individual.

He was one of Palazzo's hired goons.

When the man across the street realized Steve was looking in his direction, he averted his gaze to the clouds, as if he were absently observing the sky.

Steve kept moving toward the front door of his apartment building. He stopped just before going in and turned back once more to the man across the street. Again, the goon was observing him like a hawk would its prey. Steve gave him a cheerful little wave like one might give to a friend or colleague. The goon quickly averted his eyes to the sky once more.

It was apparent this was an attempt to get Steve to renounce his story. When Steve had last spoken to Charlie about the lawsuit, it was still being hashed out between the lawyers and courts – it was looking favorable that Steve and the Tribune were going to win. He guessed that Palazzo and the DeLuca Family were growing tired of waiting for their lawyers to make the story go away, and decided it was time to start intimidating him.

Watch yourself, Charlie had warned. *They know they don't have a chance in hell of winning this thing; they're going to start putting pressure on you.* Steve understood the risk. But he didn't scare easily, and he would not withdraw the story, nor would he be run out of town. Anthony Palazzo could send as many thugs as he liked to intimidate him. He had been intimidated before, by worse men than Anthony Palazzo could ever dream of becoming.

Steve turned away and headed into his apartment building.

He crossed the lobby to a wall of gold mailboxes. Fishing out his keys from his pocket, he opened his mailbox and pulled out his stack of mail.

Tucking the mail under his left arm, he closed the box, locked it, and headed toward the steps beside the elevator to his apartment. The elevator no longer ran. Landlord Horace claimed faulty wiring in the elevator's switchboard, and that someone was coming out to fix it. That had been three months ago. Steve had yet to see a single person work on that damn lift.

The elevator's doors were blocked off with two yellow plastic strips in an X shape. The tape was not caution tape as one would expect to find, but rather cheap Halloween decorations the super had picked up at a local party store for a buck that said **HAPPY HALLOWEEN**, and had little white ghosts in between the words.

What kind of hell am I living in?

As he headed to his apartment, his mind drifted back to the mysterious package. *Where had it come from? Why was it left for me? Who delivered it?* He pondered these thoughts while trying to keep the vile images on the video from creeping back into his brain. But that was impossible.

He kept seeing sixteen-year-old Rebecca Turner struggling against her restraints; the metal handcuffs clacking against the legs of the table were like some dark, ambient sound effect used to enhance the scene. But it was Rebecca's cries that shattered his skull and broke his heart, cries reminiscent of a wounded animal, especially when those three bastards began to sodomize her.

Steve's head snapped up, his mind torn away from his thoughts, when he saw someone move in the hallway. His defenses rose. Had the goon, who he'd seen earlier standing on the corner, come to kill him?

No.

It was only Steve's neighbor, Mrs. Estell Loomis, walking toward him from her apartment. Mrs. Loomis's purse was draped over her left shoulder, and a small floral overnight bag dangled from her right hand. She walked at a crawl, the movements of a woman whose best days were far behind.

Steve came to his apartment door just as Mrs. Loomis approached him.

"How are you doing, Mrs. Loomis?" Steve asked, trying to be polite.

"Piss off, James," she snapped. "I gotta go see the damn grandkid and watch him perform in some shitty fourth-grade adaptation of *The Wizard of Oz*. What a waste of time!"

Mrs. Loomis looked like a sweet, innocent old woman with thick white hair and a face that resembled Betty

White's, but she was a cantankerous old bitch that Steve would not want to cross.

"Sounds horrible," Steve replied.

"I'd rather piss barbed wire for a week than have to go to this." She said nothing further to him, no '*goodbye*,' not a '*see ya later, Steve.*' Nothing. The old, crabby bitch just kept strolling down the hall toward the stairs.

Steve watched her go for a few more steps and then turned back to his apartment.

As soon as he was inside, something felt off. The air was thick with an insidious presence, like one might feel in a dark room of a haunted house filled with malevolent spirits. Since the curtains were pulled, and the light was dim, Steve could not see anyone, but he smelled the heavy musk of a man's cologne lingering in the air. Someone was in the apartment with him.

It was then that Steve realized the man on the corner had been the watchdog for his partner, who had been waiting in his apartment the entire time. He had probably texted his buddy, letting him know that Steve was on his way up.

Steve moved down the short hallway into the kitchen. A man sat on the sofa in the living room; his form was silhouetted from the window behind, his face hidden in shadows. In his right hand, he held a can of soda, taken from Steve's refrigerator.

Thieving bastard stole my pop!

Steve placed his computer bag on the countertop, as he always did, and then began to open his mail as if nothing was different.

"Have you come to scare me?" Steve asked, as he tore open the gas bill. He needed to keep his hands busy and his mind occupied. He couldn't show this man, whoever he was, an ounce of fear – fear that was causing his stomach to twitch with spasms and a hard knot to form in the back of his throat.

"I'm here to give you a message from Mr. Palazzo," the man said.

Steve swallowed the knot away before he spoke; he hoped his voice didn't quiver. "Really?" *Son of a bitch, the gas bill went up this month,* Steve thought. "And what message is that?"

"You retract your story on Mr. Palazzo, and you'll be rewarded handsomely." The man took a long obnoxious sip from the can.

Annoying. Thieving. Bastard.

Steve looked up as the man sat forward on the sofa, and the light caught his face for the first time.

His blood ran cold.

Vinny "Icepick" Rossi was in his home, sipping a Sprite. Rossi was, by all accounts, one of Anthony Palazzo's top painters – a mob term for *hitman.* Rumor was, Rossi had murdered more than two dozen people, most with an icepick. It was how he received his nickname. But Rossi hadn't come to silence Steve, to drive his icepick into his throat and slowly bleed him dry, since he wouldn't retract his story on Anthony Palazzo.

If that were the case, I'd already be dead.

No. He was there to deliver a message only.

Rossi was in his mid-thirties, handsome, lean and muscular. He wore an expensive coal-colored suit and black tie. The outfit made him look more like a banker or a Wall Street broker than a hitman connected to the Palazzo Family. Steve wondered where Rossi kept the icepick in that nice suit, or did one only find out moments before their ticket was punched? Rossi's dark eyes were deadly cold, with an unflinching blackness that told Steve he had killed men for far less than what Steve had done to his boss. Those unapologetic eyes were trained on Steve now.

Steve dropped the gas bill onto the pile of discarded mail and then picked up another unopened envelope. This one was a credit card offer. He opened it and shook his head, annoyed by both the offer as well as Rossi's intrusion into his home.

"Well, you can go back to the hole Palazzo's in and tell your boss I cannot do that."

"Is that so?"

Steve nodded while he pulled out the contents of junk mail. "Yep. That's so."

"Mr. Palazzo's not going to like hearing that."

Steve pretended to read over the credit card's offer, though he only saw the percentage rate. "Can you believe that they want to charge me thirty percent interest on this card?" He glanced at Rossi. "That's robbery!"

"You're taking this too lightly, Mr. James. I warn you, that's the wrong thing to do."

Steve shook his head. "No, I'm not. Thirty percent interest is a lot of money to dish out to these clowns. Legal loan sharks, all of 'em."

"Mr. Palazzo would like to offer you some assistance," Rossi continued to push.

Steve looked at him.

"Assistance?"

Rossi nodded, smiled, rows of perfect white teeth gleamed in the dim light.

"What kind of assistance?"

"Anything you need, Mr. James."

"Really?" Steve dropped the mail on the countertop and leaned on it, rested his chin on the palm of his hand. "Well, now that you bring it up, I could use help getting that very sofa you're sitting on out of the apartment; been meaning to get a new one. If Mr. Palazzo could help me–"

"Enough!" Rossi shouted, slamming the soda down onto the end table, causing it to fizz up and run down the side of the can and onto the wooden stand.

"Hey, you said assistance."

Rossi stood, leaving the Sprite can on the stand beside the sofa. He crossed the living room with the stride of a self-assured killer, to where Steve stood by the counter in the kitchen.

"It's not wise to play games with me, Mr. James." Rossi's emotionless eyes bore through Steve, straight into his very soul.

The intent behind Rossi's dusky eyes was enough to cause a normal man to coil into a ball on the floor and beg for his life. But Steve wasn't about to do that. Sure, he was scared of what Rossi could do to him. Scared shitless, actually. Still, he had come face-to-face with evil men – truly evil men – while held hostage in a cave in Afghanistan. Compared to them, the Palazzo family was nothing more than two-bit street hoodlums. But there was another reason for Steve's brazenness: he had insurance, guaranteeing his safety from Palazzo's retaliation – at least for a little while yet.

Throughout Steve's two-year investigation into Palazzo, he had accumulated a substantial amount of evidence, evidence that helped put Anthony Palazzo behind bars. His "MOB IN PITTSBURGH" story for the Tribune brought Palazzo's money laundering scheme for the DeLuca Crime Family into the national spotlight. But not all the evidence Steve collected had been exposed in his story. Some had been withheld, at Charlie's insistence, in case Palazzo put pressure on Steve when the mob's lawsuit failed in court, which it would.

If Steve ended up missing or dead, Charlie was to release the remaining evidence to the authorities and the public. Neither Palazzo nor the DeLuca family knew about the withheld evidence. If Charlie released it, the Feds would be able to link everything back to Palazzo and the DeLuca Family without much effort.

In the old days of the mafia, contracts were put out to silence journalists from shedding light into their murky world – some were gunned down, others stabbed or blown up in car bombs. This practice was still going on, not so much in America, but in Italy, where the old ways of conducting business were resurging.

In Italy, journalists and their families were living with twenty-four-hour police protection from the mafia. In America, however, the mob fell back on its sleazy lawyers to hit journalists with defamation lawsuits, which came down on Steve and the Tribune like the fist of God once the story garnered national attention. Now that the lawsuit was fail-ing, they were falling back onto old tried-and-true tactics of the past. Steve had been offered police protection, but he declined. He wished he wouldn't have now.

"Get the fuck out of here," Steve shot back. "I find you in my home again, I won't be as polite and hospitable the next time." He took a ballsy move and stepped closer to Rossi; that musky tang of cologne he had smelled when he first walked through the door permeated off Rossi's skin. He was not about to back down from Rossi or anyone else Palazzo sent his way. He would not show them an ounce of fear, no matter how scary or intimidating the situation was.

Rossi inhaled deeply; anger and irritation flared his nostrils. His skin seemed to shrink tightly around his skull, and his jaws twitched with rage, a rage Steve knew he wanted to unleash on the smart-ass reporter standing in front of him.

Then, Rossi smiled – a friendly smile. No, not a friendly smile at all, but one that told Steve the devil just might be knocking on his door again, soon. Rossi produced a billfold from his front pocket that held several one-hundred-dollar bills and cards. He pulled one of the cards from the billfold and placed it on the counter.

There was only a phone number printed on the card.

"In case you change your mind, Mr. James."

Rossi stepped around Steve but stopped and turned back before he reached the door.

"Remember what I said, Mr. James."

Rossi then opened the door and left without saying another word.

Chapter Four

Steve packed a bag and a few toiletries for the trip. His first destination was Abbottstown, Pennsylvania. He had found a hotel online, the Abbottstown Inn, and phoned ahead and booked a room for two nights.

He had a seventy-two-hour window until his deadline. Would that be enough time to uncover what had happened to Rebecca Turner?

Steve hoped it would be.

From the top shelf of the closet, he pulled down a wooden box and placed it on the bed beside his duffle bag. There was a combination lock on the front that he quickly rolled the numbers to – 12-07-01 – the date he escaped (or had been rescued; Steve never decided which) his captivity in Afghanistan.

Opening the box, a nickel-plated .38 rested in its soft foam home. Steve lifted the revolver. He enjoyed the weight of the gun, and the comfortable fit of the stock in his palm was like an extension of his hand and arm, a deadly extension.

He slipped the gun inside the duffle bag, along with a

box of ammunition. He didn't know who posed a threat to his life. Someone was always willing to harm others to keep the truth from being exposed, especially when it came to making sure a secret, like what happened to Rebecca, stayed buried. Steve had put his safety in the hands of others once before; he would not do so again.

He then headed out to face a bleak world.

Outside, the afternoon air was brisk, and the wind brought with it the smell of snow. The sun had disappeared, and gray clouds had moved over Pittsburgh that afternoon, large and insolent, threatening yet another winter storm.

Steve looked back to the corner where he had see the goon earlier. No one was there now. But they would be back. Palazzo was going to do everything he could to get Steve to retract his story.

Good luck, Steve thought.

In his twenty-five years with the Tribune, he had never retracted a story. Even with the pressure from Palazzo and his goons, Steve was willing to take the risk to ensure the truth remained visible to the public.

Once inside his car, Steve slipped the key into the ignition. He was about to turn it over when he realized that the goon on the corner could have planted a bomb in the car. *A hit.* If they took Steve out, hopefully it would kill the story and scare the Tribune into a retraction of the article. *Had it come to that yet?*

An icy chill touched him. Gooseflesh rose across his body, and his balls withered up into him like a dying flower. He was only a turn away from his life possibly ending. Slowly, Steve removed his hand from the ignition and placed both of them on the steering wheel. He took a deep breath, trying to find his balance, his inner fortitude, and not allow Palazzo, or his goons, to intimidate him. *Easier said than done.*

If Steve allowed Palazzo and his gang to terrorize him, to frighten him, to bully him into retracting the story, then Palazzo would win. If he did retract his story, then he was no better than Palazzo or any other person who broke the law and bent the facts to suit their needs. If he died today, if the car exploded when he turned the key, Steve would at least die a martyr, standing up for his core belief that the truth must be exposed no matter the cost.

Realizing his grip on the steering wheel was so tight that his knuckles had turned white and his hands had begun to ache, Steve pried his fingers from the steering wheel and reached for a cigarette in the center console. He brought the cancer stick to his mouth with a wavering hand and lit it with the Zippo. If he were about to meet his maker, he would have one last smoke before he went.

He smoked half the cigarette before he placed his right hand back on the ignition.

A faithful man would have prayed to God for mercy or forgiveness, but Steve was not sure God would listen, nor forgive him for his biggest sin – taking a life.

He closed his eyes. A scene from the video cut the blackness with a sharp white flash, like a subliminal editing manipulation done in horror films. In his mind, he saw Rebecca helplessly bound to a table with her hands and ankles cuffed to the legs. A red ball gag had been shoved in her mouth and drawn so tightly around her face and head, that her lips had been pulled up into a grin-like smirk.

A lock of her blonde hair had fallen over the right side of her face; her left eye was full and round, the pupil large and black, the size of a dime, and consumed with terror and repulsion at what was being done to her. The sounds of her whimpers seemed to float up to Steve from some far-off place, as if he were hearing them played from an old record, static and scratchy, an unclean sound that needed to be cleansed from his mind.

A tear rolled down Rebecca's face, as thick as jelly. It was the biggest tear Steve believed he had ever seen; an awful reminder of the pain and torment she was in at that very moment.

Steve's eyes snapped open to the cold, icy reality that was Pittsburgh that afternoon. He could not allow the thought of a hit to stop him, to control him. He had put himself in harm's way in the past to seek the truth, and persevered, even when his life was being threatened at gunpoint in a cave six thousand miles away from home. He would find out what happened to Rebecca, and no one, including Palazzo, was going to stop him.

Steve turned the key.

Four hours later, Steve checked into the Abbottstown Inn. The inn sat on the corner of a roundabout intersection in Abbottstown, Pennsylvania. He had chosen the location because of the town's proximity to Hanover, which was less than five miles away. Also, Dennis Turner, Rebecca's father, still lived in town, just a few streets from the inn; he would be easy to access.

Abbottstown was small. Blink and one would be through it. There was nothing to entice visitors to come here, other than the inn, and maybe the Brand Feed Mill, sitting directly behind the inn, its towering steel silos like two metal monsters, as if they were the town's watchful guardians.

Some Kind of Truth

The Abbottstown Inn was a large three-story Victorian with a wraparound porch, which was used as an extra seating area in the summer, Steve presumed, from the tables and chairs he saw pushed against the front wall. The first floor of the inn consisted of a dimly lit dining room. A small bar area was tucked behind a wall, away from the dining crowd, which was already gathering by that hour. But the bar was empty. Steve began to salivate at the sight of the plentiful amount of alcohol bottles lining the shelves. He had not had a snort since the car started without exploding, and he had dipped into his emergency flask, thankful to still be among the living. He thought about ordering himself a drink – *one for the road*. It would help quiet the anxiety still wrecking his insides.

Instead, he decided to finish the check-in process first. He would get a drink later. A few actually, and fall asleep good and numb, with the troubles of the day behind him. He made his way to his room and phoned Amy to say that he was in town. The conversation was short and to the point. He was to meet her at the *Hanover Daily Record* in twenty minutes.

The *Hanover Daily Record* sat on the corner of Broadway and York Street in downtown Hanover. Steve turned right onto South Railroad Street and pulled his car into a small parking lot behind the *Record*, then made his way to the front. The paper operated out of a turn-of-the-century three-story red brick building that had been restored to meet the needs of the paper. *Hanover Daily Record* was etched into the stone above the entrance.

Entering the building, Steve started across the lobby to the receptionist's desk. A pretty, young woman was typing into the computer. Was she the same person he spoke to earlier that afternoon? He didn't know. She looked up as he approached the desk and smiled politely.

"May I help you?" Her voice was pleasant, bubbly, and Steve was confident she had been the person he'd spoken with earlier.

"I'm here to see Amy Richards."

"And your name?"

"Steve James."

Any recognition of his name, or their conversation, seemed to elude her. She picked up the phone and punched in three numbers – Amy's direct line – and then waited a moment for it to be answered. When the line was answered, she informed Amy that Steve was here.

She replaced the phone and looked back at Steve. "You can head up. Use the stairs over there." She pointed left to the stairwell.

"Thank you," Steve said.

Steve started up the steps and was greeted on the second floor by a strikingly beautiful woman. Her vibrant green eyes stood out like emeralds gleaming in the summer sun. Eyes so captivating that they could easily hypnotize a man and bend him to her will.

"Steve James?" the woman asked.

"Y-yes," Steve stumbled, still awestruck by her beauty and those vivacious green eyes.

"Amy Richards." She extended her hand, and they shook. "Nice to meet you."

"Nice to meet you, too," Steve replied.

He estimated that Amy was around his age, maybe a few years younger. She stood about five foot eight, thin and toned – a body sculpted from a rigorous regimen of healthy eating and exercise. She wore a white blouse with a dark skirt that stopped just below her knees; a pair of classy black and white pumps completed the outfit. Waves of reddish-brown hair that held natural body and curls fell to the middle of her shoulders.

"Let's talk in the conference room," Amy said, her green eyes flared with excitement and intrigue as she spoke.

She led Steve across the newsroom, which was empty at that hour; it appeared everyone had gone home for the evening except Amy and the receptionist. In the corner of the building, behind a glass wall and door, was the conference room with a large table surrounded by chairs. Steve took a seat at the table. Amy joined him.

"Excuse me, Mr. James, if I sound a bit apprehensive. But I can't seem to wrap my head around how Rebecca Turner's driver's license came into your possession. Nor how it was found in Pittsburgh."

Steve opened his laptop bag and pulled out the small white box and set it on the table. He did not open the lid. Amy's eyes drifted to the box, lingering on it with interest.

"Before I get into that," Steve began, lifting his hand away from the box. "I have a few other questions. Tell me how you got involved in Rebecca's case."

"Pretty simple, actually. I wanted to do a series on local cold cases. I went to my editor with the idea and he gave me the go-ahead. Rebecca's was the first story I wrote for that series."

"What made you want to write the cold case articles?"

"I'm from Hanover and was in high school when Rebecca disappeared. Rebecca's disappearance shook this community to its core. But after a while..." Amy trailed off, lost in some far-off thought; then, "It was like everyone moved on. I wanted to remind people that she was still missing, still out there. That was my motivation to start the series."

"So, you knew of her and her disappearance before writing the article?"

"Of course," Amy said. "Everyone around this area knows what happened to Rebecca Turner; it's not something people easily forget."

"Did you know Rebecca? Personally, I mean?"

She looked back at him with a measured gaze and shook her head. "No. I didn't. Though we did go to the same high school. I passed her in the halls regularly, but we weren't friends. Rebecca was two grades ahead of me and would have graduated in 2001, had she not disappeared."

Steve got the picture.

"So why didn't your article get the spotlight back on Rebecca? You just said, 'it's not something people easily forget.' One would think they would want to help find this girl."

"I don't know. The story got a few people talking, but not enough to get the entire community to put enough pressure on the Hanover PD or the DA to get the ball rolling again."

"Wouldn't they want to know what happened to Rebecca?" Steve asked.

"Life moves on, Mr. James," Amy said honestly. "So do people after a while. Twenty-five-years is a long time to ask for continued public support without answers or new leads to keep them invested."

"So, there's been no further developments in Rebecca's case?"

"None."

"What about the sheriff in Hanover? According to your article, he claims they're making headway."

Amy shook her head and her face tightened with annoyance. "Meeker's playing it safe for the public.

They're no closer to finding out what happened to Rebecca than they were when the case was still with Abbottstown PD."

"What makes you say that?"

"There are no new witnesses to question, and there isn't a stitch of new evidence. All roads to Rebecca lead to nowhere."

Steve nodded, but he knew different.

"Mr. James, you said over the phone that someone had come forward with information about Rebecca Turner, just not to me. What did you mean by that?"

Steve glanced at the box. Amy followed his gaze.

"Yesterday, when I returned home, there was a package outside my door." Steve placed his hand on top of the box. "This box."

Amy's eyes returned to Steve's, puzzled.

"Rebecca Turner's driver's license was inside," Steve said, opening the lid.

Amy grew tense with a mix of curiosity and trepidation, Steve saw as he reached inside and pulled out Rebecca's driver's license. He slid it across the table to her.

She studied the card intently; her face murky, she hesitated to pick the card up, as if touching it would pass some disease onto her. After a long moment, she reached out and lifted the license; the fine red dust fell from the plastic and sprinkled the tabletop.

"Does that look like Rebecca Turner's real driver's license to you?" Steve asked.

Amy's eyes slowly rose from the license. "It's hers. But I still don't understand–"

"Someone wants me to look into Rebecca's disappearance," Steve cut in. "That's why I received the box. But what I can't understand is why they chose me. They could have easily gone to you since you were already involved with the case."

"I wouldn't say I was involved with Rebecca's case. I wrote a follow-up story that was twenty-five-years too late. What I know is minimal at best."

"Still more than I know," Steve said.

Amy nodded. Though she knew more than Steve about Rebecca Turner's case, he knew she was just as in the dark as to why someone left the box and wanted him involved.

"There's something else," Steve resumed. "Along with the driver's license, there was a USB flash drive in the box."

Amy stiffened in the chair, her body rigid like someone had just walked over her future grave. The smooth, soft skin of her face twisted into a tight ball of disbelief.

"A flash drive? There was a flash drive found inside this box? What's on it?" Amy asked.

There was an urgency in her cadence now, one that had not been there before. Or was that fear Steve heard? He couldn't tell.

"A single video file." Steve paused, gauging if he should tell Amy anything further. "The video was the rape and torture of Rebecca Turner."

For a moment, Amy stared at him, trying to comprehend the unspeakable horror that befell Rebecca Turner. Her gaze then drifted back to the box, and her face curdled like she had just tasted spoiled milk.

"Are... you sure... it's... Rebecca?" Amy asked, stumbling over her words. She pushed herself away from the table, repulsed by the mere sight of the box.

"I'm confident it's Rebecca in the video," Steve said somberly.

Amy looked downright ill, with the pale, clammy appearance of a feverish person with the flu. Raising to her feet on quivering legs, her eyes remained fixed on the small white box, as if she feared it would suck her into its dark, hidden world.

Steve thought she might collapse back into the chair, but she kept her balance. However, she did waver from side to side a bit as she stood, like a drunk pushing themselves up from a barstool after one too many drinks.

"Are you okay?" Steve asked, unsure how to help or what had suddenly affected her. *Was it something I said?*

"I'll... be... right back."

She turned and opened the door of the conference room and walked out, leaving Steve alone and confused as to what the hell was going on. He watched her walk across the newsroom, past the cubicles where other reporters worked on their daily assignments, and then open a door along the back wall and disappear into the room beyond.

What the hell is she doing?

A moment later, Amy reappeared. In her right hand was a folded newspaper. She came back to the conference room, closed the door, and sat down.

"Before we continue, I need you to read this." Amy unfolded the newspaper, turned it around, and slid it across the table so Steve could read the headline.

KILLER CLAIMS SECOND VICTIM!
VIDEO OF VICTIM'S DEATH FOUND
WITH BODY!
by Amy Richards

Steve needed to read the headline twice to make sure his eyes had not deceived him. He felt his insides go squirmy like his stomach was filled with worms, and a cold chill shot through his body that frightened him.

He slowly lifted his eyes. Amy watched him with intense curiosity. He wanted to say something, anything, but he was at a loss for words.

"Read the article, Mr. James."

The desperate need for a drink clawed at him. He almost reached over and pulled the flask from his computer bag but held off.

Steve began to read.

The mutilated body of Martin Green, 46, a Hanover resident, was discovered Saturday morning in a cornfield by the land's owner, Joe Tully. Along with the body, police discovered a flash drive which contained on it a graphic video file of Green's murder.

Green is the second victim to have been found slain this year in Hanover.

The first victim, also a local resident of Hanover, was Kim Hooper, 45. Hooper's body was discovered last April by passing motorists (names withheld for anonymity), off Woodland Drive. A flash drive was also found with Hooper's body that captured his graphic demise on video.

Sheriff Ben Meeker provided a brief comment on the murders, saying only: "We are looking into their deaths. Right now, we have no suspects."

The article was short and to the point. There was no way this was a coincidence – two cases, both involving USB flash drives with violent videos on them? Were they connected with what happened to Rebecca?

Steve suspected Amy was not getting much information

from the local PD, just like she had not gotten much from them on Rebecca's case. For the moment, they were keeping the investigation tight-lipped until they knew more. When Steve looked up, he found Amy staring at him, probing his eyes as if the answer to all this strangeness rested there. After a moment, she spoke.

"By the look on your face, I suspect you didn't know any of that," Amy said, her eyes motioning to the paper between Steve's hands.

Still too stunned to speak, Steve slowly shook his head. What fucked-up, twisted mystery had he been pulled into?

"I..." Steve started, but words escaped him. The only thing he knew for sure was that he wanted a cigarette and a drink, and not necessarily in that order. After some time, while trying to recover from the figurative sock to the jaw, he spoke. "Are these crimes connected to what happened to Rebecca, Amy?"

"Until you showed up, I would have said no. But what are the chances of you receiving a flash drive containing a video of Rebecca Turner's torture, while two other victims turned up dead with similar videos, all within a few months of each other?"

"Highly unlikely," Steve said. "Unless–"

"Unless someone wanted you to connect the crimes."

Steve didn't like where this was leading. It made no sense. Why would he have been sought out to find what happened only to Rebecca when both her case, and what happened to these two men, were possibly connected? What was his role in all of this? *Where do I fit in? There has to be a reason. What the hell am I missing?*

"Are you okay, Mr. James?" Amy asked, noticing the ashen look on Steve's face. "Can I get you a glass of water?"

"Steve. Call me, Steve. No, thank you." Anxiety tightened his chest. "Have you seen the Green and Hooper videos?"

"No. Sherriff Meeker isn't allowing anyone to see them, outside of law enforcement, that is. I've asked – several times in fact – but he won't budge on his decision to keep the press at arm's length on this case."

Steve understood. Sheriff Meeker was only releasing essential information to the media and the public, while retaining specific details about Green and Hooper's murders. A tactic used by law enforcement to keep a possible suspect in the dark and to sift out the crazies from coming forward with a false confession, which would happen.

"Do you think Sheriff Meeker would be willing to talk to me?" Steve asked.

"I'm not sure anyone would be willing to talk with you, Mr. James – Steve."

"Oh?"

"People around these parts don't like outsiders sticking their noses where they don't belong."

"We're talking about murder, Amy. I would think–"

"Doesn't matter. No one is going to talk to you. You can try, you can go door to door asking your questions, but be prepared to have them slammed in your face."

Steve didn't like obstacles in his way while he searched for the truth. But, if what Amy said was correct, and people around the area were unwilling to talk to an outsider, then how would he get to the bottom of this story?

What's the point of my involvement if I can't get anywhere? Steve wondered.

"What do you suggest?" he asked.

"That we work together on this."

Steve studied Amy. He had no problems working with

another reporter on a story; never had sharing a by-line bothered him. But what did Amy have to gain out of all of this? Exposure. Fame. A one-way ticket out of writing for the *Hanover Daily Record* and go to work for the big-league papers like the *New York Times* or the *Washington Post*, or hell, even the *Pittsburgh Tribune*.

If they broke this story, the floodgates would be open, and with Steve's involvement, the story would gain national exposure for sure. Amy would be thrust into the spotlight, sought out by other news outlets to hear the story firsthand and to be offered possible job opportunities. It was a story that could make a career. Any reporter would want in on this investigation – Steve sure as hell would have if he were in Amy's shoes.

"Look," Amy continued, "if you're worried that I would steal the story–"

Steve held up his hand. "I'm not worried about you stealing the story, Amy. I've worked with other reporters in the past, and I don't have a problem with it. If you think no one is willing to talk to me because I'm a stranger, then I believe you. I've run into this situation before, so it helps to have someone who knows the people and area. It makes them feel comfortable." He tried to align his running thoughts. "We'll need to conduct our own investigation, do our own interviews of those involved. Do you think you could arrange that for us?"

"I believe I can set that up."

"Good."

"What about Green and Hooper?" Amy asked. "If their murders are connected to Rebecca's disappearance some-how, then we're going to need to speak with Sheriff Meeker and see those videos."

"We're going to have to link the cases before going to

Meeker," Steve said. "Without something tangible connecting them, he's not going to speak with us."

"But you have Rebecca's driver's license? The video? The box you received that they were delivered in?" Amy's eyes drifted to it again. "Isn't that enough?"

"No," Steve said, shaking his head. "We need more."

Chapter Five

Aﬀter the meeting with Amy ended, Steve returned to the Abbottstown Inn. The day had been long and exhausting, fatigue cramped his joints and the muscles around his neck and lower back. His mind felt heavy and sluggish, confused with troubled thoughts that were not easily dismissed.

Booze would help.

He stopped at the bar and ordered himself a shot and a bottle of Jameson to take back to his room. While waiting for the bottle, he nursed the shot of whiskey. There was no one else at the bar that evening, other than himself and the female bartender. The solitude of drinking alone, with only his thoughts to keep him company, was peaceful after such a stressful day.

Back in his room, Steve sat down at the desk, lit a cigarette with the Zippo, and opened the bottle of whiskey and poured himself another drink. He had made sure to book a smoking room. While sipping the liquor, he watched the blue smoke circle off the end of the cigarette hypnotically, lost in absent thoughts as the alcohol warmed his cold blood.

The reprieve from thinking about Rebecca Turner was welcome, comfortable even. But Steve's amnesty was short-lived – he had to look into the devil's work.

Pulling the laptop out of its bag, he sat it on the desk, and turned it on. Once booted up, he stared at the computer's screen, as if going further and opening the video would unleash a great wrath upon the world. Maybe it would, once the video became public knowledge, a digital plague that would sweep across the earth, bringing with it the disease of truth. *A disease someone wants spread.*

Could he stomach watching the video a second time? Steve wasn't sure. He had averted his eyes last night, unable to focus on some of the more brutal moments captured. What had he missed? There were clues hidden in the video. Steve was sure of that much. He just had to find them first.

Easier said than done.

He took another sip of the whiskey. His tongue and throat felt numb, and his fingers and toes were tingling with the alcohol's magic. His mind began to relax; the agitated demons grew still.

But the question remained: why had he been chosen to investigate this case? He was a crime reporter from Pittsburgh who had zero connection or knowledge of Rebecca Turner until yesterday. To be thrust into the middle of a twenty-three-year-old cold case, one a long way from his beat, was not only strange but categorically disturbing. Not only that, there was the possibility that the recent murders of Martin Green and Kim Hooper might somehow link back to what had happened to Rebecca.

Someone wanted him involved. Wanted him to know what happened to Rebecca. But why had they chosen him?

And, if the recent murders of Green and Hooper were connected, why had they not sent those videos over as well?

There must be a reason.

Finally, Steve opened the video file marked REBECCA on the computer. He finished off his snort of whiskey, then poured himself another. *You're going to need it*, he reminded himself. He thought about calling Charlie but decided to hold off until after he viewed the video again. He needed more than the half-ass theory about the crimes being connected before speaking with his boss.

He hit PLAY...

The video snapped on. The image was on a doorway as two shirtless men with hard, muscular bodies began to materialize from the darkness, like demons emerging from some shadowy underworld realm. Black leather masks, which resembled executioner's hoods, concealed their identities. Metal zippers made up the mouth holes. To Steve, these men looked like they had stepped out of Anthony Palazzo's S&M magazine *La Prostituée Bizarre*, which he had used to help launder the DeLuca Crime Family's dirty money.

Anger tightened Steve's chest, just like it had the night before when he first watched the video. Rebecca Turner, with her hands and feet bound, was dragged into the room. She was nude except for a pair of white underwear that had turned the color of rust and she was covered head to toe with what looked like caked-on dirt; it was hard to tell with the video resolution.

Steve wanted to look away. Wanted to pry his eyes from the computer screen as he helplessly watched Rebecca thrash around, her head jerking in odd angles, causing her long, blonde hair to flail like a nest of irritated snakes, while trying to get away from her captors. Her screams shot from the small speakers of the laptop, piercing Steve's ears as if a needle had been driven into the drums.

He reached for the volume control and lowered it to a more ingestible level. *Is there such a thing?* Steve wondered. He didn't need to have the cops called on him by a guest, thinking he was torturing someone in his room.

Looking back to the screen, he studied the room in the video. It was plastered with an ugly yellowish-green wallpaper. A single wooden red table sat under a work light suspended from the ceiling. A soft white hue in the shape of a bell glowed over the table, making the room seem dingier somehow. Behind the red table was a single window filled with the blackness of night; it had not been covered over with a shade.

Steve paused the video there. He lifted the cigarette from the ashtray and took a long drag. It tasted awful, but he did not stub it out; it was his only link to reality while he watched. With the cigarette dangling from his lips, he began to write a few notes onto the legal pad.

> *- There are no blinds on the window? Would someone not be able to see inside, to witness what they were doing?*
> *-Rebecca continues to scream without being gagged – that comes later in the video. Were they not worried about her cries being heard?*
> *-Were they in a remote location, far away from civilization? If so, where?*

When he was finished writing, Steve picked up the glass and took a sip of whiskey. He steeled himself, took a deep breath, knowing the worst was still to come, and continued the video.

For the next fifteen minutes, Steve watched in utter disgust as Rebecca continued to try to fight off her two attackers, while another one filmed the event unfolding. Eventually, she was yanked off the floor and thrown down onto the red table on her stomach. Her hands and ankles were unbound from the rope and then she was handcuffed to the table's legs; her body bent over the edge of the table in a backward L shape.

The sickness in his stomach worsened. He wanted to vomit, but more so, he did not want to watch the rest of the atrocity unfold. *What would make someone do this to her?*

Rebecca's moans began to softly fill the room then. Steve bit down on his lip, hard. He wasn't sure why he did this; maybe to ease his own mental torment, memories of his own past while being tortured and filmed in a cave in Afghanistan, or was he doing it to relate to what Rebecca was going through, as a way to feel at least some of her pain?

When Rebecca began begging for mercy, to be spared a fate worse than death, Steve felt tears moisten his eyes. He already knew these men would not listen, and Rebecca's pleas would fall on deaf ears; they only had one thing on their minds...

He took a long swallow of the whiskey. It warmed him uncomfortably and he felt his face flush. When he looked back to the screen, the second masked man on the video was climbing up onto the table. Steve reached out to the screen, as if to stop him from what he was about to do.

Foolish. There was nothing he could do but watch helplessly as the man straddled Rebecca, grabbed a handful of her blonde hair and yanked her head back violently. Tears streamed down her dirty face. Rebecca stared glassy-eyed off into the distance; the realization of what was going to happen if she didn't cooperate caused the muscles in her face to spasm and her eyes to dance wildly with fear. Small, wounded-animal-like moans seeped from her mouth.

"Stop your moaning, you fuckin' stupid cow!" the masked man said with a low, even voice.

You son of a bitch! For a moment, Steve took pleasure in vivid thoughts of what he would like to do to those three men. He would make them feel every ounce of Rebecca's pain and more if given the chance.

It was then, in a fluid-like movement, the masked man pulled the red ball-gag out of his pocket, shoved it into Rebecca's mouth and pulled it taut. He then bent and licked the side of her face with an abnormally long tongue that would have made Gene Simmons envious.

A shiny, wet residue of saliva, like snail slime remained on her flesh. Repulsion consumed Steve's entire being, and he felt himself wither, like a tulip after the sun goes down, with disgust. The masked man rose and smiled. It was then that Steve saw for the first time the chipped right incisor through the mouth hole of the mask.

Steve made a note of the chipped tooth. Then he heard the person behind the camera giggle, snapping his attention back to the video. It was a high-pitched giggle that sounded, to him, like an overly excitable schoolboy that had yet to go through puberty.

On the screen, the man with the chipped tooth produced a large Bowie knife from the back of his pants; its sharp steel blade reflected onto the leather mask. He held the large knife in front of himself, admiring it as if he were holding King Arthur's sword, Excalibur.

Steve paused the video again. He needed a break. The footage was as horrific as the first time he watched it, maybe more so now that he'd forced himself to pay attention and not look away like the night before. He needed to digest the video in bits and pieces; it was the only way to get through it.

Lighting another cigarette, his last one having burned down to the filter in the ashtray, he drew in deeply, letting the smoke steel his shaky nerves. He drained the remainder of whiskey and poured himself a third, just for good measure.

Digging into the video's origins was sure to lead Steve down some profane paths. But how far down the depravity hole was he willing to venture to expose the truth, and how much of himself would he lose in the process?

It bothered him that Rebecca's story reminded him of his own situation. Like Rebecca, Steve had also been tortured in front of a camera, by Taliban fighters trying to prove their warped views to the world. But as horrifying as what he had endured while being held hostage in a cave in the Tora Bora Mountains was, he could not begin to imagine what it must have been like for Rebecca. Where Steve had seen a light of hope, an opening that forced him to act in such a way he never thought himself capable, Rebecca must have seen none.

A sharp pain sliced across Steve's chest and he rubbed the spot just below his left nipple.

This was all a game to these men. Smiling and laughing while they tormented a helpless teenage girl who was nothing more than a warm body to abuse. And, when they were done having their fun, what had happened to Rebecca? Did they kill her? Discard her remains like animal trimmings at a slaughterhouse? These were not men. They were monsters.

There's a special place in Hell for men like this, Steve thought.

He brought the glass to his lips but was surprised to find

he had already finished the whiskey off. He did not remember taking a sip. *How many drinks am I up to now?* he wondered. *It doesn't matter. Fuck it.*

He poured himself another and took a long swallow that drained half the glass. The booze was not strong enough to dull his senses and get him through the rest of the video without feeling downright ill and pissed off simultaneously.

He looked back to his notebook and wrote:

-Man with chipped incisor (Broken Tooth) – who is he?
-The cameraman giggles like a kid – who is he?
-The second masked man has no identifiable markings – who is he?
-How did they get Rebecca there – kidnapping?
-Did she willingly go with them – did she know them?
-Did they know her?
-Was she followed the night she disappeared?

When Steve finished writing, he returned to the video.

On the screen, Broken Tooth, which Steve was now calling him, took a handful of Rebecca's blonde hair, bunched it together ponytail-like between his thumb and forefinger, and began to cut it with the knife. As he severed the hair, strands fell onto Rebecca's bare back. Rebecca tried to wiggle from Broken Tooth's powerful grasp. The sound of handcuffs clacking against the table's legs was dull, hollow, just like these men; another muffled cry seeped from Rebecca's lips, only now the ball-gag made it sound like a wet and slurpy sucking sound.

No one heard Rebecca's screams that night. No one who cared about her came to save her from a hellish nightmare.

Steve swallowed. His throat felt dry and his mouth tasted the way cigarette filters smell – smokey and sour – and his lips were sticky with booze. He knew the next morning he would awaken with what he liked to call *the morning mouth of anguish* from the previous night's overindulgences – he'd been down this road before while working a story, though none as horrible as this.

After Rebecca's hair was cut free from her head, Broken Tooth brought the tresses to his mask and inhaled deeply. Steve saw the man's eyes glaze over. The scent was euphoric, intoxicating to him, and a slow pleasurable smile became visible through the mask's mouth hole, showing the chipped front tooth once more. Then, from his pants pocket, Broken Tooth produced a large Ziplock bag and stuffed the hair inside, then resealed it and placed it aside.

A keepsake, Steve realized. *He's bagging the hair as a memento.* The realization disturbed him. How sick and twisted it was to keep the hair in a Ziplock bag, preserving its freshness. He knew scent was linked to memory more than any of the other senses. Broken Tooth didn't just want to remember this night, he wanted to relive it over and over and over.

Back on the screen, Steve noticed the camera was being mounted on a tripod, and the third man, who giggled like a schoolboy, stepped in front of the lens for the first time. Then the three men disrobed, except for their masks, and they advanced on Rebecca, circling around her like a pack of wolves to their supper. Steve felt helpless. Again, he wanted to be able to reach into the screen and pluck Rebecca off that red table and return her to safety. But when Rebecca began to scream, even muffled, they were unlike anything he had heard before.

Pressing the MUTE button on the computer, the video

fell into a thick, foreboding silence that unnerved him unlike any silence had before. The torture went on for thirty-five minutes, absent of sound. When it was all over, and not a moment before, did Steve turn the sound back on, sickened by what he had witnessed in its entirety.

It was quiet on the screen now, with exception to the heavy, labored breathing from the three men. They stood naked in the room; their toned bodies covered in a sheen of sweat and blood that glistened under the dim light above. They began congratulating one another with high fives and pats on the back, or each other's bare asses.

Broken Tooth stepped out of frame. When he returned, he was holding a lighter and a cigar. He lit the cigar and then arched his head toward the ceiling and blew a plume of smoke that filled the room. He looked like a man who had just finished a satisfying meal and was having an after-dinner smoke.

The display made Steve sick to his stomach, and a fire burned so hot inside he could have spit flames. He wanted to make these men pay for what they had done, wanted to see them suffer the same way Rebecca had.

Rebecca lay motionless on the table now. She was battered and bloody. Her chest rose and fell slowly, the breaths of a person on the verge of death. If there was any fight or dignity left in her, it had been stripped away, she lay as helpless as a wounded animal dying on the side of the road.

Steve was sure she was still alive at this point.

But what happened to you after the camera was turned off? Did he really want to know? He supposed he already did know Rebecca's fate, since she has not been seen for twenty-five years.

Steve lifted the cigarette to his lips and drew in, while

watching the man with the obnoxious schoolboy-like laugh turn around and start toward the camera. As he neared, Steve caught something he had missed the first time he'd viewed the video – his disgust blinding him to the clues on the screen by having to look away many times last night.

He snapped forward and punched PAUSE.

Laughing Boy's bare chest and flat stomach took up most of the frame on the computer's screen. Steve inched his face closer. Though the picture was blurry, soft, almost out of focus, he could still make out...

A tattoo! A fucking tattoo!

A skull and crossbones were tattooed on Laughing Boy's right pectoral muscle. Three words were written in a semi-circle over the skull and one word was written underneath. The skin art looked professional, not some homemade job done in someone's garage or basement. Nor was this jail-house ink. No, this tattoo was accomplished with care by a skilled hand.

But there was a problem. Steve could not make out what the words said. The lo-fi definition of the video was too blurry, as if he were looking at the frozen frame through oil-smudged glass.

It was twenty past eight. He knew Ricky had probably gone home for the evening. Reaching for his phone, he dialed Ricky's cell phone, hoping he had taken his home-work with him.

"Please tell me you have the flash drive at home with you right now," Steve said when Ricky answered.

"Yeah. But I haven't looked at it yet."

"I might have found something on the video. Something I need your help with."

Ricky remained quiet. Steve wondered if his hesitation

had anything to do with his understandable reluctance to watch the video again.

"Go to the end of the video – to the 55:26-minute mark," Steve said. "And pause the screen."

"Okay."

Steve heard Ricky fumbling around with his computer for a few moments. Finally, he came back on the line.

"I'm there," Ricky said.

"Can you make out what the words above and below the tattoo say?"

There was silence on the phone, and Steve felt his muscles grow tense as he waited for a response. He lit another cigarette, hoping it would quell his jumping nerves.

"It's hard to see," Ricky said. "It's so blurry from the low video–"

"What do you *think* it says, Ricky?" Steve cut him off.

More silence, thick and uncomfortable, as Ricky continued to study the video clip.

"Would you mind if I called you back? I'd like to try something to see if I can enhance the image."

That was not what Steve wanted to hear. He needed answers, now. But if Ricky wanted to try some new-fangled tech trick to help them see the tattooed words clearer, he was all for it, even if that meant he had to wait. Besides, he needed to call Charlie; this would give him the opportunity to do so.

"Sure."

He disconnected the call and then phoned his boss.

"How's it going?" Charlie said upon answering.

"Might be getting somewhere," Steve said. He filled Charlie in on some of the clues he'd picked up in the video and that he might have found something substantial with the tattoo, but that he was at a standstill until Ricky got back to him. "There's more, Charlie, though I'm not sure how, or even if it connects to Rebecca yet."

"Oh?" Charlie seemed intrigued.

"There were two other murders recently. Two men who had their deaths captured on video, then placed onto a flash drive and left with their bodies."

Charlie was silent for a long moment. Steve wondered what was going through his mind.

"Do you believe these recent murders are somehow connected to what happened to Rebecca?" Charlie asked.

"I don't have any evidence to prove or disprove they're connected at this point."

Charlie again grew quiet. Though Steve could not see his boss, he knew him well enough to know he was chewing on his lower lip while mulling the situation over; Charlie was not one who made rash, quick decisions, especially when it came to getting all the details of a story covered.

"Whatever I stumbled into might be bigger than we expected," Steve said.

"You didn't stumble into anything. You were dragged into it."

No words ever rang truer in Steve's mind.

"I'm going to need more time," Steve said.

"Yeah, I think you will. I'll push your deadline back a week, that should give you a substantial amount of time to dig into this." Charlie paused, and Steve knew what he was going to say next. "I'll have to go to the police now. We can't sit on evidence that long. The police need to know what we have, when we got it, and they'll want to talk to you."

"Can you keep them off my back, at least until I return to Pittsburgh?"

"I'll cover for you. But you keep me posted on what you find, got it?"

"I will."

There was a halt in the conversation then, as if neither of them knew what to say. When Charlie came back on the line, his voice was softer, less business-like.

"How are you holding up?"

"What do you mean?" Steve asked, while refilling his glass with whiskey.

"You know what I mean. It can't be easy for you, looking into what happened to this girl. You're close to this one, closer to this than any other story you've written before."

"What happened to Rebecca is different than what happened to me."

"Is it?" Charlie asked. "Torture is torture, no matter how, where, or who it happened to." Steve took the shot and held the whiskey in his mouth for a moment, letting it burn his tongue. "I just want to know you can handle this story. That I can count on you."

"Have I ever let you down before?" Steve said, after swallowing the shot.

Charlie said nothing.

Just then, Steve's phone beeped with an incoming call.

"Gotta go. Ricky's calling me back," Steve said. "I'll text you with whatever he found."

Steve clicked over to Ricky.

"Please tell me you have something," Steve said.

"I do. I was able to take a screen shot of the video. I ran it through a sharpening filter program—"

"What's it say, Ricky?" Steve interrupted. "I don't need to know how you did it, just what the words say."

"Above the skull it says, I STOLE THE, and the word below says, BOOTY."

"I stole the booty," Steve said, writing the words down in his notes. "Is that some kind of sick joke?"

Ricky said nothing. Was there anything to say, Steve wondered? He thanked Ricky for his time and hung up. He texted Charlie what Ricky had found and that he was proceeding tomorrow with the investigation and would also begin looking into the Green and Hooper murders to see if they were connected to Rebecca somehow. He did not, however, tell Charlie he was working with a local reporter.

He would keep that information close to his chest until he had enough evidence to convince Charlie that he had no other choice but to bring Amy onboard to help write the article. Steve knew it was deceiving to Charlie, but Amy was putting herself at risk by helping him, maybe more than himself, because she was a local and could face backlash for her involvement.

The three men who had done this to Rebecca wanted to keep their crime hidden; there was no telling what they would do to keep the truth from being exposed.

But the truth must be exposed, Steve thought angrily. *No matter the cost.* These three men needed to pay for what they did to Rebecca, both in the public eye and in a court of law. Still, the truth could be a double-edged sword that always cut both ways; exposing what happened to Rebecca would not undo what had been done to her.

He fell back onto the bed, so exhausted he was having trouble keeping his eyes open. He wondered if it was the booze, the stress of the day, or the video. *All of the above.*

As sleep began to overtake him, Steve watched the swirled plaster above his head begin to move in a counter-clockwise pattern. Soon, a black vortex appeared in the center of the swirling plaster. He felt his body and mind begin to slip into that vortex, and he did not fight when sleep took him.

Chapter Six

The next morning, Steve chewed two aspirins to dull his headache and took a long, hot shower, letting the water run over him for twenty minutes. Afterward, he dressed, brushed the *morning mouth of anguish* away, gathered his things, and made his way down to the dining area of the Abbottstown Inn.

Hunger was a far-off thought, and the headache remained, though the aspirin had helped take a bit of the edge off. He hoped a cup of coffee would clear away the previous evening's overindulgence of booze, cigarettes, and the video.

He was in the middle of pouring himself a to-go cup of coffee when his phone rang.

"Hello," he answered.

"Good morning, Steve," Amy said; her voice was chipper, awake, alive with energy and excitement. *She must be a morning person*, Steve thought. "I've made arrangements to meet with Dennis Turner, Rebecca's father, at nine. Joe Tully at ten. And Sheriff Winslow around eleven at his bait and tackle shop. I'm on my way to Abbottstown to pick you up."

"Perfect. Meet you out front."

———

Amy pulled her car to the curb in front of the Turner home, which was a two-story Cape Cod with tan siding and red shutters. The house sat on a flat grassy plot on Water Street, and a sidewalk connected the neighborhood of homes that were similar in structure and size to the Turner house.

They made their way up the stone pathway to the front door, where Amy rang the doorbell. It was answered a moment later by a tall, broad-shouldered man in his late sixties. His hair was dark, except at the temples where it had grayed. He had a square jaw with a week's worth growth of salt and pepper beard. His dark eyes were deep-set and held the painful torment of his past. He wore a pair of blue jeans, tan work boots, and an untucked red and green button-down flannel shirt.

"Hi, Amy," Dennis said. He stepped from inside the house and gave Amy a hug. When they separated, he looked at Steve and extended his hand. "You must be Steve James."

Steve shook Dennis's hand. "Yes. I'm sorry we have to meet this way, Mr. Turner."

Dennis's dark eyes grew murky and his jaw twitched, as if he were trying to suppress the inner turmoil that had been eating away at him for the last twenty-five years of his life.

"Please, come inside," he said, stepping aside to allow Steve and Amy to enter.

Dennis closed the door and then led them into the living room where he told them to have a seat on the sofa. He offered them coffee. Both Steve and Amy declined.

"Amy tells me you're from Pittsburgh," Dennis said, taking a seat in a recliner across from the sofa. "And that you're here to help with her follow-up story on Rebecca?"

Steve suspected Amy had told him that they were working on the follow-up story as a way to get an interview. It was not exactly the truth, but it was close enough and he would run with it.

"That's correct," Steve replied, pulling his notebook from the laptop bag.

"And how is it that you got involved, Mr. James?"

"It's complicated," Steve replied, glancing at Amy.

"Complicated? Complicated how?" Dennis asked, turning his head slightly while eyeing Steve suspiciously.

"Just complicated." Steve didn't want to tell him the truth about how he'd gotten involved, not yet anyway. "I want to express my condolences for your loss. I won't pretend to understand how hard these last twenty-five years have been for you and your family."

"Thank you."

"Our goal is to put the pieces of this mystery together, Mr. Turner, in hopes of finding out what happened to Rebecca, and to bring closure."

"Closure would be nice," Dennis said. His eyes drifted away from Steve to his lap, where his hands tightly gripped his thighs.

"I'm sure it would. Are you ready to start?" Steve asked.

Dennis nodded and lifted his right hand, indicating he was.

"I'd like to get to know a little about Rebecca. Would you mind telling me what she was like?"

Dennis's eyes drifted away again, lost somewhere in the past where his daughter was still alive, Steve presumed. When he returned his gaze to Steve, the pain of her absence resonated on his face; a hollow spot in his soul.

"Rebecca was a great kid. Smart. Funny. Kind. Just like her mother was." He smiled. "I remember the day she came to me and told me she wanted to be a veterinarian. She loved animals so I wasn't surprised all that much. She was planning on going off to college to study in the field after high school."

"I'll bet she would have made a great doctor," Amy said.

"I believe she would have. Rebecca had her mother's brains, that's for sure. Me..." He looked down as if appraising himself. "Not so much in the brains department."

"What was Rebecca like to be around?" Steve asked.

"She was never a problem. She was mostly happy as a child. Smiled a lot – which was infectious." Steve remembered Rebecca's smile from her driver's license photo and how it seemed to jump out at him.

"Did you ever have any problems with Rebecca when she was a teenager?" Steve asked.

"No. She really was a good kid. Better than I was at her age. But, again, Rebecca took after her mother in that aspect, thankfully. Rebecca never talked back, always did what we asked of her, worked hard in school, made her curfew when one was set. Like I said, she was a really good kid, which makes what happened even harder to comprehend."

"And your wife?" Steve asked. "Where is she now?"

Dennis's lips tightened into a small, painful grimace. "Kathy, Rebecca's mother, passed on a few years ago from stomach cancer."

This just keeps getting grimmer and grimmer, Steve thought. "I'm sorry for your loss, Mr. Turner," Steve said.

"I swear Kathy's cancer stemmed from Rebecca's disappearance. It grew inside from not knowing what happened to our daughter; it ate away at my wife little by little, leaving nothing but a skeleton of a woman by the end." His eyes were wet with tears. "My wife died not knowing what happened to her daughter, Mr. James. It was all Kathy wanted before she went – her dying wish – to know the truth so she could rest peacefully."

Steve cleared his throat. The emotional heaviness of Dennis's story weighed upon him uncomfortably. Steve had said that he wanted to bring Dennis closure, and hopefully he could, but he would not be able to do the same for Kathy Turner. It upset him immensely that he could not fulfill a dying woman's last wish.

Steve shifted gears then. "Let's go back to the night your daughter disappeared. The night of January 5, 1999. Could you tell me about your last interaction with Rebecca?"

It was not uncommon for a witness or loved ones to have trouble remembering the details before the crime occurred; people tended to block the bad stuff out just so they could continue living. But the devil was in the details, and right now, Steve needed the details.

"I saw Rebecca just before she headed out that evening, if my memory serves me correct," Dennis said. "As I recall, I hadn't seen her much that week – I was stuck working twelve-hour shifts – so when I did see her that night, it was only for a few minutes."

"Rebecca was getting ready to go to the party when you saw her?" Amy inquired.

Dennis nodded. "She was already in Kathy's car, ready to head out when I pulled into the driveway."

"Do you know about what time that was?" Amy asked.

"I believe it was around five-thirty." He paused, trying

to recall a twenty-five-year-old conversation that happened only hours before his world was turned upside down. "No! No, six, yes, six."

"Did you speak with her?" Steve asked.

"Sure. I said *hi,* asked about school and how things were going."

"Did Rebecca seem normal?" Steve asked.

"Yeah. She was upbeat and happy – her normal self."

"So, there was no reason not to let her go out that evening."

Dennis shook his head.

"Did Rebecca mention when she was planning on returning home?" Amy asked.

"She didn't. But she knew her curfew was midnight." Dennis swallowed and his throat made a grinding sound. The memory of the last time he'd spoken to his daughter was reopening old wounds, wounds that would never mend.

"Did Rebecca tell you where she was headed, or where this party was being held?" Steve asked.

Dennis shook his head slowly, still lost in the last moments spent with his daughter. "Not that I recall."

"Did that make you uncomfortable, not knowing where your daughter was going?" Steve asked.

Dennis blinked, as if surfacing from a deep trance. "You don't have kids, do you, Mr. James?"

"I do not."

"Then you don't understand that every time your child leaves your protection, you become uncomfortable. So, to answer your question: yes. Yes, I was uncomfortable with her going to the party. But..." He sighed and his eyes drifted into the past again.

Steve continued, unabashed; he had heard the parent

speech about not having kids before. "Did Rebecca go to the party with anyone? A girlfriend or a boyfriend?"

"Rebecca wasn't seeing anyone, at least, not that I knew about. But she was going to pick up her friend, Wendy Brewer, that night. They were going to the party together."

"Was there anyone else at the party that Rebecca knew? Other friends from school perhaps?" Steve asked.

"If there were other kids from Hanover High there, I wouldn't know."

"Were Rebecca and Wendy close?" Amy asked.

A shadow darkened Dennis's face, as if Amy had just brought up some taboo question that could not be spoken in the Turner home.

"You could say that. Wendy lived next door until ninety-five, when her parents moved to downtown Hanover. The girls rekindled their friendship in Junior High."

"By your tone, I get the feeling you didn't think fondly of Wendy," Steve said.

"I liked her when she was little."

"What does that mean?" Amy asked, looking irritated with Dennis's snarky remark.

"It means what it means, Ms. Richards," Dennis said. "We knew Wendy well. And when she was little, she was such a smart, funny, outgoing child. But by the time Rebecca and Wendy got to high school, Wendy had changed."

"Do you know what happened to cause such a drastic shift in her personality?" Steve asked.

"I suspect it had something to do with Wendy's home life."

"And what was that like?" Amy asked.

"Rough," Dennis said bluntly. He looked away; his eyes

softened. "Her parents were... well, they weren't the best people, let's put it that way. My wife and I wanted Rebecca to find another friend – I know that sounds selfish and cruel – but we saw the writing on the wall and where Wendy was heading. We didn't want her problems affecting our daughter, understand? But at the same time, we knew the only good person in Wendy's life was Rebecca."

He paused in thought, then continued. "We had hoped with Rebecca's influence, Wendy would make better life choices. Sadly, it didn't work. I've since heard she was mixed up with some bad people who got her into drugs and God knows what else."

"Do you have the names of these people?" Amy asked.

Dennis shook his head. "No. Sorry."

"Did Wendy tell you what she knew about that night, Mr. Turner?" Steve asked.

"Wendy wasn't allowed to speak with me directly. Sheriff Winslow kept us apart and reminded me that speaking to her could jeopardize the investigation. I didn't want to do that. I just wanted my daughter back. So, taking Winslow's advice, I kept my distance from her."

Dennis's face jumped with disgust. When he spoke again, his voice was a hoarse whisper. "But from what Winslow told me... I don't think he believed a goddamn word of her statement. Not a goddamn word."

"Winslow thought Wendy lied about what she knew?" Amy asked.

"He had his suspicions but couldn't prove them. I know he followed up with her several times but got nowhere. Wendy never changed her story and there was not one inconsistency. I would think cracks would appear in her story at some point, but they never did."

"And you, Mr. Turner?" Steve asked. "What do you believe?"

Dennis raised his shoulders, his face awash with anger. "I believe either Wendy's a really good liar, or what she told us is only part of the truth."

Steve shifted his gaze to the living room and noticed there were no pictures of Rebecca in the home. He found this odd, but not uncommon. People tended to bury bad memories, pack everything away that reminded them of their loved ones. The daily reminder was too much for some to bear.

"Do you know where Wendy is now?" Steve asked. "We'd like to speak with her."

"How would I know where she's at, Mr. James? I haven't seen or spoken to Wendy in twenty-five years; it's not like we kept in touch after Rebecca disappeared."

"You're right," Steve said. "I apologize for asking such a dumb question."

Dennis waved him off. "No need to apologize. You're doing your job – I get it. At least you two care enough about Rebecca to actively pursue what happened to her – more than Hanover PD is doing, that's for sure. It means a lot to me. And, if my wife were still here, she would tell you the same."

The room grew quiet then, and Steve instinctively knew further questions would be useless, resulting in speculative answers that would get them nowhere.

"Thank you, Mr. Turner," Steve said. "We'll be in touch if anything comes up."

"What do you know about Martin Green?" Steve asked, once he and Amy were back in the car and on their way to speak with Joe Tully, the farmer who found Green's remains.

"He was a family man, married with two kids. Owned a lawncare service called Green's Lawn and Garden. He was quite popular around town. The kind of guy that everyone knew, even if they didn't *know* him."

Steve got the picture. "Sure. So, he had no enemies then."

"You'd be hard-pressed to find someone to even speak ill of Martin Green. And that's what makes his murder even more shocking, more so than Hooper's: that it happened to such a well-respected member of our community."

"Tell me about Kim Hooper."

"Not much to tell. Guy was a loner with no family. He worked at a papermill, in the shipping department loading trucks, and lived out along Lake Marburg in a small cabin."

"Were you able to question any of Hooper's co-workers? Or Green's wife?"

"No."

"Why not? They seem like valuable sources."

"I wanted to conduct interviews. But my editor wanted me to keep the focus on the murders for the time being. Lean and factual. He said we could run a follow-up story later when things calmed down. His concern, and in hindsight I agree with him now, was for public safety. If there was a killer on the loose, the community needed to be informed, especially after Green's murder. People scared and looking for answers. Hanover's a relatively small community. So, two murders inside seven months piqued people's concerns and had the community on edge."

Last year alone there were fifty-eight murders in and

around Pittsburgh. With a murder-rate as low as two, Pittsburgh would have been celebrated for taking control of crime. But in Hanover, two murders were considered a travesty that *piqued people's concerns,* as Amy had put it.

Steve guessed he, like so many others around the Pittsburgh area, had become so accustomed to hearing about murders that a sort of disconnect had formed, making them nothing more than background noise. He suspected a part of him, a part of all of them, had grown numb to the misfortunes of others; after a while it was just another day-in-the-life of a Pittsburgher.

But people in Hanover had not witnessed such violence before, especially toward a man who held such respect in the community. The murders had shocked them, rocking their town to its foundation, upturning everything they believed about rural America to be true – that it could not happen here.

Steve had heard it said often that small-town America was safer than the cities – that small towns were *the place to raise a family.* But he knew there was no such thing as a *safe* America. *Safety is an illusion.* There was nowhere truly safe. Not the big cities. Not the small towns. A killer was on the prowl, and the streets and backroads of Hanover were the hunting grounds. Safety was an illusion for this community, reinforced by blood.

The ugly truthfulness of his thoughts bothered him. He turned his attention out the window to a pasture where a herd of cows roamed in the snow looking for bare grass to feed on. The day was dreary with an overcast sky. A cold, misty rain made the day wet and raw, and the snow-covered landscape resembled glass. He disliked cold, rainy days but found there was some strange part of him that enjoyed the tranquil stillness they possessed, like the world was cleansing its sins.

"I take it your silence means you're surprised to hear that about Hanover?" Amy asked.

"Hmmm?" Steve turned back to her. "I'm sorry. What?"

"That such atrocities could happen here, in our small community."

"Not really," Steve said frankly. He saw Amy glance at him out of the corner of her eye, looking for an explanation to his sardonic remark. When he spoke again, his voice was stark with bitterness. "It's a myth that small towns are safe."

"What do you mean?" Amy asked, not taking her eyes off the road.

"All towns have crime, even the small ones; they just don't make national news like Pittsburgh or New York might. And why would they?" Steve said in a tone that sounded as cold as it felt coming from his mouth.

"Everyone has a right to be heard," Amy said. "The crimes, and those who committed them, should be exposed to the public."

"I agree. But the problem is that small-town stuff gets lost in the shuffle; too much going on in the world for every voice to be heard, for every story to be told. The story needs to be worth reporting to get national attention. If it's not, why bother spending time, money, and resources covering it?" He remembered statistics he had read over the years of crimes across the United States that had gone unnoticed nationally. An injustice for sure. But a cold, hard fact.

He watched Amy study him for a moment before looking back to the road. He assumed she was looking for a rebuttal to his glum assessment of small-town America. Or had Steve echoed her thoughts? He wasn't sure.

"What made you become a crime reporter?" Steve then asked, changing the subject.

"Just my calling, I guess." Amy didn't elaborate further, and Steve could tell that she did not want him to push the issue.

Maybe later?

They sat in silence for a while as they drove. The passing countryside seemed endless, and Steve could not remember the last time he had seen so much farmland. He had been in the city long enough that he forgot what it was like to be outside of its concrete walls. It was a nice break to be in the country.

Amy turned off Route 194 onto a pockmarked dirt road. The car bounced and dipped in the ruts, tossing both occupants around as if they were in some lame amusement park ride that caused more pain than fun. They continued on for about a quarter of a mile before she pulled the car over alongside a harvested cornfield, behind an old F-150 pickup parked there.

"We're here," Amy said, turning the car off. She looked forward, just as the door of the pickup opened. "There's Joe."

Joe Tully stepped out of the truck. Tully was an old man. But other than his white hair and the lines in his weathered, tanned skin, one would not have been able to tell. The man looked fit for his age and moved with the grace and ease of someone much younger.

Stepping from the car, the wind blew across the field ferociously, cut through Steve and Amy's clothes, chilling them to their cores. The falling mist was like tiny glass needle-points prickling their exposed flesh.

"Steve James, this is Joe Tully," Amy said.

"Amy tells me you're from Pittsburgh," Tully said, "and

that you're here about the murders of those two boys – Green and Hooper."

"That's correct."

"You're a long way from Pittsburgh, fella. How'd you get involved in all this?"

"Luck," Steve replied curtly. "Mr. Tully, when did you find the body of Martin Green?"

Tully brought his right hand to his chin and rubbed his whiskers; he thought for a moment. "I suppose... it was about four months ago now, sometime in late November. The morning – I can't give you a specific time, 'cause I don't remember – but early, before the sun was up."

"Were you the only one who discovered the body?" Steve asked.

"I was. Thankfully."

"What do you mean?" Amy asked.

Tully glanced at her and his body hardened. "I mean, the missus wasn't with me, for that I'm truly thankful." Tully's eyes drifted to the field that seemed to go on forever, and his lips drew into a thin, tight line. "It... well, it wasn't something I would have wanted her to see, let's put it that way."

Steve followed Tully's gaze. "I see the corn's been reaped, but I'm guessing it wasn't when you found the body."

"That's correct."

"Then how did you know there was a body in the field? It's not like you could have seen it through the corn from the road, right?" Amy asked.

Tully nodded. "I usually take a drive around my property every morning. We have one hundred and two acres, and you never know who or what you're going to find out here."

"You've found people in your fields before?" Steve asked.

"Sure," Tully said. "Found a few kids smoking dope once. Another couple I found screwing – guess they couldn't wait. I also find discarded garbage like plastics, trash, tires. Cats and dogs too–"

"People leave their pets on your property?" Amy said, her voice a high-pitched whine filled with shock.

Tully gave Amy a grave nod. "Sure do. Assholes, the lot of 'em. Look, I'm a farmer and a butcher, but I don't condone cruelty to animals, even ones for slaughter. Some people just don't have empathy toward other creatures."

Steve thought of Rebecca and the three men on the video – they lacked empathy toward other creatures too.

"What do you do with the animals you find?" Amy asked.

"Take most of 'em in. Feed 'em. Nurse 'em if they need it. Try and find homes for some. Others we keep." Tully smiled; it was clear the thought of doing something bigger than himself was comforting for the old man.

"The morning you found the body, did you see anything suspicious?"

Tully thought about Steve's question, chewing on the inside of his cheek. "Can't say I did. My guess is that they dumped the body and got the hell out of here before I did my morning rounds."

"What time do you do your morning rounds?" Amy asked.

"I'm usually up around four. Out here doing the rounds no later than five usually," Tully replied. "But, like I said, I can't give you a specific time when I found the body."

"What would be your estimated time?" Steve inquired.

"I'd say between 5:30 and 5:45, if I had to estimate."

"Was there snow on the ground when you found Green, back in November?" Steve asked.

"Nope. Had been dry for a few weeks by that point."

"Were any footprints found?" Steve asked, looking at the field again. "Even if it was dry, there could have been prints in the dirt."

"I can't say that *I* saw any myself," Tully answered. "But if any were found, you'd have to ask the sheriff about that."

"How far into the field would you say the body was?" Amy asked.

"That's easy," Tulley said. He turned and pointed. "See that cross out there?"

Both Steve and Amy nodded.

"That's where I found him. There used to be a scarecrow on the cross to keep the birds away from the corn."

"Does that actually work?" Steve asked, turning back to the farmer.

Tully smiled slyly, like he knew a secret other farmers were not privy to. "Not really."

"Would you mind taking us out there?"

"Sure." Tully looked down at Steve's feet and saw he was wearing a pair of clean brown Dockers. "You're going to ruin those walking through the muck. You should be dressed more like her," he said, glancing at Amy's winter boots.

"I'll manage," Steve replied.

"Alrighty."

The cross was about a hundred yards from the road. Tully led the way. The cold mist caused the snow-covered field to glaze over with a thin crust of ice that crunched underfoot as they made their way across the field, an eerie sound in an otherwise serene place.

"I found him sitting against the cross," Tully said, pointing.

Steve walked to the cross and then looked around in all directions. There was nothing for miles that he could see: not a house, a person, a car, or even an animal, just an endless amount of open farmland that seemed to go on forever. They were a long way from civilization. With the corn obstructing the view from the road, there was a good chance the body of Martin Green might not have been discovered until it was time to harvest the corn in the late fall. *A great place to dump a body.*

"How did you know Green was in here?" Steve asked.

"I didn't," Tully replied.

Steve frowned. "Excuse me?"

"What I mean is: there's no reason for me to come in here, I just do it from time to time. I check for stuff around the cross like animals, trash... people, like I mentioned earlier. They like to hang out by this cross, especially when I had a scarecrow on it – I guess they like getting naughty while someone watches – so I check from time to time to make sure no one is partying on my property."

"What about your house, Mr. Tully?" Amy asked. "Can you see this part of the field from there?"

Tully shook his head and then turned and pointed to the west. "Our house is on the other side of that ridge. The only way to see this area is to get in my truck and drive over here."

"When you found the body, what was its condition?"

Tully looked back at Steve. His face had taken on an odd, twisted expression, as if the question were out of place, even in the context of their conversation. "Was he clothed? How was the body positioned? Were there any signs of decomposition or mauling, especially with the eyes, lips, or nose?"

"Well... I found him sitting on the ground with his back against the post like he'd fallen asleep. And he was naked as the day he came into this world, so there were no clothes, except..." Tully paused, his eyes drifted to the ground, searching the glassy surface of the snow as the vivid, horrific memory played through his mind.

"Except for the piece of twine around his neck that had the little black computer thingy dangling from it." He then blinked, as if surfacing from a deep trance, and lifted his head. His eyes were filled with horror by what he had seen.

"A USB flash drive?" Amy asked, glancing at Steve.

"Yeah. That's it," Tully said. "It looked like some home-made necklace." He then turned back to Steve. "But, as for the other part of your question... I'm not sure I understand, Mr. James."

"If the body was out here for a while, say, longer than a day, it would have shown some signs of decomposition or animal tampering."

"Even in the cold?" Amy wondered aloud.

"Sure," Steve said. "The soft tissue like the lips, nose, and eyes are usually the first part of the external body to show signs of decay, though it's slowed in the cold, but still occurs. There are also scavenger animals that pick away at the same parts first."

"They go for the easy meat," Tully said in a matter-of-fact tone.

Steve nodded. "Were there any markings on the body like that, Mr. Tully?"

"Nope. He looked like he was just sleeping one off. It wasn't until I got closer that I saw... well, I saw that he wasn't breathing and the extent of what had been done to him. I called the sheriff right away."

"What visible wounds did you see?" Amy asked.

"His toes." Tully swallowed, sickly. "All of his toes had been lopped off. Also, the entire left side of his body was covered in dried blood from a small puncture, just under the jawline." Tully touched his own throat, indicating where the wound was. "Someone wanted him to bleed out."

"What brings you to that conclusion?" Amy asked.

"As a butcher, I've slaughtered my share of animals. To put them down, we use a gun. But, to bleed the meat, you must open the animal up. A quick jab to the throat allows the heart to pump all the blood from the body before the animal dies. Someone did the exact same thing to that young man, only he was tortured before he met his end."

"So," Amy asked after they were in the car and on their way, "what did you make of that?"

Steve contemplated the question before he spoke. "I think whoever placed the body in the field was someone local. They knew Tully checked his land, and that he would eventually stumble across Green's remains and call the police."

"The murderer *wanted* Martin Green found."

"Along with the flash drive."

"Why? What's the killer's goal by allowing the police to view how these men were murdered?"

Steve had asked himself the same question. Did the killer want fame and exposure like Zodiac or Dennis Rader, the BTK Strangler – both of whom contacted the press and police about their murders with letters, boasting about their crimes? Or was there another unseen motive for the brutal killings, one no one understood?

"Maybe the killer wants us to know how the victims were murdered, so the flash drives are left with the bodies," Steve said. "His way of showing off."

"Does the killer get off on recording the murders?" Amy asked, glancing at Steve. "Is it a fetish – a form of twisted voyeurism — that gives the killer some sick pleasure?"

"Possibly. There is a voyeuristic nature to recording the murders, just like with Rebecca's video. What I don't understand is why I didn't get copies of the Green and Hooper videos too. That would have been enough to get me involved, to get my attention. Instead, I receive Rebecca's video and her junior driver's license? It doesn't make sense. Rebecca's been missing since 1999. Now, twenty-five years after her disappearance, two men are murdered on video and the footage added to flash drives, just like Rebecca's was. What's the connection between the crimes, outside of the flash drives? Are there three men, just like in Rebecca's video, on the Green and Hooper videos as well, or is it only one person?"

"There are *two* other differences. One: Rebecca is female. Green and Hooper were both males. Two: Rebecca's body was never found." Amy looked at Steve and cocked an eyebrow. "If what you believe is true, that someone local knew to dump Green's body in Tully's field so he would find it, why was it different with Rebecca? Why wasn't she found somewhere with a flash drive shortly after she disappeared? Why keep her footage hidden all these years? Why not share it with the police, like the Hooper and Green videos were?"

Steve scratched his ear and realized he needed a cigarette. He had not had a smoke since last night, just before he fell asleep, and the need for nicotine beckoned, making him feel itchy both inside and out.

"Maybe the killer, or killers, want credit for the crimes now," Steve considered. "A lot of serial killers go decades hiding in the shadows before creeping out. Maybe they've evolved, finetuned their craft, and now they want to share their work with the rest of the world."

"And, with your paper, the crimes could get national recognition. The public would eat up this outlandish story, and the tabloid press would sensationalize it further, cementing their fame in serial killer history. Like you said earlier, to get national attention the story has to be worth the resources. By anonymously dropping that box off at your place, it ensures a mind-fuck of a mystery that's bound to get attention from the press."

"You could be right," Steve said. But as the words left his mouth, something felt wrong. Rebecca's video, as horrible as it was, did not feel like the work of a serial killer looking to make a name for himself, but rather a sick perverted fantasy come to life. It was possible that one or all three of the men who tortured Rebecca, could have murdered Green and Hooper too. But to prove or disprove that idea, Steve would need to view the other videos and see if there were similarities to Rebecca's.

They were getting nowhere by speculating about the killer's motives; that was pointless and a waste of energy. If they wanted to link what happened to Rebecca to the Green and Hooper murders, then they needed cold hard facts and evidence. Steve then thought of something. "Who found Kim Hooper's body?"

"It was two people, actually," she said. "Denise Shoff and her daughter, Shelly Sterner. They were coming home from Sunday church when they drove past Hooper's burnt remains tied to a tree."

Steve looked at the clock on the dashboard; 9:45 a.m. They had an hour and fifteen minutes before they were to speak with Winslow at his shop.

"Contact them. See if they're willing to speak to us," Steve said.

"Thank you for taking the time to meet us on such short notice," Amy said as she and Steve took a seat at the dining room table of the Sterner home. "We just have a few questions about the day you discovered the body on Woodland Drive."

Shelly Sterner, a tall, slender woman with short black hair, sat beside her mother, seventy-five-year-old Denise Shoff. They were polar opposites of one another, and Steve assumed that Shelly must have taken after her father's looks and build. Denise was at least five inches shorter than her daughter and held a natural rotund build. With her white hair and chubby pink cheeks, Denise's face resembled how some artists interpreted Mrs. Claus in Christmas paintings; it was a stark contrast to Shelly's thin, almost gaunt appearance.

Shelly cleared her throat and sat up, folding her hands in front of her on the table. "I don't know how much help we'll be. We didn't really see... anything."

"Let's start with how you discovered the body," Steve said. "We'll get to the details in a moment."

"Okay. Momma, you want to go first, since you were the one who saw... it, before I did?" Shelly said, glancing at her mother.

Denise nodded and trained her sharp blue eyes on Steve. "Shelly and I were coming home from Sunday Church. Our Church is on Moulstown Road, right at the intersection of Route 116. Do you know where it is? It's a nice little–"

"That doesn't matter, momma," Shelly said, tapping her mother's arm gently. "Just stay focused."

"Oh! Pardon me. I tend to ramble off topic sometimes. Anyway, since we live on the other side of the mountain, we usually cut through Woodland Drive to come home. It's faster that way."

"And you live here with your daughter, Mrs. Shoff?" Amy confirmed.

"That's correct, dear. I've been retired for ten years and after my husband died, I couldn't take care of our home by myself. So, I moved in with Shelly and her husband when they offered."

"I'm sorry to hear about your loss, Mrs. Shoff," Steve said.

"Thank you. He was a sweet, sweet man. I miss him so." Her eyes drifted away then and Steve saw heartache play across her supple face.

"You were saying," Steve gestured with his hand for her to continue.

"Yes." Denise looked up; the memory of her beloved husband washed away. "We were coming down Woodland when I noticed something against the tree. At first, I thought it was a deer, a deer someone had tied up there. I was like *Oh, my, God, that poor animal! Who could have done such a thing and leave it hanging on the side of the road like that?* People can be so cruel to animals, ya know. And there are people around these parts that would–"

"Momma, stay focused," Shelly said again.

"Sorry. Sorry. So, as we drew closer, I noticed whatever was hanging from the tree wasn't a deer, but a person."

"How did you know that it was a person?" Amy asked. "And not a dead animal that someone left there?"

"He had a head, two arms, and two legs – that's a person," Denise said, rather straightforward. "Anyway, I shouted, 'Stop the car! Stop the car, Shelly, there's a person tied to the tree back there!'"

"And you didn't see the body?" Amy asked, looking at Shelly.

Shelly shook her head. "I was focused on the road and drove right by it."

"So, what happened then?" Steve asked.

"Well, to be honest, I didn't believe her." Shelly glanced at her mother.

"She didn't believe me! Can you believe that?" Denise said, shaking her head. "Didn't believe your own mother."

Shelly ignored her mother's accusations. "She doesn't see as well as she thinks; refuses to wear her glasses because she thinks they make her look old."

"Which they do!" Denise said with a nod. "Anyway, I see distance just fine. Reading, that's a whole other matter."

Shelly rolled her eyes. Steve got the impression that this battle over the glasses had been a raging war between the two for some time.

"Mom's mind can wander, as you can tell," Shelly said. Denise scoffed at her daughter's assessment of her mental capabilities. "I was convinced–"

"But not this time!" Denise interjected, pointing an index finger at the ceiling. "What I saw, I saw as clear as day."

"Did you go back?" Steve asked.

"Not at first. Like I was about to say, I was convinced

that she hadn't seen what she thought she saw. That it was a twisted tree limb or a trick of light that confused her."

"We did go back," Denise said. "But not until I begged her."

Shelly nodded again. "After hearing the concern in her voice, I decided to turn around. If for nothing else, than to give her peace of mind. But when I pulled to a stop..." Shelly trailed off and covered her mouth with her right hand. "It was awful."

"He was burnt!" Denise shouted out. "Looked like a crispy hotdog that was left over the fire for too long."

"Momma! Ewww!"

"Well, he did," Denise said, looking back to Steve and Amy. She shrugged.

"What position was the body in?" Amy asked.

"He was tied to the tree," Shelly said. "Upright."

"Looked like someone burned him at the stake," Denise added.

"What was he tied to the tree with?" Steve asked. "Rope? Chain? Wire? What?"

"I... I don't remember," Shelly said. Steve watched her stiffen and her face turn pale with discomfort as she searched her memory of that awful day.

"It was rope," Denise said, surprising both Steve and Amy with her clear recollection.

"Are you sure?" Amy asked.

"Yes, I'm sure. I might be old, and my mind might wander from time to time, like my daughter said, but my memory's sharp, missy," Denise snapped.

A small smile creased Steve's lips. He liked Denise. She was filled with spunk and tenacity. Strangely, she reminded him of Mrs. Loomis, his next-door neighbor, though without all the hateful bitterness.

"And you called the police after that?" Amy asked.

"We did," Shelly said. "They took our statements and sent us on our way."

"Did you see anything else out of the ordinary?" Steve asked.

Shelly shook her head. Steve could tell from her body language and how she spoke that she was uncomfortable talking about that day. He assumed that Shelly did not want to get involved, more than they already were, and feared for their safety.

"The rope wasn't burnt," Denise suddenly said. Her eyes flashed to Steve with surprise, as if a lightbulb had just gone off in her mind's eye.

Steve trained his attention on the old woman. "What do you mean the rope wasn't burnt?"

"Just what I said. The rope wasn't burnt."

"What about the tree he was tied to?" Amy asked.

Shelly looked from Amy then to Steve and then to her mother. Denise was lost in her memory; her bright blue eyes worked around in their sockets. Finally, her gaze lifted, and she shook her head slowly.

"No. Just the man was burnt. And I remember thinking then how strange it was. He was all burnt up, hair missing, skin blackened and blistered, and the smell was so thick it seeped into the car."

Steve had seen burnt bodies firsthand while in Afghanistan. But it was the smell of charred flesh and hair that he would never forget; a rancid, hot smell that had lingered in his nose since 2001 when he saw the aftermath of U.S. bombing runs, where the dead lined the desert floor; some were combatants, most were not. *Collateral damage.*

"Momma, we don't need to hear all this," Shelly said in a disgusted tone which drew her lips over her teeth.

Denise waved her daughter's comment away with a swipe of her hand, like the words were a pestering mosquito that kept nibbling away at her soft flesh.

Amy looked at Steve. Her suspicious gaze seemed to mirror his thoughts. If what Denise Shoff recalled was correct, and there was no sign of scorching on the rope or on the tree, that could mean Hooper was murdered somewhere else, just like Martin Green was believed to have been.

"There's one other thing," Denise added, her tone a bit darker, as if a shade had been pulled over her bright soul. Steve and Amy both sat forward in their seats, fully captivated with her words. "He was wearing a necklace. And this flat, bright red thingy dangled from the end."

Chapter Seven

Steve was eager to see the Hooper crime scene and wanted Amy to take him there next. But Amy said it would be beneficial if they stopped to speak with former Abbottstown sheriff, Dean Winslow, about Rebecca's case first. They would be passing his bait and tackle shop while on their way; it would save them from having to backtrack and lose time spent investigating. Steve agreed.

Once back in Hanover and on Eisenhower Drive, Amy explained that the stretch of road had been dubbed 'The Golden Mile' and that Hanover was considered 'the snack capital of the world' because of brands like Snyder's of Hanover and Utz Quality Foods.

The land between Route 194 and Route 94 was a congestion of stores, strip malls, and restaurants. Of course, there were big-box retailers like Walmart and Home Depot, as well as restaurant chains like Chili's and Red Lobster. But sprinkled in among the more prominent conglomerate corporations, and to help fill out the spaces, were mom and pop places like Winslow's Bait and Tackle Shoppe. The area was a hotbed of activity; the most life Steve had seen since he arrived.

Amy pulled the car to a stop in front of Winslow's Bait and Tackle Shoppe.

Inside, the sharp tang of fishy water and earth worms hung in the air. The smell made Steve's stomach lurch, and he realized he should have eaten something that morning before leaving the inn. He had not put anything in his stomach other than booze since he left Pittsburgh yesterday afternoon, and it was catching up to him now.

The shop was small but fully stocked with bait, fishing gear, and anything else one would need for a day on the water. It was a laid-back place with a welcoming vibe that Steve found pleasant; he could see locals supporting the shop, probably since it was owned by a former sheriff.

At the counter stood a balding man in his mid-sixties. He wore dark slacks and a tan button-down shirt. A pair of reading glasses rested on the bridge of his nose. He wrote in a ledger and had not heard Steve or Amy enter the shop. He looked over his glasses as they neared the front desk, straightened, and pushed the glasses on top of his head.

"Sheriff Winslow, thank you for speaking to us," Amy said.

Dean Winslow nodded. "You said over the phone that you're looking into Rebecca's case again?"

"That's correct, sir," Amy replied. She turned back to Steve and introduced him. "Mr. James came upon a mysterious package yesterday."

"How mysterious?" Winslow asked.

"The kind that gets dropped off at your home anonymously," Steve said.

Winslow's face tightened with uncertainty. His eyes shifted back to Amy to corroborate Steve's claim.

"It's true, Dean."

Winslow turned back to Steve. "What was in this mysterious package?"

Steve reached into his laptop bag and pulled out the small white box and set it on the counter. He opened the lid and lifted out Rebecca's driver's license and held it up for Winslow to see; small flakes of red dust sprinkled the countertop.

"This."

Winslow slipped the glasses from atop his skull and onto his face. He bent to get a closer look at the ID. Anger flashed through his brown eyes and turned them black. He stood and slipped the glasses back on top of his head; his face was a mask of grim hopelessness that reiterated his troubled thoughts. He sighed then – the sound of a defeated man.

"This box was delivered to your home?" Winslow asked.

"It was," Steve replied. He knew how outlandish his tale must sound to the former sheriff of Abbottstown. Steve slipped the license back into the box. "Along with the driver's license, there was also a flash drive."

Winslow's eyes widened. He had just made the same correlation Steve and Amy had come to yesterday. That Rebecca Turner and the murders of Martin Green and Kim Hooper were possibly connected. Winslow might be retired but Steve knew an investigator when he saw one; they always had the look of bloodhounds sniffing for a fresh scent. But Winslow's shock soon turned into dismay when he realized what this new evidence might mean for Rebecca.

"Is she... dead?" he asked, just above a whisper.

"I don't know," Steve replied. "The video cuts off before we see what's become of her."

"And what *has* become of her?" Winslow asked, his voice a sour, raspy whisper.

"Nothing good," Steve replied.

Winslow swallowed and looked away, lost somewhere between the past and the present.

"I've lived with Rebecca for so long, it's like she's become a part of my family – a lost part I hoped to either reconnect with or bury for good someday." Winslow blinked back the hurt welling in his eyes. "I'll help any way I can. What do you need?"

"Do you still have access to Rebecca's original case file?" Amy asked.

"I don't have the original file. When Abbottstown PD shut its doors, all our cases were transferred over to Hanover PD. Sheriff Meeker took over the investigation from there." Winslow reached under the counter. "However, I made copies of everything we had in Rebecca's case up until that point. After we spoke on the phone, and in light of the possibility of new evidence you told me about, I brought it along today. Figured it would help."

He pulled a manilla folder out and placed it on the counter. The file was thin. Winslow's efforts had not gained much traction or evidence in the years he'd spent on the case, Steve presumed by the size of the file.

"Don't tell Meeker."

"You have our word on that, Dean," Amy replied.

"As you can see, the case went cold quickly. I still look through it from time to time – that's why I made a copy – hoping I'll find something that was overlooked all these years later. But I never do. Never will, I suppose," Winslow said, lost in his own shortcomings as an investigator on this particular case. "I guess it doesn't matter now anyway if what you say is true..."

"It still matters," Steve said. "Rebecca still matters."

"I suppose she does."

Steve was about to start paging through the file when the door opened and two fishermen strolled in. They had just come from some local body of water; their boots were muddy, and the cuffs of their pants wet. Steve guessed they were ice fishermen by their heavy winter attire.

"If you wouldn't mind stepping into my office. I'll be in as soon as I help these customers," Winslow said, directing Steve and Amy to a walled-off space behind the front counter.

Amy closed the door while Steve eagerly got to work on the file.

The first document was a Missing Persons Report filled out on 1/6/1999 by Dennis and Kathy Turner, the day after their daughter disappeared. Sheriff Winslow had conducted only four interviews: Dennis and Kathy Turner, sixteen-year-old Wendy Brewer, and a forty-five-year-old woman, Lois Hansen.

1/10/99 – Turner Home: Interview Mr. Dennis Turner (40) and Mrs. Kathy Turner (39) at their home located at 428 Water Street, Abbottstown, Pennsylvania. Mr. Turner states that his daughter, Rebecca Turner, left their home on the night of January 5, 1999, to attend a party around 6:30 pm. According to Mrs. Turner, Rebecca was going to the party with a high school friend, Wendy Brewer (16). Mr. Turner also stated the girls were long-time friends, and at one time were neighbors, before the

Brewer family moved to Hanover. Neither Mr. or Mrs. Turner knew where the party was being held and could give no further information on the whereabouts of their daughter. They contacted the police when their daughter did not return home by midnight, her curfew, which Rebecca never disobeyed.

There was nothing in the interview that Steve didn't already know. He flipped the page. The next interview was with Wendy Brewer and took place the following day.

1/11/99 – Brewer Home: located at 905 Circle Drive, Hanover, Pennsylvania. Interview Wendy Brewer (16-year-old W/F) at her home. Her parents were present at the time of questioning.

Ms. Brewer states that Rebecca Turner picked her up at her home on the night of January 5, 1999, around seven-thirty that evening to attend a party. Wendy Brewer said the last time she saw Rebecca Turner was around midnight (Jan 5/6 1999) when Rebecca was heading to her car to leave the party. Mr. Brewer stated that Rebecca left because she did not want to stay out past her curfew, which was midnight (curfew confirmed with Mr. and Mrs. Turner; see previous page). Ms. Brewer indicated that Rebecca was not under duress when she left the party and that she was not intoxicated before getting behind the wheel.

When asked where the party was located, Ms. Brewer could not recall, and stated that she did not remember the location nor how to get there, since Rebecca had driven them and it was dark. She was also unable to describe the home's exterior where the party took place, because it was dark when the girls arrived.

Ms. Brewer also stated she did not know anyone at the party, except for her friend, John Hansen. Mr. Hansen, who hosted the party, had invited Ms. Brewer. Ms. Brewer did not know where Mr. Hansen resided, saying they were only acquaintances and had met through mutual friends. She also indicated that one of Mr. Hansen's friends had given her a ride home around two in the morning on 1/6. Ms. Brewer could not remember the name of this individual.

Reading Wendy Brewer's statement, Steve agreed with Rebecca's father that she knew more than she initially told Winslow. He wondered what Wendy was hiding and why she had not told Winslow all she knew about that night. *Is she complicit in Rebecca's disappearance?* Steve thought. *Maybe.*

He flipped to the next page and found a rap sheet on John Hansen. Hansen was from Hanover and at the time, lived with his mother, Lois Hansen, at 848 Old Jacobs Mill Road. He would now be forty-six years old.

Hansen's first offense came at thirteen when he was caught stealing cigarettes from a grocery store in Lancaster, Pennsylvania. The stunt landed him in juvie for six months with a year of probation and public service afterward. Three years later, at the age of sixteen, Hansen was again arrested, this time for a DUI while driving around in his mother's car. For that, Hansen spent another three months in juvie lock-up and another six in a drug and alcohol program. Once out, he kept his nose clean until he was twenty-two, at which time he was busted for possession of marijuana. Five grams were found on his person when he was pulled over at a checkpoint. The police suspected he had been dealing in the area but were unsuccessful in proving their theory. Hansen did a year and a half for possession before being released from the York County Correctional Facility in the fall of 1998. Since then, there had not been a peep from him, and he had no further incidents with the law, that they knew of.

Steve turned the page and found there was another interview sheet dated 1/15/1999 – it was nearly blank. This time, Winslow had tried to speak with John Hansen's mother, Lois Hansen. According to the transcript, Winslow went to the Hansen's home to locate John's whereabouts – seemed he had disappeared just like Rebecca by that point.

Lois Hansen claimed her son was out of town on work but was unable to verify where he was or what kind of work John did. Mrs. Hansen also claimed that John was home with her by eleven-thirty the night of the party and did not leave until the next day, when he headed off to his out-of-town job.

An airtight alibi, Steve thought.

"As you've just read, Lois Hansen wasn't useful to the investigation," Winslow said. He stood in the threshold of the office; his cheeks were flushed.

"Did you believe John was home with his mother by eleven-thirty the night Rebecca disappeared?" Steve asked.

Winslow hiked his shoulders. "No. But I couldn't disprove it either." He came around the desk and took a seat.

"Were you ever able to question John Hansen about that night?" Amy asked.

Winslow shook his head. "I wish. It would've cleared up a few nagging questions I had, but he fled town before I could get to him. Never did locate his whereabouts in the years I investigated the case. The guy's a ghost."

"What were those nagging questions you spoke of, Sheriff?" Steve asked.

"My biggest question was why a twenty-three-year-old man invited two teenage girls to a party – that's not normal. My second question, though I could never get a straight answer from Wendy Brewer, was how she knew John Hansen in the first place."

"Did you go back for another interview with Wendy?" Amy asked.

"I tried. But I could only do so much. I couldn't question Wendy without one, or both of her parents present. She was a sixteen-year-old child at the time, and you must tread carefully and make sure that you don't coerce a statement out of a minor – juries don't like that. I went back to the Brewer home several times over the years, hoping Wendy would eventually talk to me, but she shut me out. As soon as she turned eighteen, she lawyered-up and threatened to sue the police department if we – I – kept harassing her. I was forced to back off by the D.A. after that and leave the Brewer family alone."

Winslow took a breath and folded his hands across his stomach. "I didn't have any evidence linking Wendy directly to Rebecca's disappearance anyway."

"Do you think Wendy lied about what happened that night?"

Winslow thought about Amy's question carefully before he answered. "I've always had suspicions about the legitimacy of her statement. My instincts say she has more to tell, but you can't make a case on those. The question is: will Wendy ever come forward with what she really knows?"

Steve looked back at the file. There was nothing else to look through except color-copied photographs of the abandoned blue Ford Tempo, the car Rebecca had been driving the night she vanished. He pulled two dozen eight by ten photos from the folder and began going through them.

The first photo was a side-angle exterior shot of the Tempo. The car's undercarriage and tires were coated with dried mud. The hood and roof were dusted with dead leaves, and the windshield had a thick layer of dust coating its surface. The car had been there a while before it was discovered.

"When and how was the car found?" Steve asked.

"About two weeks after Rebecca disappeared," Winslow said. "A trucker pulled off to take a leak. Walked back into the woods for privacy, and there it was."

"The car was found on Maple Grove Road?" Steve asked.

"Just off it, about seventy-five yards into the woods, on an old forest trail. You couldn't see the car from the road, you had to be on the trail to see it."

"So, someone could've easily driven back there and hiked out," Amy said.

"Sure. One of my many working theories was that Rebecca might have been kidnapped while at a red light or a stop sign somewhere near where the car was discovered. Kidnapper gets in, demands she does what he tells her. She complies, hoping she'll make it out alive. He then does what he does with her and then dumps the car back there."

"Did you search the area for any remains?" Steve asked.

"We did. But we didn't find anything," Winslow replied.

Steve looked back to the stack of photos and flipped to the second one. This photo was a wider shot of the car, showing the forest trail cutting through the woods. It was impossible to tell the distance between where the vehicle sat and the main road in the photo; the forest was too dense.

"Whoever hid the car had to know about the forest trail," Steve said. "How else would they know it was there? You'd never be able to see the trail in the dead of night."

Winslow agreed.

Steve flipped through the next six photos; all were of the car's interior. "Did you find anything inside? Prints? Blood? Clothing? Hair?"

"Upon further investigation, it appeared the car had been cleaned before being disposed of, so we got nothing. Whatever happened to Rebecca that night, someone didn't want it coming back on them." Winslow sat up in his chair and trained his eyes on Steve and Amy with an intense stare that raised the hair across Steve's body. "And they're not going to like you two poking into the past and digging up bones."

———

They left the shop with Rebecca Turner's copied casefile. Winslow felt it was time a pair of fresher eyes investigated. Guilt twisted the retired sheriff's face as he passed the file to Steve. But he understood he was no longer able to dedicate his life to finding out what happened to Rebecca. At some point, he had to move on. Now was that time.

"Do you know the forest road where the Tempo was found?" Steve asked once they were back in the car.

"Sure. It's no longer in use. The county closed it off after Rebecca's car was discovered. Most locals think it's haunted."

"Maybe it is," Steve whispered to himself. "Let's head

there next, and then on to where Kim Hooper's body was found."

They grew quiet as Amy drove east, away from the hustle and bustle of 'The Golden Mile' of Hanover. A mutual ease had developed between them in the short time they had known one another, which Steve liked. He might have been a good crime writer and reporter, but when it came to human connection, he was not as skilled.

Amy drove on for another five minutes before coming to a Y in the road. On the left sat a small brick church that Amy pointed out was where Shelly Sterner and her mother were coming from the day they found Kim Hooper's body. An icy chill walked up Steve's spine; a strange, serendipitous feeling that everything in these cases was indeed connected somehow. Amy headed left, past the church, and up into the hills surrounding Hanover.

Ten minutes later, they turned onto Maple Grove Road. The area was desolate, with overgrown dead vegetation and towering gray trees, their bare branches like skeleton fingers reaching to the heavens, a wasteland that resembled a nuclear fall-out. About three-quarters of a mile in, Amy pulled the car into a clearing along the side of the road.

"That's where the forest road used to be," Amy said, pointing. "As you can see, it's grown over since 1999."

Steve stepped out of the car with the casefile tucked under his arm. A light mist continued to fall. The surrounding forest was still and quiet, not even a bird chirped, and the air was crisp; it stung his lungs to breathe. The remains of the forest road rested eerily in front of him, muddy, wet, and overrun with tangled briar bushes and fallen trees that blocked the path in parts. A good place to have hidden a car; it would easily disappear into the thicket, and unless someone ventured back into the woods, the car would not have been discovered.

But the car was *found.*

He began walking toward the forest road; the snow crunching underfoot was the only sound in the otherwise uninhabited forest.

"What are you doing?" Amy hollered after him.

"I want to see where the car was," Steve called back over his shoulder.

He opened the folder and pulled out the wide-angle shot of the abandoned Ford Tempo. The photo had been taken on a dry day; there was no snow on the ground nor leaves on the trees to mask the earth's natural features. But now the land was snow-covered. Finding the exact spot where the car had been was going to be tough, but not impossible. The crime scene photo revealed a wavy ridge-line beyond the vehicle. If Steve could match up the ridge-line with the angle taken in the picture, he could approximate the spot where the Tempo had been left.

He traversed over fallen trees, around the briar bushes and unseen rocks and ruts in the land that nearly folded his ankles more than once. As he walked, he compared the ridgeline in the photo to the actual ridge. It took several attempts, but eventually, Steve's persistence paid off and he was able to approximate where the Ford Tempo was originally discovered.

Steve was not looking for tangible evidence amongst the rotting trees and brush. He was twenty-five-years too late for that. However, he wanted to get a feel for the place, to understand another part of Rebecca's story.

Looking back in the direction he had come; Steve could no longer see Amy's car or Maple Grove Road. He estimated there were about seventy-five yards between himself and the main road, the forest was dense, even in the winter months, and it was impossible to see anything through the brush.

When was the car discovered? Steve wondered.

He opened the folder and paged through it until he found what he was looking for.

The report stated the Ford Tempo was found on January 20, 1999, by truck driver Rudy Carter from Manchester, Maryland. According to Rudy, he had pulled off the road once he found a clearing big enough for his truck so he could relieve himself. He then walked back into the woods, and while taking a leak, he spotted the car. Feeling there was something off about the car, he decided to call the police.

There was not much else in the report, and Steve figured Winslow had cleared Rudy Carter of any wrongdoing. He got the feeling Winslow did not leave many loose ends, or Carter would still be a suspect.

Steve then went back to the photos taken of the Tempo. It was apparent the car had been there for some time, with the number of leaves and dust on the windows, but there was one thing he found odd.

The mud.

Why were the tires and the undercarriage of the car covered in mud?

He flipped to the next photo. This photo was taken directly facing the rear of the car and showed the forest road leading back toward Maple Grove Road. There did not appear to be any tire tracks in the dirt behind the car, which meant when the car was driven back there, the road had not been a muddy quagmire.

So how did the car become covered in mud?

Then something else stuck out to Steve, something he

had not comprehended until he stood in the middle of the foreboding woods.

The Ford Tempo was facing Maple Grove Road, not away from it like it should have been if someone had driven the car in from the main road.

Strange.

Steve made his way back to Amy and got in the car. His hands were nearly frozen, his fingers so cold they felt like they were about to snap off. He put his hands against the vents to warm them.

"Do you remember if it rained around here after Rebecca disappeared?"

Amy shook her head. "I would have no idea. Why?"

Steve opened the file and pointed to the car in the photo. "The underside of the car is covered in mud. But there are no tire tracks in the dirt." Steve tried to come up with a solid conclusion for the mud being on the car, but a theory eluded him. "And why is the car facing Maple Grove Road and not away from it, like it should be?"

Amy frowned and studied the photo. "That is bizarre, now that you bring it up."

A reasonable explanation for why the car faced the road ran through Steve's mind. Had the car been turned around before it was left? Had the driver backed the car in there? The whole scene bugged him the same way being out of booze bugged him.

It makes no sense.

"How far from here was Kim Hooper's body found?" Steve asked instead.

"Not far. Maybe a ten-minute drive."

Eight minutes later, they stood together along Woodland Drive. The road was small and narrow, unpaved, created long before modern cars, and absurd amounts of traffic cluttered the highways. Woodland Drive was the type of road out-of-towners did not venture on – there was nothing around – only people who knew of its existence traveled the windy, secluded road.

"Hooper was found over there, tied to that tree that looks like a three-pronged fork."

Steve studied the area by the tree. What had been left behind by the murderer had been cleaned up, so there was nothing to see...

Except Steve *did* see something – a familiar pattern in the forest no more than twenty feet from where Hooper's body was discovered.

"Is that another forest road?" Steve asked, pointing.

Amy followed Steve's finger to the unnatural opening in the forest.

"It might be. There are forest roads all through these woods."

"Do any of them connect, or are they just dead-end trails?"

"I suppose some of them do."

Steve turned to Amy. "Drive back to Maple Grove Road and wait for me there."

Confusion danced across her face. "Why?"

"I have a theory. If you don't see me in about twenty or thirty minutes, I'll meet you back here."

"Okay?" Amy replied, still puzzled.

Steve wasn't sure what he was on to. Maybe it was nothing. Or maybe, just maybe he had put something together that everyone had overlooked. He was hopefully optimistic but knew never to count on optimism in his line of work; the truth had a way of remaining hidden.

Amy pulled away and drove off, leaving Steve alone in

the middle of the silent forest. He started up the road, past the forked tree where Hooper was discovered, and made his way to the clearing; it sure as hell looked like there had been a road there at one time. But if there ever was a road cut through this part of the forest, it was now overgrown and impassable to traffic, just like the forest road off Maple Grove.

He made his way into the woods and began following the path. Steve hiked a mile into the woods, and was about to turn back, thinking his assumption about the path had been wrong and that he had projected evidence in an effort to connect the crimes in his mind.

That was until he spotted something recognizable in the distant landscape.

The ridgeline.

Excitement grew in Steve's stomach and worked its way up into his throat forming a hard knot. He swallowed the thrill away and kept going. The path was dense in parts, unpassable in others, to where Steve had to trek around obstacles if he wanted to continue. It slowed him down. Winded him. He had to pause several times to catch his breath – *damn cigarettes*.

But none of that mattered; the excitement of the hunt pushed him onward. If what he thought was correct, he might have just linked Rebecca Turner to Kim Hooper's murder.

The path cut sharply to the left. He continued on. Once Steve was past the bend in the path, he felt his heart begin to race, and not just from the physical exertion. He recognized where he was. He had just been there only moments ago. But there was one final thing he had to check. To be sure his eyes were not misleading him. He continued on until he found his own footprints in the ice-crusted snow and stopped. He was back at the spot where the Tempo was found.

Now Steve understood why the Tempo was facing Maple Grove Road and not away from it, as it should have been. The car had been driven in from Woodland Drive, not from Maple Grove Road, as it had long been speculated.

Chapter Eight

I t was late afternoon by the time Amy dropped Steve off back at the inn. They decided to wait until morning to start again. Martin Green's wife, Audrey, was next on the list to interview; a night's rest would do both of them good, and give them a fresh perspective on the investigation.

Steve was famished and the smell of food in the dining room made his stomach growl. He decided to stop at the bar for a bite to eat and a drink – or two. As he sat down, he realized how sore his muscles were, and how much his joints hurt. A chill had crept into his body from the raw day, the kind of chill that makes one think they might be running a fever. He ordered a bowl of tomato soup and a grilled chicken sandwich with bacon, and a Jameson to wash it all down.

As he waited for his food, he sipped the Jameson and opened Rebecca's casefile and paged through it. He was alone in the bar that evening and was not concerned with someone overseeing what he was doing – besides, no one knew the real reason he was in town.

He reread the interviews taken by Sheriff Winslow but found nothing new or helpful in the transcripts. He then reread John Hansen's rap sheet. Though Hansen was wild as a youth, with drug convictions and theft charges, it did not mean he was like that as an adult. *People change. Some for the good. Some for the bad.* What concerned Steve was how quickly he had vanished after Rebecca disappeared. According to Wendy's statement, Hansen hosted the party and had invited the girls himself. Rebecca disappeared sometime after leaving the party.

The series of events were too much of a coincidence and made Hansen look suspicious as hell, in Steve's book. Though, suspicion did not prove guilt. Steve wondered what Hansen really knew about that night and if they found him, would he be willing to talk.

Steve sat the file aside when his food came and dug in. As he ate, he thought about Martin Green and Kim Hooper. He suspected neither man was murdered where their bodies were found. One would expect to find evidence of violence at the crime scenes. There was none. And the bodies appeared to be staged, at least in Steve's mind. Of course, once he saw the tapes it would help confirm his theory.

He wondered if it were possible for the three men in Rebecca's video to be responsible for the deaths of Green and Hooper. It was possible. They were savages. Steve knew of several serial killers who worked in tandem, like Henry Lucas and Ottis Tool, lovers who were attributed to an estimated six hundred-plus murders over a span of about ten years. Could that mean these guys were trying some-thing new – a twisted three-way murder spree – and trying to gain exposure through the press, like Charlie had thought? In this day and age, Steve didn't feel anything was off the table.

His thoughts shifted to Afghanistan and this led him nowhere, other than bitterness and the bottom of the second glass of whiskey. When he was finished, he ordered another round and after draining the glass, he returned to his room, showered the memories away, dressed in comfortable night clothing, and then phoned Charlie to fill him in on what he believed he had uncovered.

"Let me see if I got this straight," Charlie said. "This is so crazy it's hard to wrap my head around. You believe Kim Hooper's body was purposely left close to where Rebecca Turner's car was discovered twenty-five years ago?"

Steve flicked open the Zippo and lit a cigarette. "I do." He blew the smoke out the side of his mouth.

"Why? If the people who did that to Rebecca are the same ones who murdered the other two men, then why bring attention to themselves for something they did so long ago?"

"Maybe they're stepping out of their comfort zone and evolving into better, more proficient killers, and want credit for what they did to Rebecca as well. So, Hooper's body is left along Woodland Drive with the flash drive of his death, not far from where Rebecca's car was found."

"I'd be careful with that, Steve. It appears you're stitching two separate incidents together to create linking evidence, so the crimes look connected."

"Why else would Hooper's body have been left so close to where Rebecca's car was discovered? Someone wanted Hooper's murder to connect back to what happened to Rebecca. All three – Kim Hooper, Martin Green, and Rebecca Turner – were tortured while on video. When the bodies of Green and Hooper are discovered, they're both found with flash drives, just like Rebecca."

"But Rebecca's body has not been found. She's still classified as missing. Besides that, why was Green left in the middle of a cornfield and not somewhere more significant, as you believe Hooper's was?" Charlie asked.

Steve took a drag on the cigarette. "I don't know."

"See. There are holes big enough to drive a truck through in your theory. I'm not saying what you believe is wrong, there just isn't enough evidence to back it up. You need more. You go to the police department with what you believe, and they'll kick you to the curb and you'll never see the other videos."

"I know I'm right, Charlie."

"Knowing you're right and proving you're right are two different things."

This conversation was not going how Steve imagined. He had hoped that Charlie would be as excited as he was with the discovery. But Charlie was looking at the evidence through an editor's lens; seeing things that Steve couldn't because he was too close to the story.

Steve took another drag on the cigarette and then rubbed his eyes. He was tired and needed sleep. Maybe he *was* projecting things that were not there. He couldn't tell at the moment.

"Did you hear anything about the Palazzo lawsuit?" Steve asked, changing the subject. He heard his voice crack and wondered if Charlie had heard it too.

"The lawyers are meeting tomorrow. Trying to hash out a deal."

"What deal? There *is* no deal, Charlie. We're not retracting the story, goddamnit!"

"Settle. I never said we were. Palazzo's lawyers are just stalling for time."

Time for what? Steve wondered. *So Palazzo's goons can get to me first, beat my sources out of me, and then kill me?*

"Charlie, if anything happens to me, you have to promise you'll release the rest."

"Did something happen?" Charlie asked, his voice rising, filled with concern.

"Yesterday, two of Palazzo's goons were at my apartment."

"And you didn't bother to tell me this last night when we spoke?"

"Slipped my mind."

"Bullshit!" Charlie barked. "Things don't slip your mind unless you've had too much to drink."

Steve said nothing, suspecting his boss knew how hard he was hitting the booze.

"I think you should come home," Charlie said quietly.

"Absolutely not. I'm in this now."

"You're too close to this one, Steve."

"You're damn right I'm too close! I was on that side of the camera while being tortured. I know what that's like. I was able to get out of that hell. Rebecca wasn't." Charlie said nothing and the call between them buzzed in Steve's ear with dead static. "Someone has to be her voice, Charlie. It might as well be someone who understands what she went through."

Chapter Nine

Steve did not sleep well. He had awoken several times during the night drenched in sweat, with the nightmare of the Afghani cave playing in the dark of the unfamiliar hotel room. In the dreams, he was being tortured all over again. But unlike reality, in the dream he did not escape his captors.

A cloud hung over him as he sat silently beside Amy in her car while on their way to speak to Audrey Green. The nightmares bounced around in his mind, reminding him of what could have been had he not acted when the first shots rang out, and US Special Forces stormed the cave compound where he and Lance Corporal Lewis Brenner were being held captive.

Steve knew he should be grateful that he was able to return home, that he was lucky enough to breathe fresh air, to drink a beer at a ballgame and eat a Pittsburgh Salad. Lance Corporal Brenner didn't get that luxury.

The torment of loss. The blood on his hands. The survivor's guilt all picked away at him and turned him into the unrecognizable bastard he had become. These memories were like having a hot poker stuck in his chest, always burning away what little remained of the man he once was. It was a lot to live with.

"You okay?" Amy asked, sensing Steve's quiet distress that morning.

"Yeah." He looked at her. Concern was fixed on her face, and her green eyes held a soft compassion that he had not seen before. He felt a need to tell her about his nightmares but knew he could not. Some things were better left unspoken.

They drove on under a thick, gloomy grey sky that let no sunlight into their lives that morning. They made small talk to pass the time at first, but soon the conversation returned to the investigation. Though most of their discussion was just an endless circle of baseless theories that needed evidence to support them.

Steve enjoyed the conversation; it kept his mind off the nightmare. He found Amy to be incredibly intellectual, passionate about her work, and resourceful. She had single-handedly made the contacts needed to get them where they were in the investigation and intermediated the conversation with the locals to put them at ease with a reporter from Pittsburgh.

He wondered why Amy had not tried to pursue a more prosperous career in journalism. She had the talent and the drive to work in the big leagues, where the money and stories could, at times, come at a reporter at breakneck speed. Steve supposed Amy had her reasons – everyone did for their decisions in life.

Amy pulled into the driveway of the Green home and turned off the engine. Three cars were parked in the driveway. A white F-150 work truck with *Green's Lawn & Garden* written on the side in large green letters, a blue

Mazda3, and a black Dodge Ram. The house in front of them was a two-story redbrick colonial. The yard was meticulously manicured, and the shrubs and trees ornamented the house with perfect symmetry. Steve expected nothing less from a man who owned a lawn business.

As they stepped from the car, the front door opened and a woman that looked to be in her forties appeared. Audrey Green was cute in that small-town-girl sort of way with a full, soft face and dark doe-like eyes. She was short and chubby, but chubby in all the right places that some men find attractive nowadays. She met Steve and Amy on the walkway with a warm, but guarded smile.

"Thanks for speaking with us, Audrey," Amy said. She introduced both herself and Steve. "We're so deeply sorry for the loss of your husband."

Audrey's brown eyes grew woeful and glassy with tears.

"Thank you," she replied, blinking away the tears. "If you would like to come inside..."

They were led down a hallway decorated on both sides with photos of the Green family. Steve paused a moment to look at one of the family photos featuring only Martin in what appeared to be a hiking trip; he stood on a large boulder overlooking a valley of green trees below. He was tall and well-built. Good-looking in a boyish way with dark, brooding eyes and hair.

"Is this Martin?" Steve asked, looking down the hall at Audrey, who stood with Amy in the threshold of the kitchen.

"Yes. That's him," Audrey said.

Steve took one final look at the photo and then joined them. They went through the kitchen and then into a large living room where two leather sofas faced one another. A flatscreen television took up most of the far wall. The audio was turned down and *House on Haunted Hill*, an old black and white horror film starring Vincent Price, played on the screen. It was one of Steve's favorite movies. He loved how wonderfully dubious the film was, leading the audience down one path, when in actuality something else was going on the entire time. Audrey picked up the remote and turned the TV off.

"Please, have a seat," Audrey said.

Steve and Amy sat on the sofa opposite Audrey.

"We just have a few questions and we'll be on our way," Amy began.

Audrey shifted uneasily in her seat. To Steve she seemed nervous. Of course, questions about a murdered husband would make any wife uncomfortable.

They had decided in the car to let Amy take the lead on this interview and Steve would interject with his own questions when needed. The approach would help put Mrs. Green at ease, by speaking to a local woman that could be trusted, rather than a male reporter from out of town.

"How did you find out about your husband?" Amy asked.

"Sheriff Meeker called me," Audrey said.

"When was that?"

"The morning of November the tenth. I remember because I was on my way over to the shop to see if Martin was there. I hadn't heard from him since he left the house the previous morning and I was concerned something had happened. I called his cellphone, but he didn't pick up. I thought maybe he was over there."

"The shop?"

"My husband has a little workshop in downtown Hanover, on Hill Street. He uses the place to store his extra yard equipment and make repairs for customers' equipment. It has more space than our garage, and it's cheaper than adding a second building to the property."

"Makes sense," Amy said. "Did your husband ever spend nights at the shop before?"

"No. But, like I said, when I called his cell and he didn't answer, I thought maybe something might have happened to him while there, that he could have hurt himself and couldn't get to his phone. He works with a lot of power equipment; any number of things could have gone wrong." Her eyes swelled with tears again. "Anyway, I was headed to the shop when Sheriff Meeker called and told me to come to the station that morning."

"And you had not called Sheriff Meeker at that point to report Martin missing?" Amy asked.

"No." Audrey shook her head.

"Why not?"

"It wasn't unusual for Martin to work late sometimes and not call me. He gets wrapped up in what he's doing and loses time. Lost time, now, I guess. Past tense, I keep forgetting that."

"When was Martin usually home from work?" Steve asked.

"Around five or six in the evening on most nights."

"And you didn't call your husband to see why he wasn't home?" Amy asked.

"I fell asleep that night around eight-thirty," Audrey replied. "I'm a heavy sleeper. When I woke, it was five in the morning and that's when I knew something was wrong and called him. When I didn't get an answer, I headed out the door to the shop."

"Mrs. Green, would you mind if we searched your husband's place of business? There might be something in there that could help us with our investigation into his death."

"Absolutely. I'll get you the key before you leave."

"Thank you for that," Amy said. "I'm sure it will be helpful. If you don't mind me asking, what was your husband acting like the last time you saw him?"

"His normal self. He got up, showered, ate a bowl of cereal and left around five-thirty to head to the shop."

"Did Martin have any enemies? Anyone who might have had a business altercation with him, that would want to hurt him?"

"Are you kidding me? Martin was loved around town. There wasn't anyone who'd want to harm him."

Amy glanced at Steve with an I-told-you-so gaze. She looked back to Audrey. "What about business partners? Did he have any?"

"No. He owned the business himself."

"Did he have any employees?" Steve asked.

"He did not. The money Martin made from April to late October was decent, but we had to save what he earned to make it through the winter, until the mowing season started again. There was never enough for another employee, if we wanted to eat and keep a house over our head."

"What did he do in the off months?" Amy asked.

"He supplemented some income by fixing small gas engines and stuff like that at the shop for customers. Martin could fix or build anything. The man was gifted, truly gifted, with his hands, and had a mechanical mind that could rival Edison's, I swear." Audrey's face tightened painfully from the memory of her husband's ingenuity; something she had obviously admired about him.

"Did your husband know a man by the name of Kim Hooper?"

Audrey's eyes shifted from Amy to Steve and then back to Amy. "Was that the other man they found..." She swallowed and her throat made an audible click. "Like my husband?"

"It was. Did Martin know Kim?" Amy asked again.

Audrey shook her head. "I don't remember Martin ever speaking about him. Then again, he knew a lot of people around town, and a lot of people knew him from his business."

"So it's possible they could have crossed paths at one time or another," Steve said.

Audrey shrugged. "Sure. It's possible."

Above their heads a floorboard creaked with the weight of someone moving. Steve and Amy both slowly looked toward the ceiling.

"Are you alone, Mrs. Green?" Amy asked, glancing back at Audrey.

Audrey smiled. "No. That's my son, Austin. He's home sick from school with the flu. I should really get back to tending him. Do you have any other questions for me? I'd be happy to answer them."

Amy looked at Steve to see if he had anything else he wanted to ask. He did.

"Did you or your husband know a Rebecca Turner?" Steve asked.

The question seemed to confuse Audrey. "Maybe Martin did. I didn't. I'm not from the area like he was." She paused, thinking, then asked, "What does this Rebecca Turner have to do with what happened to my husband and the other man, Hooper?"

"We're not sure," Steve said. "Maybe nothing."

"Was he running around on me?"

"Why would you think that?" Amy asked.

Audrey's shoulders rose weakly. She looked like a defeated woman who had lived a lifetime of abuse. "Martin... well, Martin had an eye for pretty girls, especially girls younger than me."

"How young?" Steve asked, sitting up.

Audrey leveled her gaze at him sternly. "Not *that* young. Girls in their twenties. We'd been married for almost fifteen years, and after two kids, I don't look like I used to. I caught his eyes drifting a lot."

Steve studied her closely. "Did that upset you?"

"Sure. No woman wants to see their man checking out other girls, especially ones half their age. It hurt."

"Did you tell Martin how you felt?"

"No. I thought if I just ignored him, it would go away. Besides, I didn't want to come off as 'that wife,' - the jealous type."

"Did you think Martin was seeing someone else?"

"I had my suspicions, but I could never prove them. They were more like feelings than suspicions anyway. I'm sure it was my own self-confidence issues of not feeling pretty enough to keep my husband's eye on me at all times."

Steve wrapped the interview up there and Audrey escorted them to the door, passing the key to her husband's shop to Amy as they stepped out onto the stoop.

"You find the person who did this to my husband, okay? You're doing more for Martin than the Hanover Police Department is, that's for sure."

"Why do you say that?" Steve asked.

Audrey thought about the question for a long moment before she answered. "I don't know. I just get the feeling that Meeker isn't all that interested in finding out who took the father of my children away from them."

"These things take time," Amy said, reaching out and cupping Audrey's forearm with her hand.

"I just want answers, that's all." Audrey pushed a globby tear off her cheek with her fingertips. "And I'm not getting them from Sheriff Meeker."

Martin Green had converted a two-bay garage into his shop. Entering the building, Steve saw the first bay contained Green's lawn mowing and landscaping equipment, while the second served as his workshop and repair area. Next to the first bay was a small office. It was dark inside.

Opening the door to the office, Steve reached around the corner and found the light switch and flipped it on. The long fluorescent tube bulbs snapped on with a cold hum overhead; a few flickered eerily, casting the light in such a way that made the room appear to be a dismal void, where warmth and happiness were unwelcome. There was not much in the office other than a desk, a computer, and a filing cabinet. There were no pictures on the cinderblock walls. The emotional lifelessness of the room chilled Steve to his very core.

They began to search the office. Amy took the desk while Steve looked through the two-drawer filing cabinet. Opening the top drawer of the filing cabinet, Steve found it filled with paid work orders that were arranged alphabetically. His first thought was that maybe Green had done work for Kim Hooper, a repair of some sort or lawn service, so he searched through the H's but found nothing tying the men together. *It's never that easy.* He then opened the bottom drawer and found more work orders. The only difference was that those in the bottom drawer were incomplete jobs. But like before, there was nothing tying Martin Green to Kim Hooper.

"Find anything?" Steve asked, turning back to Amy seated at the desk.

"No," she said, pulling out the bottom right-hand side desk drawer only to find it filled with office supplies. Amy slammed the drawer shut and sat back in the chair, frustrated. "I feel like we're chasing our tails."

Steve nodded. He felt the same way. "What about the computer?"

Amy sat up and turned on the tower. It took a moment for the computer to come to life; the cold hard drive spinning inside sounded like a wind-up toy about to take flight.

"Go to files," Steve said, once the computer was fully booted up. "And then check out the Quick Access tab; it'll show Green's most recently opened files."

Amy moved the curser and clicked on the file icon. When the window opened there were two listings: FREQUENT FOLDERS (8) and RECENT FILES (29). Opening the FREQUENT FOLDER tab showed Green had last visited his business-related folders, of which there were eight. One folder was marked CUSTOMER WORK ORDERS, one for BILL OF SALE/RECEIPTS and another was CUSTOMERS. The remaining five were: inventory, gas/oil expenses, equipment replacement/refillables, mileage, and finally, taxes.

"Click on the one that says customer work orders," Steve said.

Amy did. The folder opened onto an Excel sheet. Here, Green had listed the names, address, phone, and emails of his customers. All were in alphabetical order, just like in the filing cabinets.

"Scroll down to H. See if Hooper's name comes up," Steve said.

Amy scrolled through the list, but Kim Hooper's name was not listed as one of Green's customers.

"Shit!" Steve spat, throwing his hands in the air.

"What now?"

"Check the recent files, see what comes up."

Amy closed Excel and then clicked on RECENT FILES (29). She began to scroll down through the twenty-nine files listed there. Steve read over the file names as Amy proceeded through the list.

"Looks like they're lawncare estimates," Steve said. "See, each one starts with ESTIMATE and then the name of the person or persons.

"Potential customers who want a quote from Green?"

"Open one."

Amy clicked on one of the files titled ESTIMATE - HAWN. As Steve had expected, it was a quote from Martin Green to a woman named Susan Hawn for his mowing services. Green had estimated the job to be around one-hundred dollars for three acres of land per week.

"Doesn't look like anything's here," Amy said.

Steve nodded.

Amy backed out of the file and was about to click away when Steve stopped her.

"Wait!"

"What?" Amy looked over her shoulder at him.

"That one." Steve pointed at the file titled CAMPING TRIP with the Microsoft Edge icon beside it. "That's a direct link to the internet. Open it."

Amy clicked on the file and the internet opened onto a website called FAKEEMAILS.COM.

"What the hell is this?" Amy asked, trying to make sense of what she was seeing on the screen. "I was expecting some sort of camping website, not this."

Steve leaned in closer.

"It's a faux email website, nontraceable to the sender and receiver." Steve studied the page closely. "Green saved the link on his computer so he could continue to use the email over and over, so the email wouldn't reset each time he went to the website."

"I don't get it," Amy said. "What do you mean by 'so the email wouldn't reset'?"

"Some of these sites have a time limit on how long the email will work – ten days, ninety days, one-hundred and twenty days – before the user is forced to create a different email address. Since we're still seeing the emails, I'm assuming Green started using the name..." Steve focused on the sent email address. "...teddybear42@dulux.com within a month of his death."

"Why would Green be sending emails using a nontrace-able account?"

"Look here." Steve leaned over the back of the chair. The smell of Amy's lavender shampoo filled his nose; a scent that was suddenly euphoric and conjured up ideas of what it would be like to run his hands through her red hair. "See this no-reply@svr1.ghostemail.com in the 'From' boxes?"

"Yeah?"

"Green wasn't just sending emails from a fake, nontraceable account, he was also getting them from one."

"How do you know all this?"

"I worked a story a few years back. A guy was scamming

senior citizens out of their Social Security checks using one of these sites. Scroll down to the first one sent by Green at the bottom," Steve said.

Amy did as she was instructed and opened the first email.

It read:

FROM: teddybear42@delux.com

    TO: no-reply@svr1.ghostemail.com

    SENT: 15:42:02

    TOPIC: Camping Trip

    K,

Is the camping trip to your pap's place still on this year? Haven't heard anything from you or Jay? Let me know so I can make plans on how to tell A.

    M

"Is it possible that A is short for Audrey and that K could mean Kim – as in Kim Hooper?" Amy asked.

"Perhaps."

"If A is Audrey, did she lie to us about her husband knowing Kim Hooper?"

Steve shook his head. "I don't think so. See how Green phrased his words – 'so I can make plans on how to tell A.' I don't think Audrey knew a thing."

"Then who is Jay?"

Again, Steve shook his head. "Go to the next email."

Amy scrolled up to the received email from no-reply@svr1.ghostemail.com.

M, Don't know. Jay's been off the grid. Be in touch as soon as I hear from him.

    K

"So why all the secrecy for just a camping trip?" Amy asked.

"'Camping Trip' is code for something else," Steve said, standing.

"What though?"

"I wish I knew."

Chapter Ten

Amy dropped Steve off at the inn around noon, at his insistence. He knew the next move he would have to do on his own, so he quickly cooked up a story that he needed to speak with his editor and fill him in on what they had found. He didn't like deceiving Amy any more than he enjoyed deceiving Charlie about her involvement in the investigation. He would have to come clean, to both of them. But now was not the time. He needed more, needed that bombshell that would open up this deep grave of injustice.

Steve was sure he was onto something. However, he needed more than just the emails they had found on Green's computer between M and K. K could be anyone. And the emails did not exactly scream foul play or incriminate Green of anything.

Audrey, Green's wife, had said her husband had an eye for younger girls, so he could have been talking to someone, maybe having an affair even, and they were sending those nontraceable emails to keep what they were doing a secret.

If Steve wanted to link Martin Green and Kim Hooper

to one another personally, and prove they were in fact corresponding through the emails, he believed there could be something substantial at Hooper's residence to solidify it.

But Steve would have to do this part of the investigation alone, since it would be an illegal search of private property. He didn't want to subject Amy to his cross-the-line tactics to get a story.

Once back in his room, he poured himself a shot of whiskey and lit a cigarette. He opened his laptop and did a quick Google search for Kim Hooper's address, which he found in a matter of clicks. 34 Racine Drive, Hanover, Pennsylvania.

He waited until dark to head out.

It took him twenty-five minutes to find Racine Drive and to locate Hooper's address. He slowed the car to a stop by the mailbox with the number 32 on the side and looked down a long, snow-covered driveway.

Hooper's house was buried deep in the woods, far from the road. He drove past the mailbox and pulled the car over, about a hundred yards from the driveway. He would hike to the house from there; this way he would not tip anyone off to his presence if the home were occupied. He didn't need the police being called on him for trespassing, or to get shot by some redneck with an itchy trigger finger and a MAGA hat.

Stepping from the car, Steve pulled on his gloves and moved to the trunk and opened it. He lifted a small emergency bag out, unzipped it, and retrieved a tactical flashlight. Steve used this particular tactical light because of its two settings, normal LED light and red. Red light helped keep his eyes adjusted to the dark and has a low visible range – a tip he had picked up while spending time with troops in the field in Afghanistan – and used it in times where covertness was key.

He turned the flashlight on and shone the red beam around the dense woods. He was alone, in the middle of nowhere, and could not see another house anywhere close by. There would be no worries about being seen by a nosey neighbor. Next, he opened the duffle bag and pulled the .38 out. Tucking the gun into the front of his pants, he pulled his shirt down over it. Zipping up the jacket, Steve turned and started back up the road to the driveway.

The air was bitterly cold and smelled heavily of pine and snow; a sweet, refreshing scent that Steve found soothing in an otherwise stressful situation. Once at the driveway, he turned the flashlight off. He did not know how far back the house sat in the woods, and again, he did not want anyone to know he was coming, so he would hike in the dark.

He followed the driveway about a quarter of a mile into the woods, only turning on the flashlight quickly to make sure he had not strayed from the path. The driveway then opened up into a large, cleared plot of land that Steve could tell, even in the dark, butted up against a lake. *Lake Marburg,* if he remembered correctly from what Amy told him.

The home was dark, silent, and still, the black structure silhouetted against the soft gray-pink sky and the eerily calm grey waters of the lake beyond. Nothing moved inside the home or anywhere else for that matter, and Steve became intensely aware of how quiet his surroundings were, like standing in the middle of a cemetery in the dead of winter.

He switched on the flashlight and shone the red beam at the house. A large two-story cabin sat before him. The

American flag hung stick-still in the night from the right post that supported the slanted porch roof. The home was in decent shape and appeared that it had been taken care of.

He was making his way up the steps of the porch when he heard the front door creak open. At first, Steve thought someone was inside, that someone had been lingering in the dark waiting for him. His hand shot down to his waist and he tried to pull the .38 out, but the hammer snagged on his pants and the gun tumbled from his fingers and fell into the snow at his feet. He shot upright and aimed the beam of the flashlight at the door, fully prepared to come face-to-face with someone looking to harm him.

But no one was there. The front door hung ajar as if the house itself were inviting him inside.

Steve breathed a sigh of relief. The frigid night air then seemed to grow colder, stinging the exposed flesh of his nose, cheeks, and chin, while at the same time biting at his skin, even through the jacket. His fingers were numb, his hands shook; the flashlight's beam trembled as it penetrated the dark just inside the open doorway.

He stood for a moment scanning the dark entrance of the house, looking for any signs of life inside. When he felt sure that he was alone, he bent and picked up the .38 from the snow and stuffed it into the pocket of his jacket. He started toward the door again. This time, he saw the door sway, the cold hinges squeaking. He realized then that his weight and movement up the steps must have dislodged it.

Entering the house, a heavy, foreboding stillness bore down on Steve like a compression blanket draped over his shoulders. And, for a moment, he wondered if Kim Hooper's spirit had returned to haunt the place, doomed to linger there for eternity, scaring those who dared step foot where he once lived.

He pushed the thought away, so not to spook himself with ideas of ghosts and goblins in a stranger's house.

Steve tried to close the front door but found that it did not latch correctly. Aiming the beam at the door handle, he saw that the strike plate was missing and the wood doorframe that it should have been attached to was broken, leaving a large chunk missing, like it had been busted open.

Had someone kicked the door in? Had Hooper been kidnapped from his home? He wasn't sure; that part was still a mystery to him. He pressed the door firmly closed and it appeared to remain there, but Steve was sure any little movement would cause it to swing open, just like it had when he came up the steps.

Turning, he aimed the beam down the hallway; paintings of streams, serene forest landscapes, and animals like deer and bear hung on the walls. At the rear of the hallway, at the very end of the flashlight's reach, was a kitchen. To Steve's left was a stairwell. And to his right was an open doorway.

He moved slowly to the room on the right, hoping not to loosen the closed front door again. Rounding the corner of the doorway, the flashlight cut the darkness and revealed what appeared to be a den. Two leather chairs faced a stone fireplace with a twelve-point buck mounted above the mantle, now bathed in blood red light. A bear rug, complete with its head still attached, lay across the floor between the chairs and fireplace. Like the hallway, there were various wildlife, forest, and stream paintings around the room, along with other stuffed wildlife that Steve presumed were Kim Hooper's hunting trophies.

He quickly swept the first floor for clues, but only found home essentials and nothing that connected Kim Hooper and Martin Green to one another. Once done, Steve made his way up the stairs.

There were three doorways on the second floor, two on the right and one on the left. Steve found the first door on the right was a bathroom, which had the bare minimum: soap, toothbrush and toothpaste, shaving cream and a pack of disposable razors.

The second door was an office. An open roll-top wooden desk sat next to the window that overlooked the front lawn. Two bookcases were to Steve's right. The first bookcase was filled with books on World War Two and the Nazis. The second bookcase contained books about hunting, fishing, camping, and other outdoorsmen activities, like hiking and shooting. To the left was a glider rocker. Next to it, a stand with a lamp on top. The base of the lamp had a painting of a deer in the woods.

Beside the lamp rested a book titled: *NAZI CONCEN-TRATION CAMPS – THE HORRORS OF AUSCHWITZ AND BEYOND.* The photo below the title was black and white and showed a pile of bodies stacked head to feet, feet to head; a horrifying reminder of the atrocities committed by Adolf Hitler and the Third Reich. Behind the glider rocker was a gun rack that held several shotguns and hunting rifles.

Steve crossed the room to the desk. Like the rest of the home, the desk was tidy, everything in its rightful place in the small cubbyholes and slots. He pulled out the wooden chair, sat down and began going through the drawers. He didn't find anything useful until he pulled open the bottom drawer and lifted out a photo album.

Laying the album on the desk, Steve opened it. On the inside there was an inscription that read HUNTING TRIPS TO PAP'S PLACE.

Pap's place! Just like what was mentioned in the emails, Steve realized. His heart began to race. Was he onto something? He hoped so.

Steve switched the flashlight to its normal setting and opened the book. The first series of photos were black and white, pictures of men in what looked like 1940s or 1950s attire – some were posed with dead bucks and other animal carcasses – and taken in front of what appeared to be an old farmhouse.

In the middle of the album the photos changed and had been taken mostly on polaroid; some were badly fading. The fading pictures reminded Steve of Rebecca's photo on the National Center for Missing and Exploited Children's website and a pang of irritation fluttered through him that he had not uncovered more of her story. That was why he was here. But it seemed the more he dug into Rebecca's past and what happened to her, the further down the rabbit hole he ventured, with tunnels veering off into a twisted dark maze that were taking him to places unknown.

As he neared the end of the book, the old photos and polaroid pictures began to shift into more modern 4x6 color images that had a higher quality of definition. Here the pictures consisted mostly of three young men. In these photos they were partying, drinking, and like some of the older photos before them, they stood beside their kills, smiling proudly by the animals they had brought down. But when Steve flipped the last page, his blood froze.

He felt his stomach lurch and tasted bile in the back of his throat. He had come here looking for a connection between Green and Hooper, but what he had just discovered not only connected them, but also Rebecca.

He closed his eyes and saw the video of Rebecca play in his mind. The two masked men lifting Rebecca's small, dirt-covered body from the floor while she kicked and screamed, trying desperately to free herself of their large, powerful hands. He saw them slap her down onto the red table in the middle of the room and then shackle her to its legs with handcuffs.

When Steve opened his eyes, he stared at a picture of two men sitting at a table; it was covered with beer cans, snack food, and cards. Both men were looking at the camera. The one on the right was ruggedly handsome with tanned, leathery skin. Even in the picture one could tell how well-built he was, with large broad shoulders and a powerful chest and thick arms. His hair was wavy and long, sandy-blond, and a beard so thick it would have made Grizzly Adams blush with envy.

To the left sat another man. His hair was dark and cut close to his skull. This guy had boyish good looks and was leaner than his pal beside him. But it was the eyes that solidified who Steve was staring at. Martin Green.

Those dark, brooding eyes seemed to sneer at the camera in thin, angry slits, as if he did not want the photograph taken; the same brooding eyes he had seen in the photograph of Martin in the hallway of the Green home earlier in the day, when they had spoken with Audrey.

He did not know who the other man was, but Steve suspected that it might be Kim Hooper, since the photograph was found in an album in his desk. Still, it was not the men in the photo that had made Steve's blood harden, but the table these men were sitting at.

It was the exact same red table he had seen in Rebecca's video.

Chapter Eleven

S teve was up early the next morning. He phoned Amy a little past seven and told her to pick him up. It was time, Steve told her, that they speak with Sheriff Meeker. Amy asked what was going on, but he told her he didn't want to talk about it over the phone and to meet him at the inn. She must have heard the urgency in his voice because she was there within twenty minutes.

Steve met her at the front entrance and escorted her up to his room.

"You want to tell me what's going on?" Amy asked urgently, as she walked into his room and turned to face him as he closed the door.

"I found something that might connect Rebecca to Martin Green and Kim Hooper," Steve said.

"What?" Amy straightened. "What did you find?"

"A photograph."

Amy glanced at him, baffled. "A photograph?"

Steve nodded.

"And where did you find this photograph?" she asked,

apprehensively, afraid of what might come out of his mouth next.

Steve knew he had to be honest with her and confess what he was up to last night. "I went to Hooper's place after you dropped me off."

Amy grew quiet and her gaze drifted to the floor, pondering something. When she met his stare, her eyes had grown sharp and darkened, almost to a forest green.

"You lied to me."

Steve said nothing. Her contempt for being lied to had cut straight through him. He had no excuse for his actions, nor did he see a reason to deny that he had lied.

"I did."

"You lied to me so you could go and break into Hooper's house?"

"Not exactly."

"Not exactly?" Her voice rose slightly with irritation and she threw her hands out. "What the fuck does that mean, Steve?"

"The door to Hooper's house was broken when I got there. It opened on its own when I walked up the porch steps."

"And you thought it was a good idea just to mosey on in?"

"It's true," Steve said. "Look, I deceived you last night. But I did so with good intent. I suspected there might be something at Hooper's house that could tie him and Green together, after we found the emails yesterday. I didn't want to implicate you in what I was doing, okay?"

Amy crossed her arms and looked away. Steve could feel the anger pulsating from her like heat thrown from a radiator in a small room. She was upset with him and had every right to be. But what Steve couldn't tell was if she was angry with him because he broke the law to obtain evidence, or because he had not invited her along.

"You shut me out," Amy steamed. "You made sure you alone made the connection.

Guess I should have told her to come along, Steve thought.

"Amy, I didn't want to implicate you–" Steve tried again, but she cut him off before he could finish.

"That's such a fucking copout! And besides, you don't make decisions for me," she said, pointing a finger at him. "You said you didn't have a problem working with someone on a story–"

"I *don't* have a problem with working with someone."

"Then why didn't you tell me what you were up to last night? Why the dishonesty? I would have come along. We could have done this together. We're a team. This is *our* story, remember." Amy's angry glare made Steve feel the size of an ant that was about to be squashed by her boot.

Taking a deep breath, he shifted his weight uncomfortably. Steve knew telling Amy the truth was going to be tough, for both of them, but he had underestimated her resentment for being excluded in the illegal search of Hooper's home. But she was right. They were a team, a good team, he realized, and he should have kept her in the know about his suspicions. He shouldn't have gone off Lone Ranger-like. Now he felt awful for not including her.

"You're right. I should have told you what I was thinking, what I was really doing last night," Steve said. He looked back to her. She said nothing and wouldn't meet his gaze; her anger and distrust of him penetrated his heart. "There's no excuse for what I did. I'm sorry."

They were quiet for a long moment and Steve could see

she was contemplating her next move. He wanted to apologize again, to beg her to forgive his ignorance.

"Amy, I"–

"Let's get something straight. I'm not some dame you need to protect. I can handle myself. From here on out we're equals in this story, got it? You find something, you uncover something, you even think of something, you share it with me first." Her eyes were ablaze, brow furrowed into a tight scowl. "You don't do that, you can kiss your taxi, your mediator to witnesses, and police cooperation goodbye, and you can figure out the story on your own. Good luck with that."

Steve lowered his head and nodded like a kid getting berated by a teacher for acting out.

"You're right. I should have let you in. Again, please accept my sincerest apology and my word that I will not cut you out of the investigation from this point forward." He stuck his hand out to her. "Truce?"

Her eyes fell to his outstretched open hand. Was she considering his proposition? Steve hoped so. He needed her now more than ever. Then she took his hand and they shook.

"What photograph did you find?" she asked.

Steve crossed the room to the desk and picked up the photo of Martin Green and the mystery man at the table.

"This," Steve said, turning back and passing Amy the photo. "The one on the left is Martin Green, but I don't know who the other man is."

"Kim Hooper," Amy replied, looking up from the photo. "So they *did* know one another."

"If that is Hooper beside Green, like you say, it looks that way."

"It's him. He's younger in this picture, but that is definitely Kim Hooper. You found this at Hooper's place?"

"Yeah. In a photo album titled 'HUNTING TRIPS TO PAP'S PLACE.'"

"That was in Green's email. *Pap's place.*" Amy said. Steve nodded. She looked back to the photo and studied it close. "This photo ties Green and Hooper as acquaintances. But I don't see how you can connect it to Rebecca by this alone. She's not even in the photo."

"No, she's not." Steve pointed at the photograph. "But the table they are sitting at is the same red table in her video."

Amy's eyes rose slowly to him. "Are you sure?"

"Yes. That's where they..." Steve trailed off. The images of Rebecca found their way back into his mind once more. He shook them away. "Anyway, I think we can go see Sheriff Meeker with what we have. But first, I need to speak to my editor, run what we have by him first. Also, I want him to know that we're working on this together, as a team." Steve winked at Amy.

He picked up his cell phone and dialed Charlie's direct line, then put the phone on speaker so Amy could hear and talk. Charlie picked up on the third ring.

"Make this quick," Charlie said. "I'm about to go into a staff meeting and a conference call with some investors."

"Charlie, I'm here with Amy Richards from the Hanover Daily Record. We have something we need to run by you."

"You have five minutes, starting now."

Steve and Amy laid out the details of their investigation and made their case as quick as possible. Charlie listened and didn't interrupt. When they were finished, Charlie agreed the evidence collected would, if nothing else, get their foot in the door to talk to the local sheriff.

"There's one other thing, Charlie," Steve said. "Amy's been working closely with me on this. Without her help, I wouldn't have gotten this far. I've agreed to share the by-line with her."

"If that works for you, I'm fine with it," Charlie replied.

Steve thought Charlie would have put up more resistance to bringing Amy on board – he was not one for surprises – but he figured his boss's mind was elsewhere that morning with trying to keep the paper afloat by impressing the investors.

"Great." Steve looked at Amy and gave her a thumbs-up.

"Get after it," Charlie said. "Keep me posted."

"Will do." Steve ended the call and turned to Amy. "Ready to go see Sheriff Meeker now?"

"You better believe I am," Amy said as a sly, cunning smile grew on her face.

A sign at the edge of Hanover's downtown area read:

Welcome To Historic
Downtown Hanover
Where Happy Living Puts
A Smile On Your Face
POP. 3550

Steve wondered what was so historic about Hanover, that

it needed to be brought up on the sign. As he gazed around the small southern Pennsylvania town, he realized that Hanover was like any other small Pennsylvania town he had ever visited. There was nothing special that made Hanover stand out, or to entice people to come live there. *You had to be born in Hanover to want to live here,* Steve figured.

It was hard to believe there was a pack of serial killers walking these quaint streets, hiding somewhere between the apple pie cooling on the windowsill and the white picket fences. The thought unnerved him, and a disquiet lifted the hair at the nape of his neck. Hanover *was* the perfect hunting ground for three killers, a place where no one would think to look.

They made their way into Center Square, Hanover and pulled the car into a parking space in front of a three-story gray building. "Hanover Police Department" was painted across the front in bold yellow lettering with a black outline. In front of the station sat a bronze statue of a figure on horseback. At first, Steve thought the figure represented the old police force in Hanover but quickly noticed the statue's attire was that of a Civil War soldier, not of a police officer.

"He's called 'The Picket,'" Amy said, noticing Steve's interest in the bronze statue. "He was erected in 1905 by famed Boston artist Cyrus Dallin, commemorating the Battle of Hanover on June 30, 1863."

"That's one day before the Battle of Gettysburg."

Amy nodded. "Because of the Battle of Hanover, and later the march through York and Battle of Carlisle, the Confederate Cavalry, which was riding north to get around the Union Army, was delayed getting to Gettysburg."

"Changing the outcome of history," Steve said, looking back at the statue.

"Indeed. And here you thought there was nothing historic about Hanover."

"That obvious, huh?"

"Just a little. C'mon."

They stepped out into the brisk morning. Steve turned and looked around Center Square. It was filled with buildings, local restaurants, and stores. There were a few people out that morning on the sidewalks, most, Steve suspected, going to their places of work in the downtown area.

A horn beeped, drawing his attention across the square. It appeared a delivery truck and a blue minivan could not decide who should go through the intersection first. The man behind the truck wheel waved the minivan through first, and then proceeded through the intersection.

Once the truck pulled away, Steve saw a black Dodge Ram with tinted windows parked across the intersection. He was sure he had seen that same truck somewhere before, but he could not, for the life of him, remember where.

He pushed the thought aside. He had seen a lot of trucks, especially Dodge Rams, while traveling around the area, so maybe he had passed it along the way somewhere. Steve turned and he and Amy headed into the Hanover Police Department building.

Inside the station, it was as quiet as a library on a Sunday afternoon. There was no one around, and Steve wondered if the place was even open. *Could a police station shut down? Not even at Christmas.* The thought dwindled when he heard footsteps approaching the front desk.

An officer walked through a doorway that led to the rear of the police station.

"Can I help–" The officer's words caught in his throat when his eyes fell on Amy. His Adam's apple bobbed, like a man trying to work up the nerve to ask a girl out. "A-Amy... h-hi." The officer's cheeks reddened bashfully.

No introductions were needed for Steve to know he was not Sheriff Meeker. The officer was somewhere in his late twenties to early thirties, and tall, around six foot three. He had a thick head of wavy brown hair, and his steel-blue eyes held the freshness of someone who had not seen much of the world.

"Hi, Jonas," Amy said, forcing a smile. "Is the sheriff around?"

"Sure." Jonas gave a broad toothy grin. "You want me to go get him?" He flipped a hitchhiker thumb over his shoulder; his right hand rested on the buckle of his belt like a gunslinger. "He's in his office."

There was a goofy, boyish charm about the handsome officer that probably made him attractive to the younger girls around Hanover – they would swoon when he drove past them on the streets in his patrol car, Steve assumed. But he also got the impression that older residents of Hanover might think of him more as a Barney Fife type of character.

"If you wouldn't mind."

"Not a problem." Jonas waved her off. His eyes lingered on Amy longer than they should have, taking all of her beauty in and locking it away for later use perhaps. Finally, he turned away, opened the door from which he came, and hurried down the hallway; the door closed behind him with a heavy bang that shook the floor.

"Admirer of yours?" Steve whispered.

Amy rolled her eyes. "Jonas Roberts has had a thing for me since we were first introduced. He can't seem to get it through his head that I'm not – nor will I ever be – interested in him."

Some Kind of Truth

Steve felt the air around Amy grow stilted. Her coldness toward her admirer was a fair assessment of Jonas's unwanted continued advancements and affection. Steve had to admit that it was fun to watch him stumble over his words – a beautiful woman had that power over a man sometimes – but to pursue Amy like a horny hound dog was crossing the ethical line, especially for an officer of the law. Amy had a right to be irritated and she should bring her concern up with the sheriff if Jonas was making her uncomfortable.

It was easy to see why Amy would not be interested in Jonas. He was a bit goofy, too young, lacked confidence and the intellectual stimulus that someone like Amy would need in her life. He was sure Jonas would eventually grow into a well-rounded man. Men had to discover who they really were, who they really wanted to spend the rest of their lives with, and usually that was not with the person they always wanted it to be. That took time, understanding, and self-exploration.

For Steve, it took viewing the war through a reporter's eyes and fighting to survive his capture. He found out exactly who he was and what he was capable of while over there.

"I'm sure his affection for you will pass once he finds the right girl," Steve said.

"Are you speaking from experience, Mr. James?" Amy shot him a smartass smirk.

Steve smiled, knowingly, but added nothing more about his own pubescent years, and the following decade, chasing after girls. He looked away from Amy when a large burly man with a thick black beard appeared in the doorway.

"Hi, Ben," Amy said, stiffening.

Sheriff Ben Meeker reminded Steve of Bluto from the

Popeye comics – big, bearded, and burly; all Meeker needed was a sailor suit. Meeker shifted his hard gaze between the two of them. A fiery contempt burned in his eyes; he did not want them here.

"It's always nice to see you, Amy," Meeker began, choosing his words carefully. His voice was deep and gruff, like listening to some old-timer tell a western story. *Manly,* Steve thought. "But when you come to the station wearing your workface, and bringing outside help, I get a little concerned." He said this with no emotion, but with a directness that was meant to sting.

A small, tense laugh escaped Amy's lips, and her face turned a shade of pink. Was it caused by embarrassment or anger? Maybe a little of both, Steve concluded.

"Ben, this is–"

"I know who you are, Mr. James," Meeker said, turning to Steve.

Had rumors started to spread through Hanover about their investigation, and made their way back to Sheriff Meeker's ears? It was possible. People talk in small towns, word gets around fast, and when the cat's out of the bag, everyone knows.

We need to tread carefully, Steve thought.

"I'd say it's a pleasure to meet you, Sheriff, but since you're so intent on being rude to us, I'll cut right to the point about why we're here," Steve said.

Meeker shifted his bulk from one foot to the other and crossed his arms over his barrel chest; he looked like a bouncer at a bar guarding the door. His jaw hardened, and he glared at Steve. If Meeker could have shot lasers out of his eyes, Steve would be nothing more than a pile of ash on the floor.

"We want to see the Green and Hooper videos."

Meeker's hard demeanor didn't waver. It was almost as if he had expected them to walk into the station that morning and ask to see the murder videos. Again, Steve wondered if someone had been watching them and reported back to the Sheriff about what they were up to.

"You think you can just barge in here with demands?" Meeker said. "I guess a hotshot reporter like yourself, thinks he can get away with such things."

Steve considered Meeker's statement for a moment before answering. He had never fancied himself a "hotshot reporter;" even the term brought up pangs of anger that made him furious.

It was a cliché to be called such a thing. Steve worked hard to not become a reporter who sought fame from other people's tragedies. Many journalists had done just that over the years to score TV, movie, and book deals. To Steve, these fame-seekers were no longer journalists. They had crossed the line to celebrity personality – especially if they got their own morning or talk show.

Though he guessed, since breaking the Palazzo case and his capture and escape in Afghanistan, he had fallen into such a category himself. Still, he would not accept how others wanted to perceive him.

"I wouldn't say that, Sheriff Meeker," Steve replied. "But I would think that you may want to exchange information with us."

Meeker took a step forward. His eyes shifted to Amy and then back to Steve, inquisitively. "What information could you possibly have that would make me share anything with you?"

"Amy and I are confident, by what we recently uncovered, that the disappearance of Rebecca Turner connects to the murders of Kim Hooper and Martin Green," Steve said.

Meeker studied Steve carefully. He was trying to decide if what Steve said was reliable, or a crack-pot theory cooked up by, what he considered, a 'hot-shot reporter' looking to boost his name further off a local tragedy.

"Bullshit!" Meeker fumed; he made his decision. "You don't have anything."

Steve tapped his bag, enticingly, like calling a kitten to pounce. "You wanna call my bluff, Sheriff? Or do you want to step down off your law enforcement high horse and help us figure out what's going on? The choice is yours."

Chapter Twelve

Meeker finally agreed to speak with them, though Steve felt it was not without reservation and distrust that he, and the crimes, were somehow going to be distorted by the media. But Steve had left him with little recourse. If Sheriff Meeker wanted to know what they had, then he was going to have to exchange information. That was the deal.

Meeker led them to a room with just enough space to fit a small table and four chairs. The room's walls were bare except for a mounted flat-screen TV. The sheriff told them to take a seat and wait until he returned.

"Well... that was tense," Amy said, once Meeker was gone.

"Yeah," Steve replied and breathed a sigh of relief. *Made it past the first roadblock.*

"Have you ever done something like that before?"

"Bargain with a cop?"

"Yeah." Amy's green eyes shone with excitement and she stared at Steve with a look of wide admiration.

He was aware of the budding rapport between himself

and Amy, even after their argument, which he took as a good sign that Amy did not hold grudges and they had moved past it. Their partnership on this case had joined them in a way Steve had not seen coming. And, he had to admit, that he had not felt so comfortable working alongside someone in years.

At the same time, his thoughts of a relationship – past this investigation – with Amy concerned him. Usually, he would never mix his professional life with his personal one. He had seen too many reporters – male and female – lose their jobs or resign because their hormones ruined their careers. Steve had made it a rule not to get personally involved with a colleague.

Still, there was something about Amy that worked Steve up inside, bending his emotions and feelings for her in an uncomfortable, yet pleasant way. What was it about her that intrigued him so that, if the opportunity presented itself, he knew he would willingly break one of his long-standing rules?

The door opened, and Meeker entered the room. He held two plastic bags marked EVIDENCE. Two case files were tucked under his right arm. He sat down across the table from Amy and Steve; fumes of anger wafted off him like heat from a summer road.

"I want to make this perfectly clear: everything we talk about today is off the record." His eyes shifted from Steve to Amy, and then back to Steve, where they remained until Steve nodded in agreement. "None of what we speak about leaves this room. Understand?"

Steve had heard the 'off the record' speech so many times, it seemed superfluous at this point. It was apparent Meeker was more concerned with his ability to publish a story than Amy's. Steve's name on the byline would surely bring awareness to the gruesome crimes.

The attention of the article would thrust Meeker, his department, and the town of Hanover into the national spotlight. Meeker shied away from that, knowing the media, especially the talking heads on TV, would scrutinize the entire investigation, while at the same time, sensationalizing it for ratings. However, Steve knew Meeker needed them as much as they needed him now, so he was willing to bend his rules, at least for the time being.

Steve and Amy understood the conditions set forth and would follow along. *For now*, Steve thought. He was going to be a wise-ass and raise his right hand, three fingers in the air and say *scouts honor,* but thought better of it. Upsetting Meeker further was a bad idea. They needed to see the other videos and that meant keeping the sheriff in their good graces.

Meeker's eyes shifted to the computer bag under Steve's right palm; his face tightened, the crow lines growing into deep fissures.

"You said you had something. What?" Meeker growled.

Steve opened the bag and pulled out the small, white box and his laptop and set them on the table. He turned on the computer, and while it booted up, he opened the box and pulled out Rebecca's driver's license.

"This was delivered to me, Sheriff," Steve said, handing the license across the table to Meeker's massive open paw.

Meeker examined the ID. "This is Rebecca Turner's driver's license." He looked down at the white box, now confused as to why a Pittsburgh reporter would have received it.

"There was also a USB flash drive inside," Steve added. "On the flash drive, there's a video of Rebecca Turner."

Meeker's eyes shot from the box back to Steve; his right one twitching uncontrollably with anger. He grew straight in the chair, took a long, irate breath, let it out slowly, then handed the driver's license back.

"Why you, Mr. James?" Meeker asked, dusting the reddish-brown specks of dirt from his hands. "Why not share that video with the police department, or–" He glanced at Amy but said nothing.

Steve shrugged. "I don't know why someone chose me to investigate, Sheriff. But what I do know is this: whoever left the driver's license and the flash drive, wanted me to link what happened to Rebecca Turner to the Green and Hooper murders."

"And can you prove this, Mr. James?"

"I'm confident we can," Steve replied. Meeker's stare hardened, and his right eye twitched again with irritation. Steve sat up in the chair. "We're willing to share what we have, Sheriff, including the video of what happened to Rebecca. But the bigger question is: are you willing to share with *us*?"

Chapter Thirteen

After the Rebecca Turner video ended, Meeker sat back in the chair, his face flaccid and ashen with disgust. When his eyes met Steve's, they were filled with hatred; the kind of hate Steve had only seen once before, in a child's eyes while being held captive in a cave in the Tora Bora Mountains.

Steve and Meeker were alone in the room now. Amy had excused herself five minutes into the viewing, visibly shaken by the brutal acts of violence on the screen. There was no way to sugarcoat the viciousness of the video. He wanted to go after her. To make sure she was okay. To comfort her. To protect her. But he kept his distance. Amy needed time to process what she had seen.

"That should be burnt," Meeker said through gritted teeth. "And so should the cocksuckers who did that to Rebecca."

Meeker's words echoed Charlie's.

The sheriff leaned into his elbows on top of the table. "What else do you have?"

Steve ran over the evidence he and Amy had collected,

and how they believed that the murders of Green and Hooper were connected to Rebecca. He then pulled out the photo he'd taken from Hooper's house and passed it to Meeker.

"That's a photo of Kim Hooper and Martin Green, Sheriff," Steve said. He did not offer his opinion on the red table, rather letting Meeker see it for himself.

"It's the same red table in the video. Where did you get this photo?"

Steve knew the question about how he acquired the photograph would come up, but luckily, before he was forced to answer, the door opened and Amy entered the room.

She was visibly shaken. Her eyes were dull and vacant; the lights were on, but no one was home. She moved to the chair beside Steve on rubbery legs that looked like they could barely support her weight. He wondered if he should help her into the chair before her legs did in fact give out, and she crumbled to the floor.

Then again, he wasn't sure he could stand himself after seeing Rebecca's video again; his legs felt about as reliable as Amy's appeared. But Amy eased into the chair, unassisted. She did not meet Steve's gaze and stared blankly at the floor, seeing everything and nothing at the same time.

"Are you okay?" Steve asked her. Amy nodded but remained quiet. He reached out and took her hand and held it, hoping the comforting gesture would help. Though he doubted it would. There was nothing in this world that could erase what she had seen.

"As I was saying," Meeker continued. "The table in Rebecca's video is the same one in the Green and Hooper photograph." A knowing glint flashed across the sheriff's sharp, hawk-like eyes.

Steve caught Meeker's look and pounced on it like a lion would its prey. "What do you know that we don't, Sheriff?"

"Before I say anything else, you need to first watch the Green video." Meeker tapped the evidence bags. "Everything will be clear afterward."

Meeker opened the EVIDENCE bag, pulled out the Green flash drive and loaded it into the wall-mounted television, then killed the overhead lights.

When the video began to play, the angle was on a dirty wooden floor, and booted feet appeared in the frame; the camera's light was the only source of illumination in an otherwise dark room. Then the boots began walking across the room.

It quickly became apparent to Steve that someone was either holding the camera or had it mounted on them as they crossed the room. The angle panned up from the floor and onto an old red wooden table, the same table Rebecca had been shackled to, the same table Martin Green and Kim Hooper had been sitting at in the photo. Various tools were laid out across it: a screwdriver, a blow torch, drill, pliers, even a battery-powered grinder and circular saw. Beside a claw-headed hammer was a black metal chisel with the end recently sharpened; the raw metal gleamed under the camera's light.

Meeker looked at Steve.

"Same table," Steve whispered.

Meeker nodded and looked back at the TV as the scene continued.

Slowly, the camera panned around on the TV, and out of the darkness a nude male figure started to take shape. Amy's grip tightened on Steve's hand.

In the video, the man's hands were bound over his head

with leather straps fastened to a wall plastered in a yellow-ish-green wallpaper. His legs were splayed, kept in place by another pair of leather straps around his ankles. The man's head hung limp, his chin resting on the left side of his muscular chest. He appeared to be unconscious. A gloved hand then came into frame, reached out, and pushed his head to the right.

What Steve saw next made him sit forward; disgust clawed its way up his throat and produced a nasty bile taste at the back of his tongue.

On the left pectoral muscle was a tattoo of a skull and crossbones. Above the skull three words were written in a semicircle, I STOLE THE, and underneath the crossbones, BOOTY.

Meeker paused the video.

"Do you see what I see?" he asked, turning back to Steve.

Steve swallowed. There was a bite at the back of his throat from the bile's sharp tang, and he glanced down to his laptop bag, where the flask was hidden safely inside. He thought about pulling it out and taking a healthy sip to wash away the awful taste and to quiet the squirming demons inside, but he didn't want to pull out the flask in the middle of the police station with Amy and Meeker in the room.

He lifted his laden eyes to Meeker and with a shaking hand tapped the left side of his chest. "The tattoo."

"It appears that way. The image in Rebecca's video is too blurry to know for sure—"

"It's the same," Steve said. "I already had my guy in Pittsburgh clean up the image."

Meeker's face was filled with disturbed, troubled thoughts of a man who finally saw someone for who they truly were. "Then that *is* Martin Green in both videos."

Steve felt just as blindsided. It was almost unfathomable how quickly the investigation had changed course. He had been driven by the belief that there were three killers walking the streets of Hanover, preying on people, trying to make a name for themselves for both their past and present crimes. But now he knew differently. Martin Green was not an innocent victim in all of this, who just happened to be in the wrong place at the wrong time, he was one of the three who had hurt Rebecca.

Meeker slid Green's casefile across the table. Steve opened it and began looking through the crime scene photos. The condition of Green's body was as horrific as Joe Tully had described it.

"Good…" Steve cleared his throat, felt his chest constrict with a jab of pain in his lower right side. "Good God."

"He suffered plenty before he met his end, trust me," Meeker said.

Looking up to Meeker, Steve found the sheriff watching him with a curious fascination that he found disconcerting.

He pulled his gaze away, unable to take Meeker's stare, and looked back to the file and began to study the photos closely. Green's toes were missing, as Tully had described, and there was a small, black puncture hole just below his jaw. Dried blood coated the left side of his nude, gray body leaning against the cross.

"He wasn't murdered in Tully's field," Meeker said. "Green was murdered wherever the video was shot. Trust me, it's all captured, every detail."

Steve studied the area around Green in the photo. "The ground is dry. Were any footprints found at the crime scene?"

"No. It was late November and the cold came early last year. Ground was already frozen by that point."

"But why was Green left in Tully's field?"

Meeker shook his head. "There's more you need to see." He glanced at Amy, who still sat in a state of shock, but he said nothing to comfort her.

Steve wondered what she was thinking, what she was feeling. She looked lost in this world suddenly, as if the reality she knew was nothing more than an illusion. He wished he could do something to ease her discomfort, to reassure her that amidst the darkness there was light. But Steve wondered if he was the right person to make such a statement. He had seen what men could do to one another, and more often than not, it appeared the cruelty of mankind dulled what little essences of good there seemed to be in the world.

Meeker started the video again.

On the screen, the person filming took a handful of dark hair and yanked the man's head upward to face the camera. The left side of Martin Green's face was bruised, the eye socket swollen and discolored. A trickle of blood ran from the left nostril, dripped off his chin and onto his chest where it made a perfectly round bloodspot, just above the tattooed 'I'. His eyes rolled around in their sockets like ping pong balls floating in a glass of water. It appeared he had been beaten and knocked unconscious at some point before his capture.

The person filming Green then slapped him, hard.

Steve and Amy both jumped at the sound. The crack across Green's face had echoed off the walls like a shotgun blast. Amy turned and buried her face in Steve's chest. He put his arm around her and pulled her close; he could feel her body trembling.

When Steve returned his gaze to the video, Green was alert, but dazed and highly disoriented. He tried scanning his surroundings in the dimly lit room, looking for a way to escape. But Steve saw the hope quickly pour from Green's face and eyes when he realized that there would be no way out for him.

"Who's there?" Green asked, looking directly at the camera, squinting through the bright light shining into his eyes.

Steve lifted his arms from around Amy and sat up. He had heard that voice before.

The camera panned away, back to the table.

"What the fuck are you doing? Why are you doing this to me?" Green asked offscreen.

The gloved hand came back into frame, running a finger across the various tools on the red table, as if to decide which one to use. The right hand clamped around the hammer, while the left picked up the chisel. There was a streak of light, and blurry images as the camera quickly turned back to Green. His pale, nude body seemed small and weak, though Martin Green was neither of these – even after twenty-five years, he was still toned and muscular.

The camera pushed in close on Green's face. His pupils were small, black pinpoints, and he looked lost in a daze of confusion and despair. The hammer and chisel slowly came up from the bottom of the screen into the frame, letting Green see the instruments that were about to be used on him.

"I want to hear you laugh, Martin," said an indistinguishable voice behind the camera.

"Laugh?" Green asked with a bewildered look.

"Laugh like you do in your videos, Martin."

Meeker paused the video again and turned back to them.

"Videos?" Steve questioned. He felt his heart speed up

and beads of sweat broke out like acne across his forehead. "Are there other videos that Green was a part of? Is that what the murderer's suggesting, Sheriff?"

Meeker lifted his shoulders, but the doubt on his face said more than he meant it to.

"If there are more videos, we haven't found them yet. We've searched both Green's home and his shop, along with Hooper's place. No videos were found at any of those locations."

"Yet, you suspected Green was murdered because of the '*your videos*' reference. That's why you agreed to speak with us. You had nothing to go on, until today when Amy and I walked through the door with Rebecca's video, which we now know ties Green directly to the 'your videos' statement." Meeker nodded but kept quiet. "Did you do a deeper search of the hard drive at Green's shop? That's where we came across the emails."

"We did. But outside of those secret emails, there wasn't anything else found on the computer."

"You didn't consider the emails suspicious, Sheriff?"

"Suspicious? Sure. But do they prove anything? No."

"They prove that Green knew Hooper," Steve said.

"No, they don't. Since there is no way to trace those emails, all they really prove is that Green knew someone he called K. K could have been short for Kim Hooper. Or K could have been short for Kyle, Katherine, or Kelly."

"But it was Kim Hooper who Green sent the emails to," Steve said, tapping the photo of Green and Hooper. "There's your proof that they knew one another, Sheriff."

"But we didn't have this photo at the time we went through Green's computer. Which brings me back to an earlier question: how exactly did you come by this photograph, Mr. James?"

"A source gave it to me," Steve replied without hesitation.

"What source?" Meeker asked, eyeing him skeptically like a dog might a piece of strange meat it finds along the road.

"A confidential one."

Meeker's jaw twitched and his eyes narrowed sharply once more. Steve was confident that Meeker knew he was lying about how he got the photograph. But it didn't matter how Steve acquired it at this point. Green knew Hooper, and Steve was able to prove it. Not only that, but the photograph also placed both Hooper and Green in the same room where Rebecca was tortured. But if Rebecca was not the only girl Green and his pals tortured, how many more victims were there? And why had the other videos not been delivered to him as well? Why only Rebecca's?

Steve sank back into the chair. He felt drained; exhausted suddenly. He brought his hands to his face and ground his palms into the sockets of his burning eyes. He needed a drink. He thought about the voice talking to Martin Green on the video. *"I want to hear you laugh, Martin,"* the voice had whispered. *"Laugh like you do in your videos."*

Who was talking to Green? Steve wondered.

There was no indication if the voice was male or female; the words had been murmured in such a way to hide the cadence. Had the video been altered to disguise the voice and throw investigators off? It was possible.

Meeker glanced at Amy and asked, "You okay? Do you need to leave the room again? You look ill."

"I'm fine," Amy murmured, as if speaking would cause her to vomit.

"I always knew you didn't have the stomach for what

they have you writing." His tone was harsh, unapologetic. Meeker's gaze shifted from Amy and settled on Steve. "She's a ray of sunshine peeking into the darkness and not liking what she's shedding light on. You get me?"

Steve understood. He thrived on the darkness of human nature to make a living. Still, he was surprised how much Meeker's opinion mirrored his own – not everyone was cut out to investigate the abyss and come out unscathed; some could, some could not. Steve knew Amy was a talented investigator and reporter, but that did not mean she could look the devil in the eye and not blink.

"The voice on the video? Did you have it analyzed?" Steve asked.

"We did," Meeker said, nodding. "It was inconclusive. No one could give me a definitive answer. Some said it was male, others said female."

Steve gritted his teeth. *Another roadblock. Fuck.*

"I noticed the murderer's hands are free in the video," Steve said.

"I suspect the murderer was wearing one of those Go-Pro-type of cameras mounted to themselves so they could record hands-free," the sheriff replied.

Steve nodded. *Makes sense.*

Back on the screen, the chisel rested on top of Green's big toe with the hammer poised above it. His cries and whimpers had turned into a hyperventilating wheeze. The sounds of a man who knew his time on earth was about to end. Miserably.

"Let me hear you laugh, Martin," the voice spoke.

Green did this time and let out a high pitch, schoolboy-like cackle that Steve instantly recognized. *Laughing Boy.* The same laugh he had heard on Rebecca's video while she was being tortured and humiliated by the other two, while Green filmed it all.

Before Green knew what was happening, the hammer came down hard onto the chisel's flat head. The sharpened blade drove through the flesh of the big toe with ease, severed the bone, and buried itself in the wooden floor underneath.

"Oh, God!" Amy screamed and buried her face in Steve's shoulder.

"That's enough, Sheriff," Steve said. "We get the picture."

Meeker stopped the video, crossed the room, and flipped on the lights. Steve was thankful; he did not want to be in the dark anymore. He needed the light, begged for the brightness of the overhead hum of the bulbs to reassure himself that he was back in the real world.

"Hard to watch, huh?" Meeker said as he came around the table. His lips were pulled into a tight grimace – or was it a smile? Steve could not decipher which.

"That's an understatement," Steve replied. He turned to Amy. "Are you okay?"

Amy nodded and sat up. She looked peaked while pushing a strand of hair away from her face.

"Can I get you a glass of water?" Steve offered.

"No. I'll be okay."

Meeker took a seat across the table from them again and asked, "Why do you think you got the video of Rebecca Turner?"

"Isn't it obvious now?"

Meeker glared at him, not saying anything.

"Someone wanted me to know what happened to Rebecca, so when I connected the crimes, and found out what happened to Green and Hooper, I would understand the killer's motivations."

A silence befell the small room. Steve sat up in the chair as an uncomfortable, but rational thought blossomed in his mind. When he glanced back to Meeker, he realized the sheriff was also bouncing his own series of questions and ideas around internally. But were they on the same page?

"I think someone's hunting those three men down for what they did, Sheriff," Steve said.

Meeker nodded and his eyes drifted back to the table where Green and Hooper's files lay. He adjusted them so they were sitting side-by-side, as if they had been out of order.

"Do you want to see the other video now, Mr. James?" Meeker asked, looking up at Steve without lifting his head.

At first, Steve thought the sheriff was being coy, a way of scaring them out of the police station, so they would not write the story. But Meeker was dead serious. His intense stare was enough to cause Steve to look away, slowly shaking his head as he did. He could take no more of Meeker's glare, nor would he be able to sit through watching another brutal killing.

"How... how bad is the other video?"

"Bad," Meeker said, unapologetically. "Hooper was slowly cooked to death with a blow torch."

Steve swallowed; his dry throat screamed for something wet and strong. His eyes drifted to the laptop bag, where the flask of whiskey was safely hidden once again. He licked his lips like a man walking through the desert, desperate for a drink of water.

Meeker looked down at one of the two files in front of him. "That's the PG version." His eyes rose and met Steve's again, searching... but for what? He slowly slid Kim Hooper's file to Steve.

Steve reached for the file and was about to open it when he saw Amy shift uneasily in her seat. She wrapped her arms around her shoulders as if to keep herself from falling to pieces. He wanted to put his arm around her again, to comfort her, to...

Love her?

The thought entered his head before he had time to stop it. He felt his face blush, and he quickly looked away, ashamed that such a thought would cross his mind at an inconvenient time.

As those thoughts of love dwindled, something else began to materialize in Steve's mind in its stead.

There was another similarity between the videos. One all of them had overlooked. *Until now.* The killer was making a horrific, yet poignant statement by torturing and murdering Green, and on camera, in that dingy room, for a reason.

"The room," Steve said.

"What?" Meeker asked, the skin between his eyebrows wrinkling.

"The room where Green was murdered; it's the same room Rebecca Turner was tortured in. Put in Hooper's video, Sheriff?"

Meeker stood, ejected the Green USB drive, and slipped in the one with Kim Hooper on it. The video began to play.

This time, the footage captured Kim Hooper's savagely beaten face center frame; it was a swollen, bloody mess that made him look like a boxer who had gone several rounds. He had been stripped nude and bound to the wall with the same yellowish-green wallpaper, just like Martin Green had been.

"There," Steve said, pointing. "Pause it." Meeker did. "That's the same wallpaper in all three videos."

"Holy shit," Meeker gasped. "You're right."

Out of the corner of Steve's eye, he saw Amy grow rigid. She turned to him, and Steve met her urgent gaze. Her large, green eyes bore deep into his soul, imploring Steve to understand what she was silently trying to say.

But what was she trying to tell him?

"I hate to cut this short, but Steve and I really need to get going," Amy said, looking back to Meeker.

Meeker's face tightened with apprehensive thoughts, thoughts that deepened the creases in the center of his forehead even further.

Amy jumped to her feet as Meeker and Steve rose from their chairs.

"What's the sudden rush?" Meeker asked suspiciously.

"Steve needs to get back to Pittsburgh by five. He has a deadline to meet." Amy faced him. "Right?"

"That's right." Steve faked a smile, but he had no plans on being back in Pittsburgh this afternoon. *What is Amy up to?* he wondered.

Meeker watched Amy incredulously. He had noticed the difference in her body language and the sudden angst to leave. His cop intuition was piqued.

Not good!

"Thank you, Sheriff," Amy said. "For everything."

Meeker replied with a gruff grunt. He walked past them to the door and opened it. Amy went through first. Meeker watched her pass; his right eye twitched with irritation again. Amy kept her head lowered, unable to look into Meeker's black hawk-like eyes as she walked out of the room. Steve followed. But Meeker's large mitt grabbed him by the elbow, stopping him.

"I don't know what wind just blew up her skirt, but you two stay out of this investigation. Am I making myself clear, Mr. James?" Meeker's eyes were hard as iron and his jaw set like granite. His gaze then shifted down the hall to Amy. "I've known Amy since she was a little girl. I'd hate to find out something happened to her because she couldn't let me handle this."

Steve said nothing as he pulled his arm free of Meeker's grip and headed down the hall.

———

They were back in the car before Steve spoke.

"You mind telling me what that was all about back there?" he asked, lighting his first cigarette of the day. "We were getting somewhere. Maybe about to prove that Hooper was on Rebecca's video as well."

"I know where the videos were filmed," Amy said.

"What!" Steve hollered; the smoke caught in his throat, causing a small coughing fit. When his throat cleared and the hacking subsided, he asked, "Where? And how on earth could you know, Amy?"

"The videos were made in an abandoned farmhouse. My friends and I used to play there as kids. My uncle had a small hunting cabin off Moulstown Road. Behind the cabin, there were trails all through the woods. One trail led back to the farmhouse." Amy looked at him gravely. "I recognized–"

"The wallpaper," Steve said.

Chapter Fourteen

According to Amy, the farmhouse sat two and a half miles away from the nearest road, in a valley surrounded by fields and woods. The only way to get there was on foot.

Steve was not dressed for such a trudge, nor had he brought the proper clothes along. Amy stopped at the Wal-Mart on Eisenhower Drive so he could pick up a pair of boots, heavy work pants and jacket, gloves, and a hat. Afterward, they returned to Amy's house to change.

Amy's home was a 1980s style rancher on the outskirts of town. Inside, a small hallway led to the kitchen, dining, and living room areas. A door stood open in the middle of the hall, with a sign above it that said Powder Room.

"You can change in there," Amy said, pointing to the bathroom.

He quickly changed into the heavier clothes and boots. Once dressed, Steve pulled the .38 out of the laptop bag and slid it into the front pocket of the jacket; the bulk of the jacket hid the gun well enough that no one would notice it on him.

Reaching back into the bag, Steve pulled out the flask and was about to take a sip when he caught his reflection in the mirror. He no longer recognized the grizzled face, nor the sorrowful eyes staring back at him. Once, a long time ago it seemed, his eyes were bright blue, alive with hope and vigor for the future. Now, they were a dull gray, consumed with the pain and torment of a man who had seen too many atrocities to bear.

Steve unscrewed the cap and took a sip from the flask. A dribble ran down his chin, and he wiped it away with the back of his hand. Revulsion washed over him. He knew he depended too much on alcohol to cope. He needed to stop drinking and face his past – face what he had done, what he *had been forced* to do in that cave while held hostage. But drinking those memories away was easier than facing them. Steve was not proud that he understood this about himself, but he was unsure he could change.

He returned the flask to the bag, turned off the light, and opened the bathroom door. Heading to the kitchen, Steve thought he would find Amy there waiting for him, but she wasn't.

The kitchen was to Steve's left and the dining room to the right; a small table sat next to the sliding glass door that overlooked the patio and backyard, now a glossy white surface of frozen snow. An island separated the kitchen and dining room.

Amy's home was decorated with Americana wall hangings and knickknacks, some most likely bought at second-hand stores and flea markets. The decorations gave the place a warm, welcoming feeling that Steve enjoyed. The air smelled of honeysuckle and reminded him of summers as a kid and the Fourth of July. He wondered if that had been Amy's objective.

Pulling out one of the barstools, he took a seat at the island when a movement caught his eyes.

He looked up, past the kitchen, to another small hallway that led to the bedrooms. At the end of the hall a door with a mirror attached to it hung open. It was positioned at such an angle that he saw Amy inside, undressing.

Steve quickly looked away. Embarrassment warmed his face. Shame for his actions, even if they were a mistake, made him feel worse, like a pervert for wanting to continue to leer at Amy in her underwear. He would not be that kind of man.

He stood and moved into the living room where he noticed a framed article from the Pittsburgh Tribune above the fireplace. In the center of the article was the World Trade Center on 9/11, captured moments after the second tower was struck by Flight 175. The headline in large bold letters read: **NEVER FORGET**. Below, in much smaller lettering was the byline: **by STEVE JAMES.**

It struck Steve odd that Amy would have an article of his hanging above her fireplace. But what bothered him more was which article it was. His NEVER FORGET story had been the hardest piece Steve had written for the Tribune in his twenty-seven years with the paper, and still, to this day, it choked him up when he reread it. *The day the entire world changed. The day I changed,* he thought.

The memory of the attack outside the wire on December 1, 2001, flashed across Steve's mind with such force it caused an internal shudder through his body. He had been traveling with a group of ten soldiers from the 1st Battalion, 8th Marines between Kandahar Air Base and Gardez Air Base, when the first of a two Humvee transport was struck with an RPG. The explosion of the first transport killed the five Marines inside instantly and sent shrapnel into the second vehicle – which Steve was in – decapitating the driver, and mortally wounding both the gunner and communications operator.

The second RPG, fired only moments after the first, struck the ground directly in front of the vehicle Steve was in. The explosion lifted the Humvee off its wheels and threw it onto its right side, tossing Steve and the two remaining Marines around like ragdolls in a metal container.

By the time the dust settled around the upturned Humvee, and while the men inside – bloodied and bruised — tried to regain their bearings, the assault had begun. Gunshots coughed through the dry air, echoed off the cliff walls, bullets pinged against the Humvee's armored plating.

Lance Corporal Kyle Brenner – whose leg was broken when the Humvee flipped – and Private Lewis Lomax tried to defend the onslaught of Taliban soldiers surrounding the transport. Their efforts were futile. The fighting had ended before Steve realized he was being pulled from the wreckage by Taliban fighters. With the desert still of warfare, and the blood of dead U.S. Marines soaking into the sand, only Steve and Lance Corporal Brenner were alive.

Steve had not been injured in the attack, other than a few bumps and bruises and a laceration along the left side of his head that bled profusely. He and Brenner were captured and taken to a complex cave system in the Tora Bora Mountain Range, where both were tortured for information and eventually used as a bargaining chip against the U.S. Government.

Because Steve was a journalist, the Taliban forced him to recite their demands from a typed transcript while being videotaped. The gist of the transcript was simple: release known Taliban terrorists and leave the country. If the U.S. did not comply with these demands, then he and Lance Corporal Brenner would be executed for the world to see.

The Taliban kept part of that promise.

Steve threw the memory from his mind as the demons in his belly began to squirm around like maggots in a bowl. The thirst – the need – for booze came on strong, as it always did when he thought about that fucking cave, about what had been done to him and what they would eventually do to Lance Corporal Brenner. His hand inched down to the side of the laptop bag, feeling the outline of the flask under the course material – his solace.

A moment later, Amy appeared, now dressed in winter clothing. Steve was in the living room by the fireplace looking at his article framed on the wall.

"You knew me before we met," he said, turning to Amy as she neared.

"Yes." A bashful smile creased her lips, and her cheeks reddened. Her voice was soft, reticent. "I've been a fan of your work since college."

Steve was surprised that he had "fans" but was pleased to hear his writing had inspired someone. After all, wasn't that what every writer wanted – acceptance of their craft?

Amy ran a nervous hand through her hair, pushing a strand away from her face. "I guess I should have told you when we met the other night that I was a fan, but I didn't want to come off unprofessional. But my insides were screaming. I couldn't believe I was speaking to, let alone going to be working with, someone I looked up to." She giggled. "You must find me... strange?"

Steve shook his head. "No, not at all. I think it's neat."

"Really?" Amy beamed.

"Sure."

"Your article on Anthony Palazzo was some of the best crime writing I've ever read. How you connected everything together and put Palazzo right in the center of it all was fantastic reporting. Are you going to write a book about your investigation?"

"No. I'm not planning on writing a book." *At least, not on Palazzo,* Steve thought. But there was another story that publishers were after from Steve.

His memoir of what happened in Afghanistan.

Steve had been offered a seven-figure book deal before a single word was written, from some of the most prominent New York-based publishing houses. He had yet to accept any offers, wanting to have a finished manuscript before entertaining such a lucrative deal, a deal that would change his life.

He had started the memoir but had yet to finish it. The memories were still too raw, too emotional to tackle, to face. He had only made it ten pages into the manuscript before giving up and diving into a bottle of Jameson just to forget everything he had written, everything he remembered about those ten hellish days in captivity.

"Ready to go?" Steve asked, changing the subject before Amy asked any further questions, especially about Afghanistan, which he knew would follow. They always did.

Amy pulled the car over by a large pasture. Dead and yellowed cut corn-pikes protruded through the ice-crusted snow like skewers through pieces of meat. With inches of packed snow and ice, along with the steady, pestering wind and freezing drizzle, their trek to the old farmhouse would be miserable. Beyond the field, about two hundred yards from the road, a plot of dense woods ran along the top of the ridge; the trees swayed back and forth as if praying to some unknown deity.

"The farmhouse sits just over that ridge, past those trees," Amy said.

The thought of the slog through the ice and snow made Steve pause. He wanted to retreat back to his hotel room, or to the comfort of the warm hotel bar. But he opened the car door and stepped out; the thrill of truth drove him forward, as it always did. The air whipped over the field with a ferocity that nearly pushed him off his feet. He pulled the hood over his head and tightened the drawstrings; it did little to keep his ears warm.

Amy came around the car. Her hood was pulled over her head in a way that made her resemble a skier at a mountain resort about to hit the slopes. The thought of being at some charming ski resort, sipping whiskey with coffee while soaking in a hot tub with Amy was better than being in the middle of nowhere hunting down clues.

"Ready?" she asked.

Not really, Steve thought. But he nodded that he was, whether he liked it or not.

The hike across the uneven turf to the top of the ridge zapped their energy quick. The temperature had risen, and the rain had softened the snow and ground beneath their feet. They sunk into the muck, their boots collecting ice and mud that weighed them down as they tried to traverse their way through the corn-pike rows without tripping over them. By the time they reached the top of the ridge and made their way through the dense patch of woods, they were gasping for air and exhausted.

Standing on the ridge, they looked down at the valley

below. The farmhouse was tucked quaintly in the middle of the field with snowy, rugged hills surrounding it. The house was old, built sometime in the latter part of the 1800s, judging by its wooden construction; it looked relatively intact and structurally sound, even for its age.

The view was serene. Steve had to admit that even with the farmhouse's age, the home and land surrounding it looked quite peaceful, a place someone could retire to and not have to worry about the outside world.

"This... this... is... something else," Steve said through deep, fatigued breaths. He bent over, put his hands on his knees and coughed. He needed to quit smoking but knew he would not stop until it killed him.

"Yes." Amy sucked in a large breath of her own; the air whistled through her teeth. "I've always been fascinated with this place. The house has a strange aura about it, like it wants people to live there."

"Is... it... haunted?" Steve craned his neck to look up at her, his hands still on his knees while he sucked wind.

"Not that I know of." Her voice grew serious when she spoke again, "Only with memories, I suppose."

The hike to the house was easier since it was all down-hill. However, Steve's feet slipped out from under him twice before reaching their destination, and he fell once on his side, and once straight down on his ass so hard pain shot through his entire body. He felt like such a klutz. Each time he had fallen, Amy helped him back to his feet. *She thinks I'm a moron,* Steve thought. But if Amy did believe this, she kept her opinions to herself.

They approached the house from the west, by the ruins of a barn that had long since been torn down. The stone wall foundation remained, and large wooden beams – that once held the roof – were piled inside the foundation's walls. Outside the foundation was a large stack of oak panels, grayed from years of exposure to the elements – the barn's walls.

The farmhouse was about twenty yards away from the ruins. A covered porch with cinderblock walls took up most of the home's west side. A single window and a door leading to and from the farmhouse was under it. Next to the porch was a tree that must have been there over a hundred years, its thick and twisted branches blowing this way and that, creaking spookily in the breeze. The trunk was the size of a whiskey barrel and three large knot holes resembled a face – two for the eyes and one for a nose. The bark just under the "nose hole" had twisted at such an angle that it appeared the tree was grinning evilly, as if possessed by some malevolent spirit that cursed this land.

"That's a scary-looking tree," Steve said, almost afraid to get closer fearing it might reach out and pull him into its mouth with one of its warped limbs, like in the film *Poltergeist*.

"That's Sam."

Steve looked at Amy sardonically. "Sam?"

"Yeah. We named the tree when we were kids."

"Oh?" He knew there had to be more to the story.

Amy laughed and shrugged. "We were kids with vivid imaginations."

Steve understood. Being an only child, all Steve had sometimes was his vivid imagination. Even as an adult, sometimes all he *still* had was his vivid imagination to get him through the day.

Moving onto the porch, Amy went to the door, while Steve cupped his hands on the window and peered through the old, wavy glass into the house. It was dark inside the farmhouse, but Steve could make out a kitchen. The place was a mess with old pizza boxes, paper plates and cups, and wadded-up napkins littered around the counter and floor. Someone had been using or living in the farmhouse from the looks of it.

"I thought you said this place was abandoned," Steve said.

"It is."

"Doesn't look that way to me."

Amy's face grew curiously grim. Steve met her by the door, reached down, and turned the knob. The door was unlocked, and the latch popped free. The door swung open on its own with an eerie *creeeeeeak*. They stepped inside; the wooden floor groaned under their weight. The place smelled old and musty, unlived in. There was an unpleasant warmth inside those walls that should not have been there if the place was abandoned. The fragrance of death faintly lingered in the air.

"You smell that?" Steve asked.

Amy nodded.

Unease squeezed Steve's insides. He was sure this was where Rebecca had been tortured, and more recently, Green and Hooper had met their horrific ends. He could smell blood in the air, could taste burnt flesh on his tongue, and death clung to his skin like a film of slime. Amy was right, the house did have an aura. An unsettling one. Only misery and death were welcome inside these walls now.

They crossed the kitchen to the once-white counter; it was yellowed with age and covered in a layer of dust and grime. The sink was filled with used paper plates, cups, water, soda, and Pabst Blue Ribbon beer cans. Next to the sink was the stove. It was old, at least dating back to the 1960s, and like the counter, it was dirty and the paint had peeled off in long sheets and rested on the floor.

Steve began going through the top cupboards while Amy searched the bottom ones. Inside the upper cabinets were extra paper plates, cups, bowls, and plastic utensils. Several unopened snack food bags and boxes had been invaded by mice; little black mouse turds spotted the shelves. Amy found several cases of water and soda in the bottom cabinet.

Turning from the counter to the refrigerator, Steve opened it. Inside it was stocked with beer – more Pabst Blue Ribbon. The place was not as abandoned as someone wanted it to appear from the outside.

A stone fireplace stood in the center of the room. Steve kneeled by the hearth and began to examine the inside for anything suspicious. Half-burnt logs rested on the metal dog grate; the slightest warmth emanated from them.

"Someone was here recently," Steve said, looking back to Amy, who stood by a doorway that led to the front of the house.

He picked up a small, half-burnt log and began to sift through the black soot and ash residue, hoping to find something useful. He pushed the charred wood away and then started digging down into the ash pit below the dog grate.

The more ash Steve churned, the more contents he began to unearth from the pit.

Amongst the ash were five melted VHS tapes; the magnetic tape inside lost to the flames. There were also five DVDs and five flash drives – both of which were broken before being tossed into the flames, so no one could recover what was on them. Steve then excavated several blackened plastic cards, melted and warped around the edges. Whatever had been on the cards was unidentifiable now.

"Looks like someone might have been burning evidence," Steve said. He stood and dusted his hands off.

"We should check out the rest of the house before whoever did that comes back," Amy said, waving for Steve to follow.

She had a point, Steve realized. They did not need to be caught snooping around the house and get into an altercation. He pulled out his phone and snapped pictures of the fireplace for documentation, and then replaced everything to make it appear undisturbed.

Standing, he turned and followed Amy down a hallway, the wooden floor pockmarked with holes. Steve was unsure if the floor would support their weight; the wood looked warped and sagged ever-so-slightly in the center. But it held, despite its appearance.

Two windows were on the righthand side of the hall. They gave an unobstructed view of the snow-covered hills and the wooded ridgeline from which they came. On the left side of the hall, an opened door led to a stairwell hidden between the walls. Steve poked his head inside the stairwell and looked toward the second floor. Two bedrooms were at the top of the stairs. The stairwell seemed to magnify the sounds of the driving wind pushing against the house and the rain tapping against the roof.

Steve was surprised the old farmhouse was so dry and warm inside. He assumed whoever was using the place had made the proper repairs to keep the elements from getting in while, at the same time retaining the farmhouse's outside uninhabited appearance to deter nosey visitors from entering.

They continued on to the front of the house. A door at the end of the hall led back outside. On the left was a large entryway that led into the living room.

The smell of death was stronger in this part of the house.

In the living room, an old green sofa sat in the middle of the room, with the stuffing scattered across the floor. A size-able wooden wire holder had been turned on its side and used as a makeshift coffee table. It was covered with porno magazines, empty beer cans, and an ashtray filled with cigarette and cigar butts. Take-out containers and crumpled napkins were littered around the makeshift table.

In the corner, sitting on a rickety lawn chair, was a small CRT television and VCR/DVD combo. Both were plugged into the wall, to Steve's surprise. *There's power to this place?* Beside the retro entertainment set up were two doorways, both blocked by darkly stained wooden doors.

"Where do those doors lead to?" Steve asked.

"The one on the left goes to the basement. The one on the right..." Amy trailed off and glanced at Steve expressively.

The room, Steve knew.

Amy crossed the living room to the door on the right, while Steve sifted through the trash and dirty magazines for anything useful. While examining the stack of porn magazines, Steve was surprised to discover one he had not expected to be there at the bottom of the stack. *La Prostituée Bizarre. La Prostituée Bizarre* was the S&M magazine published by Anthony Palazzo, under his S&M Solutions Publishing banner.

Anger ignited inside Steve, elevating his blood pressure. Palazzo's reach was far and wide, spreading like an infection to the rest of the world.

There was nothing beneficial on the table other than jerk-off material and junk, making Steve wonder what was really on those napkins crumpled around the table. A shudder ran through his body, and he felt dirty. *I need hand sanitizer.* He wiped his hands on the jacket to clean some of the filthiness from his flesh, and then backed away to take a few pictures on his phone.

He was in the process of snapping pictures when Amy screamed.

His hand went to the front pocket of the jacket and gripped the .38's stock tightly. He spun to find Amy standing in the doorway of the room on the right, an appalled gaze fixed on her taut face. Tears welled in the pits of her eyes.

Steve started across the room, while his heart hammered against his sternum, and a thin sheen of sweat broke out across his body. He wet his lips; they were cracked, and his saliva burnt the split skin, but Steve hardly noticed as his eyes tried to comprehend what he was seeing past Amy. When he stepped into the doorway, Steve was shocked at what he saw. And smelled.

The room was smaller than it appeared in the videos. He wondered how three hulking men, a table, and Rebecca all managed to fit in there at once. He was not claustrophobic, but it seemed like the walls were quickly closing in around him.

A few things stuck out to Steve right away, confirming they were in the right place where all three videos were filmed: The yellowish-green wallpaper. The workman's light dangling from the ceiling, that had cast the bell-shaped hue over the table in Rebecca's video. And the single window in the center of the room that faced the rolling countryside. Escaping this place would have been impossible for Rebecca, and for Green and Hooper, Steve realized. *There was nowhere to run to.*

He tried the push-button switch on the wall, but the light did not come on. *Odd,* he thought. The room had been lit in Rebecca's video. Had there been a power source then? Steve believed there was.

The smell was atrocious inside the room; the warmth of the house lifted the shit and piss, blood and burnt flesh smell out of the wood, turning the stench into a singular odor that made his eyes water. He understood then that Amy's tears had not been brought on by what she had seen inside the room, but by the harsh tang of decay and defecation.

In the left corner of the room, there were two leather straps bolted high on the wall, and two by the floor. These straps had been used to bind Martin Green while he was tortured and eventually murdered. A large spot on the floor was covered in dried blood. Fecal matter speckled the floor and walls in large dark splotches, as if it had exploded from Green when he died.

More of the same leather straps were mounted at the top and bottom of the wall, directly across from where Green was murdered. The only difference here was the wallpaper and plaster were burnt away and had fallen to the floor in crispy, dark patches; the house's wooden bones were scorched black.

Kim Hooper's final moments were spent bound to that wall.

The amount of pain Hooper experienced before death came to collect him must have been unfathomable; being slowly cooked must have been excruciating. Steve had seen countless innocent people burnt while over in Afghanistan. The lucky ones died instantly. Those who didn't suffered immensely. It was one of the many reasons he was glad he had not watched the Hooper video.

The third corner of the room had two more sets of leather restraints fastened to the wall. This was where the final victim would be bound, tortured, and eventually murdered. But who was this mysterious person?

Sitting along the front wall, directly to his right, was the table Rebecca had been bound to. The once bright red paint had chipped off, exposing gray-brown wood underneath. On top of the table were various tools that had been turned into instruments of death. The hammer and chisel were a frightening sight – the very tools used to sever Martin Green's toes lay ominously patient, waiting for their next taste of human anguish. Beside the hammer and chisel was the screwdriver that punctured Green's jugular; its metal shaft coated in what looked like brown paint, but it was actually Green's dried blood coating the steel.

Steve swallowed and he wished he would have brought the flask. He just had a glimpse into the third victim's bleak future and didn't like what he saw, even if he deserved what he had coming to him. He turned back to Amy; her face was twisted in a strange way that bothered him.

"You okay?" Steve asked.

"This was the room they raped her in, Steve." Amy's eyes began to water, real tears this time. "So, they were brought back here to be..."

"Tortured and murdered," Steve concluded. "Just like Rebecca was."

Amy pushed a tear away; the emotional weight of the room and what happened there was unbearable. She moved to the window and stared across the white hills, lost in her own thoughts.

"It must have been awful for Rebecca," Amy spoke, her voice remorseful. "She screamed until her voice was hoarse. But no one would have heard, even if they had not gagged her. Not out here, cut off from the rest of the world. She must have felt so alone, so far from home. Imagine what must have been going through her mind when..." Amy lowered her head sadly.

They were quiet for a long moment, with the rain tapping against the glass and the wind blowing across the open expanse outside, which caused the house to moan a soft protest. There was nothing Steve could say to make the reality of where they were any easier. But he would see to it that what happened to Rebecca was brought to light.

Steve began to take pictures around the room, making sure he covered everything before he stepped back into the living room and turned to the other door, the one that led to the basement. He reached out and turned the doorknob. The old knob made a cold, metallic squeak, the kind of metal-on-metal screech that gave one goosebumps.

The door opened slowly to a black abyss.

Steve opened the flashlight app on his cell phone. He shone the beam into the darkness. The light revealed wooden stairs that led down to the basement's dirt floor. The foundation wall stood only about a foot away from the last step. Large chunks of plaster had fallen from the walls and lay in a crumbled pile; the exposed stacked stone behind the plaster looked like the ribs of a rotting carcass.

Steve inched his foot onto the first step, testing the strength of the wood. It bent slightly under his weight.

"Think they'll hold?" Amy asked.

"Only one way to find out. But we should go down one at a time. It'll put less stress on the steps that way."

She agreed.

Steve went first, taking the steps with caution, testing each one before he applied his full weight. Each step seemed to have its own unique vociferous sound as he descended into the underworld. But none of the steps gave way and they held Steve's one-hundred-and-seventy-five-pound frame. Once on the dirt floor, he turned and waved Amy down, assuring her the stairs would not buckle under her weight. He held the light at such an angle that the stairs were lit as Amy descended.

Taking Amy's hand, Steve guided her down until she was safely on the ground beside him. He then shone the beam around the room.

The basement was half the size of the house. Steve assumed this was because the kitchen had been added on to the home later, probably sometime in the 1930s, when kitchens became the norm inside homes. Large support beams, still with the live edge of bark, hung low enough that both Steve and Amy would have to be careful not to bash their skulls as they moved about the basement.

In the far corner was a seven-thousand-watt generator connected to the farmhouse's power box. The generator's exhaust was attached to a homemade filtration system that vented the toxic fumes out the side of the foundation wall. It was a crude design, but efficient; Steve did not smell any lingering fumes.

"They put the generator in the basement to cut the noise," Steve said. "Green's wife did say her husband was a genius with his hands."

"Pap's Place," Amy said. "Just like Green referenced in his email to Hooper. And the photo album you found at Hooper's house – Hunting Trips to Pap's Place. This is Pap's Place."

"Right."

He turned his attention back to the room and moved the light along the wall until it fell onto a four-drawer dresser that looked to be from the early twentieth century. On the floor beside the dresser, was a chain and padlock.

Steve made his way across the room to the dresser,

mindful of the beams overhead. He bent and picked the padlock off the floor and examined it. The U-shaped clasp had been severed with something sharp, most likely a bolt cutter. The lock and chain had, at one time, been used to keep the dresser's secrets sealed. By running one end of the chain through the insides of the circled handles of the dresser and then looping it back around the outsides of the handles, the chain was able to be secured by the padlock, preventing the drawers from opening. Steve replaced the lock where it was on the floor and took a picture.

With the chain and lock removed, Steve tried to slide the top drawer out, but the drawer twisted as he pulled, snagging it. The dresser tipped forward on its front legs and caused the layer of settled dust on top to rise and form a thick, moon-dust-colored cloud around him. He coughed and waved a hand in front of his face, fanning the dust away.

When the dust settled, Steve wiggled the drawer back into place, then pulled it out slowly this time, so it didn't twist and become hung up again. He looked inside.

Empty.

He moved onto the second drawer and gingerly slid it out. But like the first one, this drawer was also empty.

Pulling out the third drawer, Steve found three leather S&M masks inside – the same executioner-type hoods seen in Rebecca's video. The light caused the metal mouth zippers to gleam eerily, like shiny metal teeth.

Amy came up beside him and hooked her right arm around his left. Disgust emanated from her. He wanted to say something, anything, but there were no words for what they'd found, there were no words – written or spoken – that could make what they had just discovered digestible.

Steve snapped a picture of the masks.

He then opened the bottom drawer and found it filled with S&M torture devices. There was no pleasure to be found in this drawer, only pain.

"Gross," Amy said with revulsion. "Why were they keeping this stuff locked up down here?"

"In case anyone stumbled across the place," Steve said. A thought then materialized in his brain, as alarming as a slap to the face. "The killer spoke to Martin Green. *'I want to hear you laugh, Martin, just like you do in your other videos.'* Do you think..." Steve looked back to the dresser. "... that the other videos were in this dresser at one time?"

"From what you found in the fireplace earlier, I'd say so. After Green and Hooper were murdered, someone came back and burnt all the evidence connecting them to this place."

Steve looked back to the chain and the padlock on the floor and asked, "But why cut the lock? Wouldn't there have been a key?"

"I don't know," Amy said, lifting her shoulders. "But I think we've seen enough. We should leave."

"Agreed."

Steve took a final picture of the contents inside the dresser and then closed the bottom drawer. Together, they carefully made their way back to the steps, and one-by-one headed up to the first floor.

They had just gotten to the landing of the basement stairs when the kitchen door *creeeeeaked* open, and the sound of heavy booted feet stepped into the farmhouse.

Chapter Fifteen

Steve grabbed hold of Amy and pulled her into the murder room and closed the door slowly, to keep the hinges from squeaking. He pressed himself and Amy against the wall beside the door, so if it swung open into the room, they would be concealed behind it, giving them a chance at a surprise attack if needed.

He felt Amy's trembling body against his, and her breaths came in heavy, rapid pulls that heaved her chest up and down, almost to the point of hyperventilation. Her gaze remained fixed on the grizzly horror of the room before her, afraid she might end up like Rebecca.

Steve would not let that happen.

"Take it easy," he whispered into her ear. "Just breathe."

Amy closed her eyes and tried to focus on her breaths. In through the mouth, out through the nose.

"That's it," Steve whispered. "It's o–"

There was a metallic *click* as the latch on the door gave way, and it began to slowly open, the hinges making the smallest *squeak, squeak, squeak* as the door inched closer and closer to Steve and Amy's bodies.

Steve's chest seized tight with fear. He slipped his hand into his pocket and found the comfort of the .38's handle. His index finger wrapped around the trigger, ready to take down whoever was on the other side of the door if need be.

The door continued to open toward them; the soft *squeeeeeak* of the hinges seemed louder than before in the otherwise quiet home, coming closer and closer before stopping, almost touching Amy's nose.

Booted feet stepped into the threshold of the doorway. The wooden floorboards crackled.

But the figure did not move past the door.

Whoever was in the house, on the other side of the door, no more than inches from Steve and Amy, just stood there looking around the heinous murder room. Was there an admiration for the room and what had happened there, or were they disgusted by what they saw, as Steve and Amy had been? Steve's grip on the gun tightened.

The person took another step forward; the floorboards under Steve and Amy's feet rose slightly with the added weight. Then they moved to the edge of the door but did not step past so Steve could see their face; instead, the person held their position just out of view.

Who are you? Steve eased the gun from the jacket pocket, his finger caressing the crescent shape of the .38's trigger. Had they been followed? Were he and Amy's movements around town being watched, their activities monitored?

Possible. Likely, even.

Steve had sensed earlier that Meeker knew he was in town before their meeting at the police station that morning. Someone else could have found out what they were doing and sent the dogs after them. There was a murder to cover up, and someone did not want what happened to

Rebecca, and what they were doing at the farmhouse, exposed. How far were they willing to go to keep their secret buried?

Steve already knew the answer.

The floorboards creaked again when the person turned and started away from the threshold, the footfalls echoing in the quiet stillness of the abandoned farmhouse, heading back to the kitchen. Soon, the footsteps softened and then disappeared altogether.

Steve remained still. To step out from behind the door now was a bad idea. They had to wait until he was sure it was safe.

Amy looked at him, her eyes asking, *What now?*

After a few moments of silence, Steve felt it was prudent to move. They needed to get out of that house and back to the car, fast, before whoever was just there found them. He stepped out from behind the door with caution and trained the .38 in front of him. No one lingered in the living room. Whoever had been snooping around was gone.

"C'mon," he said, reaching for Amy's hand. "We need to get out of here."

"Who do you think that was?"

"I don't know."

Steve led them through the living room to the wall that separated it from the hallway, where he paused and peered around the corner, down the hall. The hallway was empty, and the door in the kitchen, which led out to the porch, hung open and rocked back and forth with the outside breeze and tapped against the wall. There was no one else in the house as far as he could tell.

"Let's go," Steve said. He took hold of Amy's hand again and led them down the hallway.

But something was wrong.

The door to the stairwell was closed.

It had been open when they walked past it earlier. Steve remembered looking up the steps to the second floor when they first entered the hallway and –

Before Steve could rationalize why the door was closed, the stairwell door burst open, and a towering figure charged at him. A full-faced ski mask and goggles hid the features, and a thick, black snowsuit concealed the form of the body underneath. There was something long in the gloved hands, something that was being drawn back over the shoulder.

Amy screamed.

Steve had but a moment to react. He brought the .38 up, thumbing the hammer back in the process, and leveled the barrel at the approaching figure. His index finger was already applying pressure to the trigger when the masked figure swung whatever was in those gloved hands across Steve's knuckles. A flash of intense, crippling pain shot through Steve's right hand and up his forearm, and his finger reactively pulled the trigger from the pain.

The gun went off.

The shot was as loud as cannon fire. The round spat from the barrel and found its way into the far wall; the plaster exploded on impact and fragments of wood, horse-hair plaster, and a thick, white dust kicked into the air.

The figure swung again. This time the object connected with the nose of the gun, knocking it from Steve's hand. The swing had enough power that it forced Steve off balance and almost caused him to fall face-first into the window.

"Steve!" Amy screamed from behind.

Steve quickly regained his balance, stopping himself before he crashed through the window. He turned just as the figure brought the wooden oak plank – Steve realized it was from the stack of wood outside the barn – up over their shoulder, poised to connect across his skull this time.

The pain in Steve's right hand was exasperating, as surges of heat flashed up his arm and into his elbow in spasmatic, fiery spurts. He was unsure if his hand was broken. But broken hand or not, Steve had to do something, or end up with his skull bashed in.

Instead of dodging away from the oncoming blow, Steve lowered himself and dove into the masked figure's midsection before the strike could be delivered. He pushed forward with his legs as hard as he could, pumping his muscles with every ounce of energy that his body could muster, and drove the assailant back into the doorframe of the stairwell.

A male voice grunted under the mask when his back connected with the wooden doorframe.

Steve took a step back and scanned the floor for the gun, only to find the .38 lying between himself and the masked figure.

He lunged for the gun.

But just as Steve's hand was about to wrap around the wooden stock, the masked figure stepped forward and kicked the gun away. It slid across the floor, bounced off the wall, and then fell through one of the holes into the basement below.

The masked figure then reared back, again with the wooden plank, and swung. Steve saw the blow coming and turned into it so his shoulder and upper back would take the brunt of the impact. He knew the strike was going to hurt, but did not fathom how much pain he would feel when the board connected, like he had just been hit by a thousand wasps stingers all at once.

The power behind the swing was enough to knock Steve forward and cause him to fall face-first onto the hardwood floor, kicking up a haze of old dust and dirt that got caught in his throat and caused him to cough.

The masked figure, thinking he had the upper hand, stomped toward his prey. His hands flexed on the wooden plank like an abusive teacher about to take pleasure in punishing an insubordinate student with a giant ruler.

Steve rolled onto his back as pain coursed through his body; he felt as if he'd just survived a car accident and was crawling from the wreckage. He coughed again. His chest felt heavy, constricted; the taste of copper filled his mouth – blood, his blood. The wallop with the wooden plank across the back must have damaged some of the blood vessels of his lungs, causing the blood in his mouth when he coughed.

The masked figure stepped forward and raised the plank over his head with both hands. He looked like someone at a carnival swinging a mallet at the High Striker game, trying to get the lead puck to ring the bell at the top. There was a wildness in his eyes; they wanted to see death. A deep, angry, guttural – almost primal – holler exploded from somewhere behind the mask. He brought the plank down, aiming for the center of Steve's forehead, in a wide arc that was sure to connect.

Steve saw the final blow – the killing blow – coming at him in slow-motion, as if he were in a Sam Peckinpah film. He rolled to the left just before the massive plank caved his face in.

The board smashed into the floor. The floorboards jumped from the impact, and a piece of wood splintered off and shot across the hall, bounced off the windowsill, and fell to the floor.

Steve rolled onto his back and then kicked out, hard.

The heel of his boot connected with the masked figure's shin. The man screamed out, his cries muffled under the mask, and staggered backward while grabbing at the injured leg.

Turning on his stomach, Steve began to crawl, trying to put as much distance between him and his attacker as he could, when he looked up and saw Amy. She was not standing helplessly by but instead, charging at their aggressor, armed with the very hammer that had been used on Martin Green.

Amy ran at the masked man without an ounce of fear. A tribal-like scream erupted from her throat, the hammer poised back over her right shoulder like an Indian warrior about to bury a Tomahawk into a soldier's skull. She closed the gap between herself and the masked man with ease, and just as he looked up from his injured shin, Amy brought the hammer down across the front of the mask.

There was the sickening crack of steel meeting plastic, and a muffled *ohofff* escaped the masked man's mouth. He went down to one knee, dazed from the blow; the heavy plank fell from his hands. Amy heaved the hammer back over her shoulder again, this time intending to finish him off.

But the masked man shot to his feet quicker than Amy had expected. He had been stunned from the hammer's blow but was not out of the fight. His large, gloved hand caught Amy's wrist mid-swing, and he drove her back into the far wall, pinning her there. He then twisted her wrist in a downward angle. She cried out in agony. The hammer slipped from her hand and fell to the floor with a heavy *clack*.

Steve got to his feet. Across the hall, he watched helplessly as the ski-masked man took a handful of Amy's long red hair, yanked her head back, and then slapped her across the face with the back of his right hand. The impact drove her to the floor hard enough that the house shook. She lay on her side, dazed, holding the side of her face.

"Fuckin' stupid cow!" the masked man screamed. He moved in on Amy, positioning himself like a soccer player squaring up to kick a winning goal.

Steve saw the oak plank on the floor and went for it, just as the masked man was drawing his booted right foot back, intending on burying it in Amy's gut. Steve leapt for the board, heaved it back over his right shoulder, and swung it as hard as he could at the masked brute.

The board connected across the man's broad chest. He stumbled backward, clutching his torso. Steve charged at him and swung the board again, this time hitting the attacker across the left shoulder. The man hollered under the mask and grabbed at his shoulder as pain seized his body and he staggered backward.

"How's that feel, fucker!" Steve wheezed.

He swung the board for the third time and caught the masked man on the side of the skull. The plastic of the goggles shattered, and pieces of them flew across the room and scattered on the floor. The man stumbled drunkenly toward the window, clutching the side of his head.

Before he had time to react or recover from the blow, Steve sat the plank in the crook of his right elbow, since he couldn't hold onto it with his right hand, and gripped the board with his left hand as hard as he could. He charged at the attacker again and planted the wooden plank into the man's upper chest, just below his jaw, and pushed with all his might, propelling him into the glass window with enough force that it exploded on impact.

Shards of glass scattered everywhere, and they rained

down with a *tinkling* sound. The masked figure fell through the window to the snow-covered ground five feet below, onto his back. The wooden plank, which caught on both sides of the window frame, stopped Steve's forward momentum, preventing him from going out the window too.

With his adrenaline surging, Steve wanted to jump out the window and continue his attack, but Amy's soft moans drew his attention back to her. She was trying to push herself up, but the slap across the face had stunned her to the point that she couldn't stand without assistance. When Steve looked back outside, the masked figure was already on his feet, staggering across the snow to a snowmobile parked a few feet from the old barn ruins.

Steve turned from the window and went to Amy, instead of pursuing. Even if he wanted to chase after their attacker, he was in no shape to do so. He was winded and physically drained. He felt lightheaded, and his stomach churned uncomfortably like he was about to hurl. Besides, Amy's injuries were more important to tend to than trying to apprehend whoever had just attacked them.

He knelt beside her and helped her sit up. She winced with pain. Her eyes held the glassy, far-off gaze of someone who just had their bell rung.

"Are you okay?" Steve asked, keeping a firm hand on her so she did not collapse back to the floor.

Amy's right hand was on the side of her head, pressed firmly against her ear, as if to keep her brain from leaking out. The slap across the face had disoriented and confused her, maybe even caused a concussion, but there was no way to tell without seeing a doctor.

"I-I think..." She spoke but stopped when she tried to move her right wrist. "Ow!"

Outside, the snowmobile fired-up; the high-pitched

whine of the engine broke the quiet. Steve was surprised that they had not heard it approach the house. Then again, they had been preoccupied with other things, and in the basement when it arrived. The engine revved to life and sped off until it was nothing more than a small drone in the distance. Soon, the sound faded into oblivion, and the quiet befell them once more.

Steve took Amy's injured wrist and looked it over. There was no visible contusion or swelling that he could see. That was good. It meant her wrist had not been broken, but it might be badly sprained. He reached up and lightly took her chin in his hand and turned her face. A large, red bruise below her right eye was beginning to swell – she would need ice to reduce the inflammation; discoloration was sure to follow.

Tears caught in the cups of Amy's eyes, but Steve knew she would not allow their aggressor the satisfaction of her torment. He helped her to her feet. She was wobbly but managed to stand. With Steve's assistance, he guided her back to the kitchen, where he leaned her up against the counter.

"I think we need to get you to a doctor," Steve said, worried.

Amy shook her head slowly, the motion nearly making her fall over. Steve reached out to support her.

"No, I'll... be okay," she replied, trying to sound reassuring.

"Are you sure?" He had seen people become concussed from far less of a blow than Amy had taken.

She nodded. "Just give me a few minutes."

It took Amy at least ten minutes to regain her wits and stability. When she was able to stand on her own, she looked at Steve and asked, "Are *you* okay?"

Steve nodded. The pain in his hand had already begun to subside, and he could once again move his fingers, but making a fist was impossible. There would be residual pain that evening, but nothing booze couldn't fix. He was lucky his hand had not been broken when the board connected across his knuckles.

He helped Amy back out to the porch and eased her down on the brick wall. She needed to rest before they began their hike back through the muck to the car.

Steve turned his attention to where the snowmobile had been parked. The tracks in the snow indicated the snowmobile had spun around in a one-hundred-eighty-degree turn before it headed back over the hill from which it came. He thought about following the tracks but decided against it; they were in no position to chase, nor get into another quarrel. One was enough.

His focus then shifted to the footprints in the snow. There was something odd about them.

"What are you looking at?" Amy asked.

"The footprints," Steve said. "See. There are two different sets. One set of tracks lead from where the snowmobile was parked to the barn, and then another set from the barn back to the house."

"But there's nothing over there."

"Then why walk that direction?" Steve asked, looking back at Amy. When she had no reply that satisfied his curiosity, he began making his way toward the barn.

Following the footprints, Steve came to the side of the barn ruins where a stone archway, that at one time led inside, still stood. They didn't lead into the ruins of the barn, as he would have expected them to, but continued around the back. Steve followed. Once at the end of the foundation wall, the footprints took a sharp right and headed out into the center of the open field.

What's so important out here that someone would walk through the snow, ice, and rain for?

He was going to find out.

The wind blew harder across the open expanse of the field, stinging Steve's exposed flesh; his nose, cheeks, and ears were so cold they burned. Snow and ice gathered on his boots, weighing him down like before, and quickly zapped the remainder of his energy. He was tired from the fight and was running at this point on adrenaline alone, huffing and puffing like a seventy-year-old man drudging through the icy slop. He wanted to be inside – preferably in a warm bar – out of the bitter wind and rain, away from any physical activity. Still, the thrill of what he might discover strangely warmed him and carried him on.

The footprints led to a small mound in the earth, though it did not appear to be a natural incline in the field created by Mother Nature. The packed snow and ice camouflaged the mound from a distance; neither Steve nor Amy had noticed it when they came in from the west.

The tracks continued around the mound to the front, where two green metal doors led into a hidden underground chamber.

"That wasn't here when I was a kid," Amy said. Steve hadn't realized she'd been following him; he'd been too consumed with where the tracks led to notice her.

A padlock secured the doors. Steve pulled it, but it didn't budge.

"What now?" Amy asked.

"Wait here." He turned around and hurried back to the house. Several minutes later, after searching around in the dark basement, he returned with the .38.

"Stand behind the mound," he told Amy.

Amy moved to the back of the mound, while Steve took position beside it. Firing directly at the front of the padlock was a bad idea; the bullet could ricochet off the metal door and back into him. Instead, Steve would shoot across the locks clasp, severing it like an artery.

But when Steve went to thumb the gun's hammer back, he couldn't. Some internal mechanism within the gun had broken when it fell into the basement.

"Shit!" Steve grumbled. "The hammer's jammed."

Amy came out from behind the mound and joined him by the metal doors.

Steve popped the cylinder and ejected the bullets into his palm. He then closed the cylinder, took the gun by the nose, and swung the butt as hard as he could into the padlock. He repeated the process several times, bringing the butt of the gun down, over and over into the padlock. But other than leaving a small scuff on the outside of the lock's shiny surface, there was no damage to the padlock's integrity.

Steve, panting with fatigue, stared at the padlock furiously. He took a deep breath and then pursed his lips tight with irritation. He needed to know what lay behind those green doors. There had to be a way to remove the padlock.

Think, Steve, think!

He slipped the gun back into the jacket's pocket.

"We need something to break the lock," Steve said.

"We should leave this be and come back later."

"We can't. Whatever *is* down there might not be here when we get back."

Amy nodded with a shiver. She knew Steve was right. If the person who attacked them had been the one destroying evidence, they would return and whatever was behind those green doors would be removed, if incriminating.

"What about the hammer?" Amy asked. "Would that work?"

Steve realized which hammer Amy was referring to, the same one used on Martin Green.

"It would, along with the chisel."

Amy turned, and was about to head back to the house when Steve stopped her.

"I'll go. You rest here a moment," he said.

He made the sloppy trek back to the house once more. His legs burned with exhaustion and his lower back had twisted into a painful knot that Steve envisioned looking like a wet, twisted washcloth being wrung-out by invisible hands.

Steve found the hammer on the hallway floor and picked it up. Feeling its heft, he realized it must have taken a lot of strength to swing. He wondered how Amy had done it so effortlessly during the attack. Steve supposed fear and adrenaline played its part. A chill passed through him suddenly, and gooseflesh rose across his body with the realization that he was holding the very object that was once used to inflict torment and pain.

Pushing the images of Martin Green's severed toes aside, Steve grabbed the chisel from the table and then made his way back out to meet Amy by the mound.

"Are you sure this is going to work?" Amy asked.

"I believe it will. A few years ago, I did a story on a burglar and how he was breaking into locked sheds in the rural areas around Pittsburgh. His tools." Steve held up the hammer and chisel.

Steve placed the chisel on top of the base of the lock, raised the hammer and brought it down. He swung the hammer repeatedly; the striking of metal on metal echoed across the open field with cold isolation. *Ding! Ding! Ding!* He continued to swing the heavy hammer into the chisel until, finally, the metal U broke free from the lock's body. Removing it, he pulled open the door.

Reaching into the front pocket of the jacket, Steve pulled out his cell phone and opened the flashlight app. He shone the beam into the darkness below. A flight of stone steps appeared to lead nowhere at first, a black hole, but as the beam penetrated the dark, it revealed the red-dirt floor of what seemed to be a homemade root cellar.

Amy inched closer to him. She wrapped her arm around his and pulled him into her, like a girlfriend might while watching a scary movie. Her body quivered and her teeth clacked together from the extreme cold, and the fear of what lay in the black chasm of the root cellar.

"Are you sure you want to go down there?" Steve asked.

Amy nodded, though it was hesitant. "I-I have to."

Steve supposed she needed to see into the darkness, just like he did.

They began down the stone stairs. As they progressed into the root cellar, a strange, foreboding sense of dread began to make Steve's stomach roll uneasily.

They came to the bottom of the steps and stood in a twelve-by-twelve room built of cinderblock. The air was thick with the musty smell of settled dirt, from being closed. When was the last time someone had been down here? The cellar was built long after the farmhouse, judging by the modern construction material used.

"Martin Green was a landscaper; he could've built this place," Steve said. He bent and scooped up a handful of the red dirt. It fell through his fingers like fine sand. "It appears to be the same dirt that was on Rebecca's driver's license."

"God... is she... down here?" Amy asked.

Steve stood and dusted his hands off. He then moved the light's beam along the back wall until it fell on several oblong stacked shapes that seemed to materialize out of the darkness.

Steve froze, his blood turning to ice.

"What is that?" Amy asked, peering through the dim light.

"Stay here," Steve replied.

He started across the small room; the phone's light bounced with each step, making the shadows move on the cinderblock walls hauntingly. As he neared, Steve's suspicions of what he was looking at deepened, and a cold shiver passed through him.

He took a breath of the musty air and steeled himself for what he suspected he was about to find. Pushing himself forward, even though he didn't want to, Steve moved closer until he gazed upon a pile of what looked undeniably like body bags – homemade body bags.

"What is it?" Amy asked, her voice closer now, almost directly behind him.

Steve turned; the light flashed off the walls and onto Amy, who stood only inches away now. He could see her eyes were wide, even in the murky light, bugging out of her skull.

"Stop," Steve warned, holding up his hand.

Amy's gaze shifted from Steve to the bags on the floor and remained fixed there. "Is that..." Her words caught in her throat at the ghastly sight.

"Yes," Steve replied, turning back around. "I believe so."

He knelt beside the bags. Three bodies were on the bottom, and two were on top – stacked head to feet, feet to head. The heads, feet, and waists had been bound with several strips of silver duct tape, keeping what was inside together, keeping it all in.

The bodies reminded Steve of the Nazi concentration camp book he had seen on the stand at Hooper's place. The black and white cover photo of the dead, malnourished prisoners that had been systematically executed and then stacked for mass cremation or burial. Steve tried to swallow, but a lump had formed in his throat.

After a moment, he turned back to Amy and handed her the light. "Hold this, please."

"What are you doing?" she asked.

"I need to see inside," Steve said, turning back around. "I need to know..."

"Leave it alone, Steve. We found what we came for. It's time to call Meeker and let him handle this."

Steve turned back to face her. "We can't trust Meeker, Amy."

"Yes, we can. The sheriff's a—"

"No," Steve cut her off. "Someone knows what we're up to. He knew we were coming to talk with him today. He wasn't the least bit surprised when we showed up. Someone informed Meeker what we've been up to. And just a few moments ago we were attacked, almost killed, and surely would have been had we not acted. We're being watched. We're being followed. Someone out there knows the truth about this place, and they're willing to kill to keep those secrets buried."

"Are you saying you believe Sheriff Meeker is... involved?" Amy asked in a tone that suggested she couldn't comprehend the idea that Sheriff Meeker could commit such atrocities.

"I'm saying we can't trust anyone at the moment. We're not safe. And we need to keep what we know, for now, to ourselves. At least until we know who's on our side and who isn't."

He could see doubt in her eyes. She was not fully on board with his idea but gave him the go-ahead with a small, unsure nod.

With Amy now holding the light, Steve turned back around and reached out with both hands. His fingers brushed the plastic; it was cold and brittle and crunched like ice under his touch. Taking the plastic in both hands, he could already feel the shape of a human skull underneath. Steve tore it apart.

The light caught the corpse in a way that made the shadows cascade across the pale, dead skin like flowing water as Steve tore the bag further.

What skin was left on the skull was patchy, most of it eaten away by decomposition. What flesh remained had hardened, mummified, and was the color of ash under the light. Two black, empty eye sockets stared into the afterlife. The jaw hung open, as if locked in a forever scream. And for a moment, as Steve revealed more, he thought he heard a scream escape the open mouth – the cry of a woman – sending goose pimples across his entire body. A dirty strand of tangled black hair fell from inside the bag and brushed Steve's arm – a feeling like having a snake slither across his bare flesh.

Steve revolted and fell back onto his ass, both frightened and repulsed by what lay in front of him. His muscles clinched systematically, and he felt a strange tightness in his chest that he assumed could only be the physical manifestation of terror.

"Is that..." Amy began. "Is that... another woman?"

Steve's gaze was fixed on the screaming skull, particularly on those two black sockets where eyes had once been.

Now those empty, black sockets stared absently into noth-ingness. Disgust oozed from every pore of his body. This was someone's daughter, sister, niece, aunt – a person that had been left down here to rot away like a discarded animal carcass.

"Let's get out of here, Steve," Amy said, helping him to his feet.

"Hold on a moment." He pulled away from Amy and moved back to the bags and began tearing them open, exposing the faces of the victims underneath, or what was left of their faces. When Steve was finished, five bodies in various stages of decay lay exposed, but most had already skeletonized with only patches of dried skin and hair clinging to their dirty skulls.

Steve took the phone from Amy and began to take pictures; he needed to make sure everything was documented.

"We need to get out of here, Steve."

He agreed this time, and handed the phone to Amy so she could lead them out of the root cellar and back to the surface world.

Turning, he began to follow her when something became entangled on his foot, almost tripping him. He stopped, unable to see what was wrapped around his ankle.

"Amy, hand me the light."

Amy turned back. She looked antsy and eager to leave but handed Steve the phone.

He aimed the beam at his feet and found another black plastic bag had wrapped itself around his left foot. Like the other homemade body bags, this one also had silver duct tape on it. But unlike the others stacked along the back wall, this one was empty.

"What is it?" Amy asked.

"Another bag," Steve replied, perplexed. He bent and picked the bag up. It was old and ratty. Strands of the duct tape, coated with red dirt on its adhesive side, hung off the bag like streamers.

"Steve," Amy said, pulling his attention away from the bag before he could examine it further. "Leave it. Let's go."

Steve nodded. He was about to follow Amy out of the root cellar and back into the cold, brisk air when something fell from within the bag. The object hit the top of his foot and slid off into the dirt somewhere.

"Shit!"

"What? What is it?" Amy asked, turning back.

"There was something inside the bag," Steve said, searching the floor for whatever fell from the bag. "Shine the light over here, please."

Amy directed the beam at the floor and caught something shiny in the red dirt almost instantly. Steve bent and pulled a stainless-steel necklace from the soil. A half-dollar sized round pendant swung like a pendulum. Upon further inspection, the pendant was separated into three round stamps. In the center pendant – the smallest— there were three letters etched into the metal: HHS. The middle pendant had another etching: CLASS OF 1999. On the third and largest pendant, was an inscription: FOLLOW YOUR DREAMS.

Amy pointed to the letters. "Hanover High School?"

"Rebecca's?" Steve asked.

Amy lifted her shoulders. "The only way to know for sure would be to speak with Dennis again, see if he can confirm the necklace as his daughter's."

"Then that's where we head next."

Once outside, Steve replaced the lock on the root cellar's green door. The padlock would appear undisturbed from a distance, but once up close, it would be apparent that someone had broken it.

Steve wanted to be nowhere near this place when it was discovered that someone had been in the root cellar and had found what was meant to stay hidden.

Chapter Sixteen

Steve insisted Amy see a doctor, but she refused. He decided not to push the issue – that wasn't his place. Once back at the Abbottstown Inn, they decided to meet back up in an hour, both wanting to clean up before they spoke with Dennis Turner.

Inside his room, Steve poured himself a stiff drink from the bottle he purchased at the bar. Unsurprisingly, he had polished nearly half of it already. *The demons were thirsty.* After finishing the drink, he stripped the heavy clothing and tossed them in the corner on his way to the shower.

He turned the water as hot as he could stand it, washed his hair, and scrubbed his skin twice to remove the grimy feeling that lingered, and then stood under the spray. The hot water felt good, especially on his cold joints and stiff muscles of his back, where the two by four had connected. He flexed his right hand a few times, the knuckles swollen and sore, but the pain was manageable.

After twenty-five minutes, with the hot water nearly extinguished, Steve stepped out of the shower and toweled off. In the mirror, he turned to see a large, multicolored bruise across his back in the shape of the wooden plank that had struck him. The bruise was not as bad as it appeared, and he no longer had the coppery taste of blood on the back of his tongue.

Good.

He got dressed in a pair of black jeans, a black under-shirt, and a dark grey button-down shirt.

Not thinking, Steve lit a cigarette and drew in deep. The smoke hit his lungs like he had just breathed fire. He coughed. *Stupid!* He might no longer taste blood in the back of his throat, but his lungs had been bruised. He stubbed the cigarette out and eased himself down into the chair by the desk.

He needed a moment to himself, a moment to reflect on what had happened that afternoon and put things into perspective.

Steve and Amy both agreed not to call Sheriff Meeker about their discovery at the farmhouse. There was the possibility their attacker had been aware of their investigation from the start, and had followed them to the farmhouse, hoping to silence them there.

But how? Steve wondered. No one, outside of him and Amy, knew where they were going after they left the police station, not even Sheriff Meeker. Had they picked up a tail? Was it after they visited Meeker at the police station or before? Steve didn't know and he was not taking any chances. At this point, everyone needed to be treated as a suspect, even those inside the police department.

We're not safe, Steve had told Amy. *And we need to keep what we know, for now, to ourselves. At least until we know who's on our side and who isn't.*

Another thought occurred to Steve then, one he liked less but he could not deny its plausible possibility: that their attacker could have just stumbled upon them by accident, while he was in the process of purging all evidence of the crimes. And when he found Steve and Amy there that afternoon, snooping around the farmhouse, it caused him to panic and react with violence.

Steve's thoughts then shifted back to the bodies discovered in the root cellar. There were five bodies in total; all of them wrapped in black trash bags and sealed with duct tape. Except, there were six homemade body bags found. Could that mean there had been six bodies down there at one time? Had it been Rebecca's, since they found the necklace inside?

If that were true, then what happened to her body?

Had this mysterious person relocated it? Had they been in the process of removing all of the bodies from the root cellar that very afternoon? The field surrounding the farmhouse was vast; there were any number of places a body – or bodies – could be buried. But, if the sixth victim were buried before the snowfall, locating it would be impossible without cadaver dogs or ground penetration radar.

Steve knew the only way they could prove this was to bring Sheriff Meeker into the fold. But he just didn't trust him, especially after what happened at the farmhouse. He worried if Meeker was involved, he would jeopardize their investigation as well as their safety.

Steve was lost in thoughts of what to do next when his cell phone chimed with a text message. It was Amy saying she was waiting out front.

He grabbed his things and headed out the door.

"You said you had new information on Rebecca's disappearance," Dennis Turner said, turning from the door and leading Steve and Amy into his home.

Steve nodded. "We do, Mr. Turner. But before we get to that, I have a few questions I'd like to ask you about the night Rebecca disappeared, if you don't mind."

Dennis lifted an eyebrow skeptically. "Why not show me what you discovered first?"

Steve had expected the reply. "To be honest, Mr. Turner, if we show you what we have, you may not be able to continue with the interview. And we must clarify a few things first."

"Okay," Dennis said apprehensively. "Whatever you need."

"The night your daughter disappeared. Do you remember what Rebecca was wearing?"

Dennis thought about the question for a long moment; his eyes danced back and forth in their sockets. "A wind-breaker, a black Nirvana t-shirt, and a pair of khaki pants, the kind with the big pockets along the sides."

"What about a necklace?" Amy asked. "Do you remember her wearing a necklace?"

Dennis shook his head. "I don't. Sorry."

Steve reached into the laptop bag and pulled out the dirty necklace and passed it to Dennis.

"Is that your daughter's?" Steve asked.

Dennis studied the necklace, his eyes soaking up every curve, every letter and number as if it were the last thing he was going to see. Then a single tear slipped from his right eye and rolled down his cheek; he pushed it away with the back of his hand.

"It looks like Rebecca's," Dennis said. "But then again, there were a lot of girls who bought similar ones that year.

The school offered them as graduation gifts, with personal inscriptions for a few bucks more, as I recall."

"Is this what was inscribed on your daughter's necklace?" Steve asked, holding the pendant in his palm so Dennis could see.

"Yes."

"So, there's a good chance this is your daughter's necklace then?"

Dennis nodded. "W-where did you find it?"

Steve felt Amy's eyes drilling into the side of his face, a hot penetrating stare that burned his flesh. He knew she was wondering how much he was going to tell Dennis Turner about what happened to his daughter.

"You asked me before, Mr. Turner, how I got involved. I told you then it was complicated. I was not lying. The necklace was delivered to me, along with her driver's license, anonymously," Steve said, still unable to disclose what he knew really happened to his daughter. "Someone wanted me to look into your daughter's disappearance."

"Why you? You're from Pittsburgh and have zero connection to Rebecca. Why would anyone come to you to investigate her case? I don't understand what's going on here."

"Neither do we," Amy said. "But we're trying to get to the bottom of it."

Chapter Seventeen

"We need to find Wendy Brewer," Steve said, once they were back in the car. "She was the last person to see Rebecca. She might be able to confirm if Rebecca was wearing the necklace or not that night."

"On it," Amy replied, her fingers already typing away at her phone's keyboard.

Using the online white pages, Amy was able to locate Wendy in a matter of minutes. Steve remembered a time, not too long ago, when trying to find someone took both physical and mental work. Now, all one had to do was punch the name into a search engine on the internet. How times had changed.

"Found her," Amy said, smiling. *Boom. Done. Easy peasy,* Steve thought. "She's married and goes by the last name Miller now. She and her husband, Todd, live just outside of Dillsburg."

"How far is that from where we are?"

"About a forty-minute drive."

"Let's go."

"Should we call first?" Amy asked. "There are two phone numbers listed – one's a cell, the other is a landline."

"No. We tell Wendy we're coming, she'll either refuse to speak with us, or it'll give her enough time to cook up another story about what happened that night. Let's catch her by surprise."

Amy nodded, put the car in gear, and headed north toward Dillsburg, Pennsylvania.

Forty-five minutes later, they pulled into the Miller driveway. The home was an early 1980s cream-colored bi-level in a development. The place had seen better days; it was not rundown like the farmhouse, but the Miller home needed a few thousand dollars' worth of repairs to give it curb appeal. A beat-up green Toyota Corolla sat in the driveway; it seemed the lack of proper upkeep spread to the car as well.

They made their way up the walk to the front door. Steve reached out to ring the doorbell, but the button was broken and hung from the housing, the wires exposed to the elements. *Can we say, 'fire hazard.'* He knocked instead.

From inside the home, footsteps approached the front door. When it opened, a woman stood there. She was deathly thin and frail, a look brought on by years of substance abuse. The hardness of her life was etched onto her face in a roadmap of torment and anguish; the deep stress lines and cracks made her looked twenty years older than she was.

Her skin was white, almost gray. Her black hair was

long and dry, reminding Steve of hay on a scarecrow's head. She wore a long Guns & Roses tee-shirt that fell to her knees. The swell of her small breasts was nearly non-existent; she wore no bra, and her nipples stood out like bullets under the shirt. Old, dingy slippers covered her feet. Her brown eyes shifted between the two reporters, wondering who they were.

"Wendy Miller?" Steve asked.

"Yes?" she replied, baffled why two strangers were standing outside her home.

"My name is Steve James. This is my colleague, Amy Richards. We're reporters looking into the disappearance of Rebecca Turner. We were wondering if we could ask you a few questions about the night Rebecca disappeared?"

Wendy grew rigid. Her guard instantly rose.

"I already told you people what I know, and I don't have any more to say on the matter."

Wendy went to close the door, but Steve placed his fist against it, preventing her from shutting it.

"I understand that, Mrs. Miller. However, we want to hear your side of the story." He forced a smile. "We just want to clarify a few things."

Wendy stared into Steve's eyes, searching for something in them. *What?*

"Does it really matter at this point?" Wendy spoke, crossing her arms over her small breasts. "I mean, it's been twenty years–"

"Twenty-five years."

"Huh?"

"Twenty-five years, Mrs. Miller," Steve reminded her, feeling his face redden with irritation. "It's been twenty-five years since Rebecca disappeared."

"Oh! Has it been that long already?" She ran a hand through her dry hair, nervously. "My memory isn't as good as it once was. Not sure how much help I'm going to be."

"We'd still like to try," Amy said. "Maybe you'll remember more once you start talking about that night."

Wendy leveled her gaze on Amy, appraising her as if she were a lost friend or relative – someone she had known in the past but was unable to place now.

"Why do you look familiar to me?" Wendy asked, squinting her eyes, as if that would help her foggy memory.

"We went to the same high school," Amy said.

"You graduated with me? I can't remember most of my classmates if you did."

"No. I said we went to the same high school, but we didn't graduate together. I was a few grades behind you."

"Oh." The wheels were visibly turning in Windy's mind, trying to place Amy's face. She shook her head as if shaking away an unpleasant thought. "Nope. Drawing a blank."

"It doesn't matter," Amy said. "What does matter is what you saw the night Rebecca disappeared."

"I'm not going to be much help. My memory isn't what it used to be."

"You already said that," Steve said.

"See." Wendy smiled. "Told ya."

"We'd still like to try," Amy pressed.

Wendy continued to stare at Steve and Amy as if they were pests that needed to be squashed. She didn't want them at her home and certainly didn't want them asking questions about the night of Rebecca's disappearance.

What does she have to hide? Steve wondered.

Seeing no other options – not that Steve and Amy left

her with any wiggle room – Wendy conceded and stepped aside, allowing the reporters to enter. She closed the door and led them to the living room at the top of the steps, where they took a seat on a sectional sofa.

Steve had expected the inside of the house to be a nightmare, but it was surprisingly clean and smelled of pecans from a candle burning in the kitchen. He had also expected to find drug paraphernalia lying around the house. Joints. Coke dust. Needles and burnt spoons. He saw nothing of the sort. Had Wendy kicked her drug habit?

"We only have a few questions, Mrs. Miller, so we'll be quick," Steve said.

"Okay," she replied, apprehensively.

"On the evening of January 5, 1999, what time did Rebecca pick you up?"

"I'd say..." Wendy thought for a moment. "I'd say around six-thirty or six-forty-five."

"And that was at your parents' home, correct?" Amy queried.

"Out front of it, as I recall, yes."

"Do you remember what Rebecca was wearing?" Amy asked.

"Now why in the hell would I remember that?"

"It was a tragic night, Mrs. Miller," Amy said. "Your best friend disappeared. It's not something that's easily forgettable."

Wendy lifted her shoulders. "Meh."

"Let's be more specific," Steve said. "Do you remember Rebecca having a class necklace?"

Wendy took a moment to think before responding. She slowly nodded her head. "I think I know which one you're talking about. They were offerin' 'em in school, for graduation. I remember hers having three pendants, I believe."

"Yes. That's the one. Did Rebecca have it on the night the two of you went to the party?"

"I can't remember. But I know she had one for sure. Her folks bought it for her. She could have had it on that night for all I know."

We're getting nowhere, Steve thought. But he wasn't ready to give up just yet.

"What time did the party start?" Steve asked instead, hoping the shift in gears would kick something loose in Wendy's fuzzy memory.

"I'm not sure there was a set time. It was a show-up-whenever kind of thing."

"Who invited you girls to the party?" Amy asked.

"My friend, John," Wendy replied, looking to Amy. She was still trying to place Amy in her mind, connecting the dots between a very murky past and the present.

"John Hansen?" Amy asked.

Wendy nodded.

"Have you spoken to John lately?" Steve asked.

"Nope. Not in a long time," Wendy said in a matter-of-fact tone. "Don't plan to, either."

"You have harsh feelings for Mr. Hansen?" Amy asked.

"You could say that."

"Why?" Steve asked.

Wendy looked away, lost within the inner torment, a torment that had controlled her life for a long time.

"I don't want to talk about my relationship with John. Besides, that's not why you're here," Wendy said.

"Fair enough," Steve replied. "Back to the night Rebecca disappeared. Do you remember where the party was being held?"

Wendy shook her head. "I do not. It was dark."

Steve glanced at Amy. Her eyes flared with frustration,

and her lips drew into a thin, straight line. She suspected Wendy was lying, as did Steve.

Reaching into his pocket, Steve pulled out his cell phone, opened the gallery app, and found one of the pictures he had taken of the exterior of the farmhouse on their way back to the car.

"Is this the place?" Steve asked, passing the phone to Wendy.

She took the phone and studied the picture carefully. If Wendy recognized the farmhouse, her face gave nothing away.

"Could be." She handed the phone back. "It was very dark, so I didn't get a good look at the outside." She hesitated, thinking. "What I do remember was how muddy the ground was. Ruined my Doc Martens that night, which pissed me off."

"Muddy? It was muddy where you were?" He turned the phone around so Wendy could see the photo of the farmhouse again. "As you can see, this place sits down in a valley, far away from the road. The only way to get there is to hike in or drive. Did you walk to the farmhouse, is that how you ruined your shoes?"

Wendy shook her head. "No. Rebecca drove us through the field, that much I remember. Muddied up her mom's car pretty bad, as I recall. Rebecca was worried about going home with the car looking like that. I told her it was just mud and would wash off – all she needed to do was stop at a carwash before going home. It wasn't a big deal, except to my Doc Martens."

But she never made it to a carwash, let alone home, Steve thought. He knew when the Ford Tempo was found abandoned along Maple Grove Road, its undercarriage and tires were coated with mud. Steve had figured that maybe the mud had come from the forest road where the car was dumped, but when he saw there were no tire tracks on the forest floor, he figured the mud had come from somewhere else. Now they knew where.

"And what time did the two of you get to the farmhouse?" Amy asked.

"I don't remember."

"Take a guess," Steve said.

"I don't remember," Wendy shot back.

"What about the guests attending the party that evening?" Amy asked.

"What about them?"

"Do you remember who was there that night?"

"I don't. Other than Rebecca and me, most of the people there were John's friends."

"Did you know any of John's friends?" Steve asked.

"A few."

Steve glanced at Amy; the shock on his face reflected her own.

"We were under the assumption that you only knew John Hansen at the party."

"That was just something I told the police," Wendy said, waving it off as if it were no big deal.

"Why would you do that?" Amy asked. "Your statement could have helped, had you been forthright with the police from the beginning."

"Don't patronize me, honey," Wendy snapped. "I had my reasons to keep my mouth shut."

"And what were those reasons, Mrs. Miller?" Steve asked.

Wendy inhaled and let her breath out slowly. Steve

could tell she was growing tiresome of the questions. All she wanted was for them to leave so she could climb back into her hole and forget about Rebecca.

"Look, I didn't want the police to know, nor for my father to find out that I was hanging around a bunch of older guys. Okay. There, I said it. I was sixteen at the time, and John and his friends were in their twenties. If my father would have found out.... Had I told the police everything, they would've pieced it together and arrested John for having sex with a minor. So, I told the police that I didn't know anyone other than John, who I only knew from my neighborhood and that he had invited me."

"He lived around you?" Steve asked.

"No. But John hung around our neighborhood. That's how I met him."

"How did you and John meet?" Wendy frowned, and the crow's feet around her eyes deepened into fissures. She was still hiding something, Steve believed. And he thought he knew what it was. "John supplied you with drugs, didn't he?"

"Fine. Yes. John was also my drug dealer. I used to buy coke and weed off him when I was in high school. It wasn't all the time. Just some to get by. To deal with teenage angst, ya know." She shrugged. "We hit it off and started fucking."

"Colorful," Amy said, sitting up in her seat. "So, when did you dump him? Or did he dump you after you aged out of usefulness?"

Wendy leveled her gaze on Amy, a look that could kill. "As I've already stated: I don't want to talk about my relationship with John. And besides, it's none of your goddamn business why we split."

"Why don't you want to talk about—"

"We understand, Mrs. Miller," Steve quickly interjected. "That's a personal part of your life, a part you wish not to speak of. We'll move on and keep our questions to Rebecca. Is that okay?"

Wendy nodded, but her feathers were ruffled.

Looking at Amy, he saw she was fuming. He should not have interfered with her questions, but he worried if the contention between the two women continued, they would lose the only first-hand witness to the events of that night. They needed to tread carefully to not upset Wendy before she told them about Rebecca's final hours.

"So, you knew some of John's friends that were there that night?" Steve continued.

"A few."

"Were any of them named Martin or Kim?" Steve asked. Wendy's eyes snapped up to him as if he had just scraped her nerve endings with a sharp blade. "Were their names Martin Green and Kim Hooper? Were they there that night?"

"Maybe."

"Well, they were or they weren't. Which is it?"

Wendy mulled over what to say next. She shook her right foot back and forth nervously, as some teenagers do when they're in trouble. Steve was sure she knew both Martin Green and Kim Hooper. He just had to get it out of her, placing both men there the night Rebecca disappeared.

"Look, Wendy, we know you're scared. But I assure you that you will remain an anonymous source in all of this. You have my word on that. I can keep you safe."

"Keeping my mouth shut has kept me safe all these years. Why should I trust you?"

"You shouldn't," Steve replied. "But you should trust

that we're trying to get to the bottom of what happened to your best friend. Don't you want to be free of that burden, Wendy? To know you don't have to go through the rest of your life looking over your shoulder in fear?"

"Yes, I knew them," she finally said.

"Were they at the party that night?" Steve asked.

Wendy nodded.

"What were they like?"

"I only met them a few times. But they were P-O-S, just like John." Wendy looked off, again lost in her memories.

"P-O-S?" Amy asked.

"Pieces of shit," Wendy spat.

What happened between John Hansen and Wendy Brewer that tainted her opinion of him and his friends so? Had the three of them done something to her that no drug in the world could mask, causing a lifetime of guilt and pain that resulted in years of substance abuse and mental torment?

"You know Martin Green and Kim Hooper are both dead?" Amy asked.

"Sure. I heard. Such a loss for humanity."

For a split second, Steve saw a moment of peace cross Wendy's weathered face, as if a significant weight had been lifted from her shoulders. But, as fast as that look came, it vanished even quicker.

"I'll send daisies to their families," Wendy added emotionlessly.

"You don't seem upset by their deaths," Amy said.

"Should I be?"

Amy glanced at Steve, agitated. Her questions angered Wendy Miller more than they helped. Whatever disdain Wendy had for Amy bubbled like a boiling cauldron inside.

"You told the police Rebecca left around midnight that evening. Do you know why she left?" Steve asked.

"Wasn't Rebecca's thing. Drugs and alcohol were going around – she wasn't into that scene."

"But you told the police that she didn't want to stay out past her curfew," Steve said.

"That too. Rebecca was a good person, probably the best friend a girl like me could ever have. She didn't belong there. Both of us knew it. But... I begged her to come."

"Why did you beg her to go with you, Wendy?" Amy asked.

"Because I didn't want to go by myself."

"You said you were dating John Hansen, sleeping with him, why would you be afraid to go to a party that your boyfriend was throwing?" Steve asked.

"Who said he was my boyfriend?" Wendy answered.

Steve was puzzled. "I'm sorry. I was under the impression that you two were–"

"He was my dealer and we were fuck buddies, nothing more."

Steve was sure Wendy was fabricating parts of her story. There were hints of truth mixed in with the lies. But she was not being completely forthright with them. What secret was she keeping guarded, or rather, who was she protecting? Herself? Hansen? Another player in the mix that they knew nothing about?

"So, why didn't you leave the party with Rebecca when she was ready to go?" Steve asked.

"I was too fucked up and passed out on the sofa. I couldn't go home in the state I was in. My father would've tanned my ass... if he stopped there."

"You stayed with John and his friends that night at the farmhouse?"

"No. One of John's friends took me home when I was sober enough to walk."

"What time was that? And who took you home that night?" Steve asked.

"I don't remember."

"You don't remember what time it was, or who took you home?"

"Both."

"When did you find out Rebecca had disappeared?" Amy asked.

Wendy thought for a moment and then lifted her shoulders. "A few days later, when the police came to my house asking questions."

"And you told the police that Rebecca left the party at midnight," Steve confirmed.

"Yeah."

"But you were unable to give the police a description of where the party was held."

"Yep." Wendy motioned to Steve's phone, the photo app open, the picture of the farmhouse on the screen. "If that's the place, I'll take your word for it."

"Let's go back to what you said earlier; that you didn't want to go to the party by yourself. Could you explain your reasoning in better detail for me?" Steve asked. "Were you afraid of John and his friends, is that why you wanted Rebecca to go with you?"

Wendy shifted in her seat uncomfortably, like she'd been poked by something sharp. Maybe it was a memory of something that had happened to her while she was with John and his friends that caused the reaction.

"Sure, I was afraid of them. They were bad dudes. John, Kim, and Martin were into some pretty wild shit at that time – shit I didn't want anything to do with. But I wanted to show John that I was a tough, badass girl, ya know. I was sixteen and rebelling against society and my worthless, neglectful parents. I asked Rebecca to go with me that night because I didn't know if any other girls would be there or not, and I didn't want to be the only girl at an all-male party – catch my drift?"

"What 'wild shit' – as you put it – were John and his friends into?" Steve asked.

"I never asked. I didn't want to know, to be honest."

"But you knew they were into... something?"

Wendy nodded. "More of a feeling, ya know."

"Why didn't you want to know?" Amy asked.

Wendy thought about the question for a long time, weighing her options on what she should tell them. When she spoke, her voice was low and raspy. "Because sometimes, Ms. Richards, not knowing the truth is better, it's safer. Now, I think I've told you two all that I know, and I'd like you to leave."

They left Wendy's house and headed to a diner just off Route 74 that they had passed on their way to the Miller home. Inside, they took a booth that overlooked the parking lot. The rain had tapered off to a light shower, but the day was still miserably cold. *A great day to spend in bed*, Steve thought. *With a good book and a stiff drink.*

The diner was small, warm, and cozy; the air smelled of grease and cooked meat fat – not the kind of place a vegetarian or vegan would be found in. There only five other people in the diner that afternoon, so the place was quiet; it was the kind of greasy spoon Steve could see himself eating at more than a few times a week. They ordered coffee and two specials – meatloaf and mashed potatoes.

"I didn't appreciate you cutting me off back there," Amy said.

The remark caught Steve off guard. He knew he had upset Amy when he intervened with her questioning of Wendy Brewer. It had not been his intention to upset her, but the intervention needed to be done.

"I'm sorry," Steve replied. He wasn't above admitting when he was wrong. "I should have handled that differently. But I was afraid we were losing her. She didn't like you, Amy. She didn't like you at all, for some reason. If she had shut-down, or kicked us out, we'd have gotten nothing out of her."

"You don't know that," Amy retorted angrily.

"You're right. I didn't know that. I should have let you continue and not interfered with your questions." He sat back in his seat, finished with the conversation, and looked out across the wet parking lot.

"You made me look incompetent," Amy said, her voice sharp with discouragement and annoyance.

"Look, the interview was going south. The contention between you two was so palpable I could have cut it with a knife. I made a judgment call to keep us in the witness's good graces. It wasn't a personal attack against you. I swear. I've been in my share of combative interviews over the years, and I'm telling you, if what I saw between you two would have continued, it would've turned ugly fast."

"Are you apologizing or giving me a lesson?"

"Both. You want to be a crime reporter, Amy, then you not only have to dig-in like a tick, but know when to let go, too. Questions don't dictate the outcome of the interview; the responses, however, do."

Amy sat back in her seat, the wind taken out of her sails. She seemed to understand where Steve was coming from and that he needed to intervene and course correct to save the interview. But all this really showed him was how green she was as a reporter.

Steve didn't want to fight. He was tired and hungry. Needed a drink and a smoke, which he'd had neither of for some time. He decided to shift the trajectory of the conversation.

"Let's lay out what we know about Rebecca's last hours before her disappearance," Steve began. "On the night of January 5, 1999, Rebecca goes to a party with Wendy Brewer. She's last seen around midnight, according to Wendy, leaving in her mother's Ford Tempo. The Tempo is later found abandoned on Maple Grove Road. The inside was cleaned of trace evidence, but the outside is still covered with mud – mud from the fields surrounding the farmhouse?"

"Possible," Amy said. Her voice still held a twinge of anger. "But we'll never truly know if the mud on the car was picked up from the field or somewhere else between there and where it was found."

Amy was right, he knew. There was no way for them to know if the mud on the car came from the fields surrounding the old farmhouse without forensic analysis to match soil samples. Steve doubted that had been done twenty-five-years-ago, as the technology was still relatively new. Taking a sip of his coffee, he wanted to Irish it up and wondered if the diner had liquor.

"If you want my opinion," Amy said. "I think our best link to Rebecca never leaving the farmhouse is the necklace. Both her father and Wendy confirmed that she had one just

like it; she could have been wearing it the night of her disappearance."

"He also said there were several other girls who got the
exact same necklace."

"But other than Rebecca, there are no other disappear-
ances around that time."

Again, Amy was right. The necklace had to belong to
Rebecca, and she had to have been wearing it that night. He
took another sip of coffee. A thought then rumbled across
Steve's stormy mind. "How did Wendy know Rebecca left
around midnight?"

"She saw Rebecca before she left."

Steve shook his head. "No. She didn't. Wendy told us
she was passed out on the sofa that night, remember – she
said one of John's friends took her home when she woke
around two in the morning – two hours after Rebecca had
left. If that's true, then Wendy couldn't have seen Rebecca
leave the party."

Amy's eyes grew wide. "Holy shit! You're right." She sat
up in her seat, visibly excited. "If Wendy didn't see Rebecca
leave because she was passed out, then how did she know
Rebecca left at midnight?"

"Someone fed her that nugget of information."

"Who though?"

"Let's go find out."

Steve threw a twenty down on the table and they
quickly exited the diner and made their way back to the car.
They were about to get in when Steve stopped, his attention
pulled across the parking lot.

"What is it?" Amy asked, noticing Steve's far-off gaze.

"Don't turn around," he whispered. "Pretend we're
talking."

"Okay."

"There's a black Dodge Ram with tinted windows just over your left shoulder, about twenty yards away."

"So?"

"I saw that exact same truck outside the police station this morning. And, I believe I saw it somewhere else we were, but I cannot for the life of me place where."

Amy went to turn around, but Steve stopped her.

"Don't. Don't move. We *are* being followed."

Amy swallowed and he saw a tremor pass through her body. "So, what now?"

"Switch spots with me. As we pass the front of the car, hand me the keys as if I'm going to drive."

"Okay. But what are you going to do?"

"Let whoever is behind that tinted glass know we're onto them." Steve saw a moment of perplexed fear cross Amy's face. "Trust me."

Amy nodded and began to move to the front of the car.

"Yeah, I can drive," Steve said, speaking louder, making sure the entire parking lot could hear, including the person inside the Ram's cab.

At the front of the car, Amy handed off the keys to Steve, and as he was about to round the front of the car, like he was going to the driver's side, he quickly changed directions and darted toward the Dodge Ram.

The Ram's Hemi engine roared to life. Whoever was behind the wheel realized their cover had been blown. As Steve neared the pick-up, the Ram shot from the parking space, the rear tires squealed and spit up wet gravel. It fishtailed out of the parking lot and back onto the road and headed south, away from the diner.

Running out onto the road after the Ram, Steve hoped to get a license plate number, but the truck was already too far away.

Steve was confident he'd seen that Ram before seeing it that morning, parked outside of the police station. He just wished he could remember where.

By the time they got back to Wendy's home, an old Chevy pick-up was parked beside the beat-up green Toyota Corolla. Wendy's husband, Todd, must have returned home.

They hurried up to the front door. Steve rapped hard, making sure to get the occupants' attention. A few moments later, a large, husky man opened the door.

Todd Miller's long, gray beard rested on top of his beer belly. He wore a stained wife-beater t-shirt that was a size too small for his meaty frame. His belt was undone from his blue work pants and dangled open by his thighs. He was chewing something. The smell of recently microwaved food – hot plastic and preservatives – came from within the house. Todd swallowed before speaking.

"Can I help you?" His voice was deep and ruff, the kind of voice that could put the fear of God into a man's soul if he were to get angry.

Steve looked past Todd to the top of the steps where Wendy stood. She looked emaciated and pale, a scared frail woman who was doing everything she could just to get through the lousy hand life had dealt her.

Steve pushed past Todd into the house, nearly knocking him down the steps that led to the lower part of the bi-level home.

"Hey!" Todd shouted, grabbing hold of the railing to keep himself from falling. "What the hell!"

"The night Rebecca disappeared, you didn't see her leave the party, did you?" Steve growled, pointing at her.

"Get out of here," Wendy shot back. "I already told you everything I know."

"Bullshit!" Steve hollered. "You never saw Rebecca leave that night because you were too fucked-up and passed out on the sofa."

"Get out of my house!" Wendy screamed and turned away, as if turning her back to him ended the conversation.

Something ignited inside Steve. He bolted up the steps, pulling himself up by the railing. The big man followed close behind, his footsteps boomed on the stairs like a giant as he chased after Steve.

"Why did you tell the police that you saw Rebecca leave at midnight, Wendy? Why didn't you just tell them the truth? Why didn't you tell them that you had passed out?"

"I told them what I knew."

"The fuck you did!" Steve bellowed.

"Steve." Amy was behind him now, in between him and Todd, who fumed like an agitated bull about to gore the matador. Had Amy not been standing between them, Steve knew he might have ended up in the hospital or worse—dead.

"You covered up the truth to save your own ass, Wendy. You turned your back on the only true friend you ever had in your pathetic excuse for a life."

"Fuck you!" Wendy said, turning back to him, tears in her eyes. "You don't know anything about me or my life, or what I went through. You don't know."

"Then tell me," Steve pleaded, his voice softer now. "Help me understand what the hell happened to Rebecca that night. Please, Wendy." Steve lowered his voice – calm, even, everything's alright. "Tell me the truth."

The room had grown heavy, still, and hot with flared emotions. Steve had not wanted the visit to go this way. Something inside him fractured with Wendy's refusal to speak to them again; her blind willfulness to not accept responsibility for her lies and the repercussions they had caused, enraged him so badly that he had wanted to slap the truth from her lying lips.

"I don't know what happened that night," Wendy began. "I'd smoked a few jays and was drinking. At some point, I passed out on the sofa. When I woke, John told me Rebecca had left around midnight."

"John Hansen told you Rebecca left at midnight?" Amy asked.

"Yes." Wendy nodded. Her face was flushed, and her eyes were swollen and red, wet with tears. "I told the police what John told me – that Rebecca left at midnight."

"So, you never actually saw Rebecca leave the party," Amy said.

"No," she uttered and pushed a tear off her cheek. "I didn't." She brought her hands to her face and began to cry into them.

"You two out, now!" Todd barked.

Steve turned and headed for the stairs; he did not acknowledge the big man as he passed him.

"Rebecca never left the farmhouse that night, Wendy," Steve said, turning back to face her.

Wendy looked up from her hands; a tear ran from her right eye, rounded her chin, and dripped off to the floor. "How do you..."

"Because I've seen a video – *we've* seen a video – of what they did to Rebecca, to your best friend. She screamed for help, Wendy. Begged for someone to save her as Martin Green and Kim Hooper – along with a third unidentified man, possibly your pal Hansen – tortured and raped her on camera."

"I didn't have anything to do with that," Wendy said indignantly, as if speaking the words aloud cleared her of any wrongdoing.

"And you didn't do anything to prevent it, either."

Chapter Eighteen

Their next stop was the home of Lois Hansen, John Hansen's sixty-five-year-old mother, who might be able to shed some light on her son's whereabouts. She lived in a rundown trailer in the middle of nowhere. Her home was in such disrepair that it looked like it might fall in on itself at any moment. The once-blue siding had faded to almost white and had begun to rust around the top and bottom. The front windows were stained from excessive cigarette smoke; some were cracked and resealed with duct tape to keep the cold out. The wooden porch was rotting and gray. Steve guessed it would not be long until the porch came down under its own weight, if the trailer itself did not come down first.

Inside the trailer, a ragged curtain was pulled aside, and a white-haired woman – who resembled a fairytale witch – peered out the window to see who had pulled into the driveway. The woman scowled with displeasure at the unexpected company.

As Steve got out of the car, the front door opened, and the woman, who had been watching from inside stepped onto the porch. A lit cigarette dangled from her mouth, the smoke taken by the breeze.

"Can I help you?" the white-haired lady asked sharply. "You're interruptin' my stories."

Steve put on his best smile. It was the trusting, innocent smile of someone much nicer than Steve supposed he was.

"Hello, Mrs. Hansen, my name is Steve James. This is Amy Richards. We're with the Hanover Daily Record. We were wondering if we could ask you a few questions about your son."

"You're here about my Johnny? Why?"

"We think he may know something about the deaths of Kim Hooper and Martin Green," Amy said. "We understand they were friends of his. Have you seen him?"

Lois stared at the two reporters with disdain; her brow pinched taut with distrust. She pulled the cigarette from her lips with two yellowed fingers and blew a plume of smoke out the side of her mouth in a snarky gesture.

"I haven't seen him," she answered, crossing her arms over her chest, defiantly.

"Does John still live here?" Amy asked.

"Only when he's in town," Lois said, uncrossing her arms and bringing the cigarette back to her lips.

"And where is he now?" Steve asked.

"Working."

"Where does he work? Maybe we can visit and talk with him," Steve said.

"Not possible," Lois replied.

"Oh? Why's that?" Amy asked.

"His job requires him to move around a lot."

"What does John do for a living?" Amy asked.

"This and that," Lois said, bringing the cigarette to her lips again and taking a puff.

Steve stared at Lois Hansen skeptically. Her story was so thin he could easily see through it, and her cryptic tone was frustrating. He wanted to grab hold of the old bat and shake the truth from her; she knew more than she was telling them, that much was evident. But how much of her son's extracurricular activities at the farmhouse was she privy to?

"I don't know any more than that. Now, you two go on and get out of here. And don't you come back." Lois flicked the cigarette into the snow, where it sizzled out.

Steve pulled a card from his wallet and handed it to her. "Call me if you hear from John, or if there's anything you'd like to speak to us about."

Lois snatched the card from Steve's hand, turned, and headed back inside the trailer without saying anything further. She slammed the front door hard enough to shake the rust from the trailer's roof and sprinkle the snow a cinnamon color.

Steve and Amy returned to the car, miserable that they had gotten nowhere with Lois Hansen. Inside, the car had already cooled. Amy started it and got the heater going again.

"Now what?" Amy asked, shivering.

"Can you find me Lois Hansen's number?" Steve asked, his eyes locked intently on the trailer, seeing past the steel exterior, fantasizing about what might lie within.

"For what?"

"We need to get her out of the house. Once she leaves, we're going to break in and see what we can rummage up."

"That's illegal. If we get caught–"

"Then let's not get caught."

"But if we do and she calls the police..." Amy stopped, looked at the trailer. "There has to be another way."

"You said before you didn't want to be cut out of the story. If you want to expose the truth, Amy, sometimes you have to cross lines you normally wouldn't for the story." Steve wished there were another way to keep her conscience clear, but he couldn't see a better strategy.

"Lois Hansen knows the whereabouts of her son. I'm sure of that much. There's a good possibility we'll find something inside that could help us locate him. And, hopefully, link him back to the farmhouse and Rebecca."

Amy seemed to get the picture and agreed, though Steve could tell she was still uncomfortable with the plan.

Tough.

Moving the car about a quarter of a mile from the Hansen's driveway, Amy parked it behind a mound of plowed snow. She then looked up Lois Hansen's phone number, again using the white pages, and recited it to Steve. He punched the number into his cell and made the call. Lois picked up on the first ring.

"'Ello?" answered a dry, raspy voice.

"May I speak to Lois Hansen, please?" Steve said, deepening his voice, hoping the disguise would get her to take the bait. Though he prayed she didn't have Caller ID, or his plan would go to shit fast.

"Speakin'."

No Caller ID, Steve thought. *Perfect!*

"My name is Joe Westenhouse, I'm with the United States Postal Service. I'm calling because a certified letter was sent to you a few weeks back, and we have not heard from you. We were wondering if you were going to come pick up your mail."

"I didn't get any not-if-i-ca-tion," Lois said, sounding out every syllable of the word.

"It says here one was sent. Hmm? Maybe it got lost or

247

misplaced by the mail carrier. It happens. Anyway, if you could come down to the post office, we could take care of this matter easily. Just need your signature."

"You need me to come down there now? My stories are on."

"I'm afraid so. All unclaimed mail gets destroyed today, and I would hate to see that happen when it can be prevented. It'll only take a moment of your time."

Lois expelled a whoosh of air. "A'right, I'll be down."

"Thank–"

Lois hung up on him.

"Well..." Steve said, looking at the phone. "That was rude."

They sat for twenty minutes before Lois Hansen's car eventually pulled onto the road and drove off in the opposite direction. She had not noticed Amy's car sitting just down from her driveway behind the plowed snow mound.

"Let's go," Steve said, opening the door.

They quickly made their way to the driveway. By the mailbox, there was another small mound of plowed snow that Steve and Amy ducked behind. Their position gave them an unobstructed view of the trailer, while keeping them hidden from possible prying eyes inside.

But the trailer was still, as if it were abandoned.

Great!

When Steve thought it was safe to move, he nodded to Amy, and they made their way up the driveway.

Coming to the rickety steps of the porch, Steve took them fast, trying not to think about the structure collapsing under his weight. But they easily held.

A window was to Steve's right and he cupped his hands around his face and peered through the dirty glass but saw no one inside the trailer. He then moved to the front door, reached for the doorknob, and began to turn it. To Steve's surprise, the door unlatched and swung open into the home.

"Well, that was easy," Amy said.

Entering the trailer, it was clear why the place had not been locked up.

It was a pigsty.

Dirty dishes clogged the sink and overflowed onto the counter and under the cupboards. Paper plates, pizza boxes, used food containers, and Styrofoam cups littered the small table in the center of the kitchen. A sour garbage smell lingered in the air, mixed with the pungent odor of cigarette and cigar smoke.

"And I think *I* live messily," Amy said, her nose wrinkling up.

The living room was in worse shape. The coffee table was covered with more junk: used drinking glasses, some still with liquid inside, and plates stained with dried food. An overflowing ashtray was filled with cigar and cigarette butts, and a roach clip held the butt of a joint. Ash smeared the table around the ashtray. The sofa and two recliners were old and worn. It looked like they had been there as long as the trailer. The carpet was badly stained from multiple spills, dirty feet and shoes traipsing across it over the years.

The trailer's unkempt interior was reminiscent of the farmhouse. To Steve, it appeared the same disheveled mind had resided in both.

"C'mon."

They moved past the living room and down a small hallway. The bathroom was on the left. At the end of the hall was the master bedroom. From the unmade floral bedspread, Steve presumed this was Lois Hansen's room.

He stepped into the room. It was as messy as the rest of the home.

Confident there was nothing in the master bedroom that would be useful in obtaining John Hansen's whereabouts, Steve turned back to Amy. She stared at the second door on the right side of the hallway. A sign on the front read: GO THE FUCK AWAY.

"Charming," Amy said.

Steve pushed open the door, and a heavy whiff of cigar smoke hit him in the face. The smell gagged him. It wasn't the pleasant smell of fine cigar tobacco, which Steve enjoyed and often partook of himself, but the cheap kind that tickled your nose and made your skin and hair smell like woodchips, and left a bad aftertaste in your mouth for days.

When Steve entered the room, he understood he was not just stepping into John Hansen's life, but also into the man's sick and twisted mind.

The bedroom was covered with Satanic Metal band posters. Steve had never heard of these bands. The band members were heavily tattooed and looked like they all needed to take a shower. Obscene pictures of nude women were taped in between most of the posters. The images had been cut or torn from magazines; most were from the S&M smut world and depicted painful acts of violence. The photographs were hard to look at.

The bed was unmade, the covers and single pillow ruffled from the last time someone had slept there. The floor was covered with dirty clothing – a pair of shit-stained underwear had been thrown in the corner and left – and trash littered the floor so thick the carpet could not be seen.

Lois said her son had not been home for a while. *He's working.* That could have been the truth. There was no way to tell the last time John Hansen had been in the room or slept in the bed.

They began to snoop around the room. Steve checked the nightstand while Amy searched the closet.

The lamp and shade on top of the nightstand were covered with a thin piece of red fabric. Steve flipped the light on, and an eerie red hue befell the room that made him think of blood – Rebecca's blood that seeped from her battered face after those three men were done having their way with her on the video. The nightstand was covered with junk: empty beer cans – Pabst Blue Ribbon, just like they had found at the farmhouse, plastic forty-four-ounce pop cups, like those picked up at a convenience store, as well as porno magazines, a bottle of lubricant, and wadded up used tissues. An ashtray held a half-smoked cigar, and ground marijuana leaves dusted the floor beside the bed.

One of the three men in Rebecca's video smoked a cigar. Steve remembered him lighting it up after they were done having their way with Rebecca. *Was that man John Hansen?*

Opening the top drawer of the nightstand, he found several boxes of unused condoms, a few sex toys, along with other lubricants – some flavored – and a string of large red beads. Anal beads. A trifling thought entered Steve's mind: *Had Hansen used the anal beads on himself?* He shuddered and closed the drawer and moved to the lower one and opened it. This drawer was filled with the S&M magazine, *La Prostituée Bizarre* – the same magazine he'd discovered at the farmhouse – the same magazine Anthony Palazzo produced. Steve pulled one of the issues out and thumbed through its pages.

Unlike the glossy paper of higher quality porno publications, if there was such a thing, *La Prostituée Bizarre* was cheaply produced. The pages were black and white, printed on low-cost paper that yellowed and cracked within a few years. The images inside were horrid, lude acts of violence and torture, mostly against young, innocent-looking girls.

He closed the magazine and studied its cover. Below the white letters of the title was a woman sitting on the floor. A ball gag was stuffed in her mouth. Her face was pouty, and mascara ran down her wet cheeks and dripped onto her bare breasts. Her left arm was wrapped around a man's leather-clad leg, as if she were submitting to his will; the girl looked up at him through watery, merciful eyes.

Steve then realized he had seen something while paging through the vile magazine, something he had taken in but had not registered until now. He flipped a quarter of the way into the magazine until he found the page he was looking for, and then stopped and stared at the man in the leather mask in the photo.

The photograph contained the same nude young woman who was on the cover, bound to the wall with leather restraints – she couldn't have been older than eighteen. Her hands were tied above her head. Her ankles bound. Her legs splayed apart. The picture reminded Steve of how Green had been bound in the farmhouse, just before he met his grizzly, yet suitable end.

Something hung from between her legs like an alien creature trying to invade her body. It took Steve a moment to realize that it was an electrified dildo; the wires held by the sizable brute standing in front of her, smiling wolfishly – a car battery rested at his feet. The girl appeared utterly terrified. The photograph was hard to digest, but it was not the girl, or what was being done to her, that interested Steve.

It was the beast holding the wires and wearing the black

leather mask with the open mouth hole, inflicting the pain and punishment while smiling, as if this was the most fun he had ever had.

Steve couldn't see the man's full face to know who hid behind the mask. But that didn't matter. He knew who was behind the mask from the open zippered mouth hole.

Broken Tooth.

"Son of a bitch," Steve said aloud.

Amy turned back to him. "What?"

"He worked for S&M Solutions before the FBI shut it down for money laundering."

"Who? And what's S&M Solutions?" Amy asked.

"S&M Solutions is one of Anthony Palazzo's subsidiary companies that published these types of magazines and videos." He held the magazine up for her to see.

"Palazzo started the company to help wash the De Luca Family's drug money. On paper, it looked like Palazzo's fortune was earned in a legitimate publishing company – though a smutty one, but still a legit business all the same. The IRS could do nothing about it because the money was "clean," so-to-speak, and he was paying his taxes. But in reality, Palazzo would produce the magazine and videos cheaply, using the De Luca crime money, under the banner of S&M Solutions. The product would then be distributed to retailers and online porn sites that sold smut, cleaning the investment money while pulling in a profit for both parties."

Steve thought for a moment.

"That was until I came along and exposed all Palazzo's dirty tricks to the world." He pointed to the photo of the brute in the black mask. "That's the same person in Rebecca's video. See, the broken tooth."

"My God," Amy replied, shocked. "He was at the party the same night Rebecca was? Who the hell is this guy?"

Steve shook his head. He folded the magazine and slipped it into his back pocket. Having proof that Broken Tooth was the same man in the video and the magazine, would be useful later.

Amy turned back to the closet and began going through it again, while Steve made sure the dresser looked the way it had before. He restrained himself from taking any pictures. There would be no proof that he and Amy were ever there.

"Steve!" Amy called. She turned around with a shoebox in her hands.

He crossed the room and looked into the box. It was filled with small plastic baggies. He lifted one out. A name was written on the front in black marker: JANE. Inside was a lock of black hair, and it had been taped shut, as if to preserve its freshness. Removing another baggie, he saw the name ANN was written on the front; it also contained a lock of hair, only this one was tan. Steve then pulled three more baggies from inside. All contained hair in different shades and colors. The names LIZZY, SIDNEY, and WILLOW were written on the outside of each.

Five baggies. Five bodies in the root cellar. Five VHS tapes, DVDs and USB drives found burnt in the fireplace of the farmhouse.

But there was one more baggie inside the shoebox.

Steve pulled out the last one. A lock of blonde hair lay at the bottom. The name written on the outside was...

REBECCA.

Steve's eyes misted over, and he felt his insides drop like he was on a rollercoaster. Rebecca had never left the farmhouse that night. And she was still there, possibly buried somewhere on that property, and the only person who could show them where she was, was possibly John Hansen.

A rage unlike anything Steve had felt before, burned

inside. He wanted justice for what they had done to Rebecca, for what they had done to those other five girls. The truth of what happened at that farmhouse, at Pap's Place, needed to be exposed, and Hansen publicly and judicially convicted. Steve wanted to do that for these poor souls; be the voice for the voiceless. It was all he could do now.

"John Hansen and Broken Tooth are the same person, Amy," Steve said. He felt the hairs on the back of his neck stand on end, and his heartbeat skyrocketed through the roof with both excitement and disgust. *Holy shit,* he thought. *Holy shit!* He pulled out the copy of *La Prostituée Bizarre* from the hip pocket of his pants. "John Hansen was working for S&M Solutions." Opening the magazine, he found the picture of the girl bound to the wall again. He pointed to the chipped incisor of the masked man holding the wires. "That's Hansen."

Amy took a step forward, her eyes the size of saucers. "My God. Steve, do you know what this means?"

Steve nodded. His thoughts turned bitter, and he desperately wanted – no, needed – a drink. He had thought he was finished with the Palazzo story. Now he knew different. He had just scratched the surface of Palazzo's crimes, and this could be the worst.

Outside, a car door slammed.

Lois Hansen had returned.

Chapter Nineteen

Steve moved up the hallway from the bedroom and peered around the wall. Through the ratty curtains in the living room, he saw Lois Hansen coming up the porch steps.

Turning, Steve motioned for Amy to head back down the hall, just as Lois entered the trailer, pausing just long enough to kick her snow-covered boots against the doorframe. They quickly slipped into John Hansen's bedroom and closed the door, undetected.

As Lois moved about the trailer, the place rocked with each footstep. Any movements they made, Steve knew, would need to be made carefully so as not to give themselves away.

"We can get out the window," Amy whispered.

Steve agreed.

Amy moved across the small bedroom as if she were walking on eggshells, which she was in their current situation, and made her way to the window next to the closet. Reaching up, she undid the clasp holding the window in place, and then went to lift the window...

Nothing.

The window would not budge, as if it were frozen shut.

She glanced over her shoulder at Steve; hopeless terror cemented upon her face.

He motioned for her to stand by the door and listen for Lois, while he tried the window. Maybe he could get it open and they could get the hell out of there.

They switched places delicately.

Steve took hold of the window and tried to lift it, but like Amy, he could not get the window to move.

"It must be frozen shut," Steve said quietly.

"How are we going to get out of here?"

Steve tip-toed back to the bedroom door, where Amy now stood. Again, they switched places, and he placed his ear on the smooth wooden surface of the door and listened. Outside the room, Lois Hansen continued to move around the trailer, mumbling unintelligible words that made no sense to anyone other than herself, maybe about having to go to the post office only to find out there was no certified letter for her to sign.

A phone rang inside the trailer, as loud as an air horn.

Both Steve and Amy nearly came out of their skins. At first, they thought one of their cell phones had just given them away. But they quickly realized the ringing had come from outside the room, somewhere else in the small trailer. Their eyes met with relief. Steve smiled. Amy did the same, but almost burst out laughing; the tension in the air so thick it was almost funny to her. She cupped a hand over her mouth to stop herself.

"'Bout time you call me back, boy. Where the fuck you be?" Lois asked, then listened momentarily as the caller spoke on the other end. "I didn't know yous was back in town."

An uncomfortable silence enveloped the room and Steve found the air had grown thick and hard to breathe. If Lois *was* talking to her son, then that meant John Hansen was back in town. Had he been the same person who attacked them at the farmhouse? The one following them in the Black Dodge Ram?

"Is she talking to John?" Steve whispered.

"Ahuh. Look, shut up. There were a few reporters here this afternoon lookin' for yous. I believe they think yous have somethin' to do with Martin and Kim's deaths, just like that fuckin' Sheriff Meeker – that son of a bitch."

Amy nodded. "I believe so."

"Yous better not show you face in town. 'Dees reporters and da sheriff, theys got a hard-on for yous again boy, just like with that Turner girl. They sure yous did it."

More silence while Lois listened to the caller's reply.

Again, Steve wondered what she knew about her son's activities at the old farmhouse. Was she culpable in the crimes? Was that why she lied and told the police John was home with her by eleven-thirty the night Rebecca disappeared? Or did her motherly love blind her to the monster she had raised?

It didn't matter at the moment. Right now they needed to figure a way out of the trailer, without Lois's awareness of their presence. A task that was anything but simple. Trying to escape the small trailer without making a sound was a treacherous game, like Russian Roulette, one that Steve didn't want to play.

"Yeah. I'll let yous know what I hear. Rumors are already starting to leak back to me – yous know how Hanover is, can't keep a secret."

Except for your son and his friends, Steve thought bitterly. *They can keep a secret just fine.*

"'Kay. Bye."

Lois ended the call and started back down the hall. Steve and Amy steeled themselves, waiting for the bedroom door to fly open and Lois to yell, '*Got ya!*' but she walked past her son's room and into her own.

They breathed small sighs of relief.

Lois was in her bedroom only a moment before she returned to the hall and passed by John's bedroom once more.

Then, there was silence. Dreaded. Disturbing. Silence.

Steve reached down and took the doorknob and began to slowly turn it. Amy reached out and stopped him. She shook her head; her eyes were wide with lucid fear.

No, she mouthed while continuing to shake her head.

"We need to see where she is," Steve whispered.

Amy considered Steve's opinion. Realizing there was no other way, she relented and lifted her hand from Steve's.

With great ease and stillness, Steve inched the door open, just enough so he could peek through a small crack between the door and the frame.

Lois Hansen was in the bathroom now, standing in front of the sink, her reflection cast in the mirror. She was in the process of balling her stringy white hair on the top of her head and pinning it there. If Steve were to open the bedroom door now, Lois would surely see them. They would have to wait her out if they...

Lois then turned away from the mirror and moved further into the bathroom, out of Steve's view. He heard the shower curtain flung aside, the metal rings making a *clinking* sound as they slid along the bar and collided into one another. The sound of running water came next, followed by the powerful spray of the shower head.

"Let's go!" Steve said.

Steve pulled open the bedroom door, and he and Amy stepped into the hallway, carefully, with feather-light feet. He closed the bedroom door and inched them down the hallway, making sure to hug the wall so they were not seen in the bathroom mirror if Lois Hansen turned around. Steam had begun to billow out from inside the bathroom and rolled around the top of the doorframe.

As Steve neared the open bathroom doorway, he caught Lois Hansen's reflection in the mirror again. This time her back was to him, and she was in the process of stripping her clothing, her wrinkled backside exposed in all its moonful whiteness.

He thought she was going to step into the shower, but Lois surprised him by turning back around, her old, sagging, nude body fully on display in the mirror.

Steve sucked in a gulp of air; he was sure they had just been seen in the mirror. He pushed himself and Amy back into the wall, out of view of the mirror, hoping Lois had not seen them when she turned around.

After a moment of undisturbed silence, Steve lifted his head from the wall. Now he could see in the mirror that Lois had ventured back to the shower and was stepping in. She turned back once more to pull the shower curtain closed.

"C'mon," Steve whispered.

They made their way to the front door and exited the trailer without Lois Hansen being the wiser.

On the drive back to Abbottstown, they were quiet. Amy was visibly shaken from the whole ordeal that afternoon; her hands trembled on the steering wheel as she drove. She had gotten a glimpse into the mouth of madness and did not like what it revealed.

Steve knew this feeling all too well; it was uncomfortable pulling back the curtain to expose the ugliness that was human nature. He had learned, to some extent, how to deal with his more unfavorable discoveries. But there were times in his career where he had been left rattled himself – more than a few, actually.

After dropping Steve off at the Abbottstown Inn, they made plans to meet later that evening at the Sky View, a restaurant and bar on the other end of Hanover.

"What's the attire?" Steve asked.

"Business casual," Amy replied with a wavering smile that somehow seemed appropriate for the craziness of the day.

"Okay. I'll meet you there around six."

Steve was about to turn away when Amy called to him.

"I don't want to talk about today," she said. "Just dinner and drinks, no work talk. I... I just need to step back from this for a few hours, if that's okay with you?"

"Sure."

Steve understood Amy's need to escape their day. It had been anything but normal. Sometimes it was best to let the investigation go, even for just a few hours, and get your mind on something else, like dinner with a colleague.

Amy waved. "See you tonight."

"Bye."

Steve closed the car door and watched Amy pull away and drive off through the roundabout. Again, he wondered if it was a good idea to get involved with her beyond the story, even just for dinner. The more Steve dug into this investigation, the murkier and more perverse the paths were becoming. How far was he willing to take Amy down the rabbit hole of debauchery before telling her she had to turn back?

Would she turn back? he wondered. When the darkness gets inside, it stays, it grows, it feeds and needs to be fed – there was never enough to fill its gluttony.

He turned around and headed for the inn.

Steve's room felt uncomfortably cold when he entered. He cranked the heat and then opened the bottle of Jameson and poured himself a drink. He took the glass to the desk and sipped it; the liquor burned his chapped lips. He lit a cigarette – his first in hours – and let the smoke calm his frazzled nerves. He did not cough this time, which was good, meaning there was no permanent internal damage to his lungs – at least from the board; his smoking was another matter. His right hand still throbbed slightly with pain, but the booze was already dulling the stiffness.

He decided to call Charlie and fill him in on what they had discovered so far.

"Tell me you have something good," Charlie said upon answering the phone.

"Not enough to go to print yet," Steve replied. "But I got a lot."

"Tell me," Charlie said, sounding eager now, unlike earlier when he wanted the Tribune to have nothing to do with this story.

Steve filled him in on the details.

"Holy shit," Charlie breathed when Steve had finished.

"There's more, Charlie," Steve said.

"Oh?"

"John Hansen was working for S&M Solutions."

An eerie quiet befell the phone line.

"Does Palazzo have something to do with all this?" Charlie asked in quiet awe when he came back on the line.

Steve thought about the question for a long moment. There was some linking evidence, like the hiring of John Hansen for *La Prostituée Bizarre*, but did Palazzo have any knowledge of what was going on at the farmhouse? Palazzo was a bad guy who had done a lot of evil things, including murder, to keep his crimes secret. But raping and torturing innocent girls for videos was not among his dastardly deeds, as far as Steve was aware.

"I'm not sure. Maybe. Maybe not."

"If Anthony Palazzo can be connected to this, it's just another nail in his coffin."

"But something isn't adding up," Steve replied, pouring himself another shot of whiskey. "Palazzo has never hurt a woman before–"

"That we know of."

"True. But why would this mysterious person want me to expose what happened at the farmhouse now, especially with Palazzo already in jail awaiting trial?"

"To make sure you connect it all back to him, and so he rots behind bars for the rest of his life. Maybe it was a side business for him, a way to make more money and not have to share it with the De Luca Family."

Steve shook his head, even though Charlie couldn't see him. "I don't think so. Why risk it? Palazzo's income from S&M Solutions was legit, even if it was funded with DeLuca crime money. He wouldn't want this kind of filth ruining that business – which it would if word ever got out."

"I see," Charlie said. "But he employed Hansen."

"Hansen's an S&M freak. He gets off on inflicting pain and punishment on women. Why not employ someone who enjoys what they do and make it look authentic for the consumer? But maybe Palazzo's movies and photoshoots weren't enough for Hansen, maybe he wanted more than Palazzo could offer."

"Of what?"

"Of the rough stuff."

"So, you're telling me you believe these three guys were making their own videos behind Palazzo's back, and what... selling them on the Dark Web or something?"

"I don't think so. I've found no evidence pointing in that direction." Steve grew quiet then. He picked up the glass and brought it to his lips but didn't throw it back. "How'd they find the other five girls? I know these women were not locals of Hanover because there are no other women missing from the area. So, they had to be from out of town."

"Maybe they invited these girls back to the farmhouse. It's not hard to get someone to go with you if you offer them something in return that they desperately need. Money. Food. Drugs."

Steve thought Charlie was onto something. There were people in this world who were desperate and would do anything to get what they needed, including going to an abandoned farmhouse with three strange men.

"But where would they find these girls?" Steve asked.

"That's easy," Charlie said. "The photoshoots."

Steve sat up in the chair. *The photoshoots! Of course. Hansen would have had direct access to girls while working for S&M Solutions.* Steve had done enough research into S&M Solutions' business practices to know what type of girls they tended to hire: those who were desperate for two things – cash and drugs. Or both. These girls would do whatever was asked of them, including pornographic photo-shoots and movies. Hansen could have easily manipulated these girls back to the farmhouse with the promise of drugs and money and they would have willingly gone.

"We'll need to prove that, Charlie. And the only way to do it is to get the names of the models who worked for S&M Solutions."

"Then that's what you do."

"Has Ricky said anything to you about the video?"

"Nope."

"Okay. Let me give him a call."

Steve disconnected the call and phoned Ricky.

"Hey, Steve," Ricky said, answering.

"How'd you make out with the video?"

Ricky sighed heavily into the phone. "I went over it several times like you asked, looking for inconsistencies, places where it could have either been manipulated digitally or altered by a clever cut. I found nothing of the sort. Nor have I found anything that would give us more clues as to who did this to that young lady, outside the tattoo on the one guy's chest."

The air deflated from Steve's lungs like he had just been punched in the chest. He had hoped that Ricky would have spotted something incriminating on the video, some link that would put them on the right path to solving this mystery. But that was not to be.

"Damn," was all Steve was able to say; anger tightened his throat, making forming words nearly impossible.

"Sorry, bud. I wish I had more."

Steve took a sip, but the liquor didn't quell the smoldering embers inside. When he spoke again, his voice was filled with regret and the heavy emotion of a tired man. "I thought for sure you'd find more on there."

"Me too. But it just isn't there, Steve. What you see is what you get."

"Thanks, Ricky," Steve said, defeated. "I owe you for this."

He ended the call.

The further he dug into this godforsaken case, the more questions arose. What was he missing?

The images of the five dead girls wrapped in plastic bags and stacked on top of one another in the root cellar, worked its way back into Steve's foremost thoughts. How did they end up at the farmhouse without anyone noticing or reporting them missing? Was it as Charlie suggested? Were they from the photoshoots? Girls who had no past and no futures? Girls who were desperate for money and drugs? It was very possible. Likely even. But he would have to prove that, and the only way was to...

He pushed the thought from his mind before it could fully form, unsure if he wanted to walk that tightrope.

From the beginning, someone had been pulling his strings like a crafty puppeteer to get him to investigate. They wanted him to know what Rebecca had gone through and that those responsible were paying for their transgressions in blood.

But what did Steve possess that another reporter didn't?

There had to be a reason why he was chosen. The question had been bouncing around his head since he opened the box, but he was no closer to figuring out why someone wanted him to unravel this mystery than he was when he began.

What Steve did understand was this: whoever wanted him involved had a specific motive. But what was that motive?

His cell phone rang. The number was from an UNKNOWN CALLER.

"Hello?"

"Back off," whispered a gruff voice.

"Excuse me?" At first, Steve thought the caller had the wrong number.

"Leave town, Mr. James, or I promise you'll end up dead and buried."

"Who is this?" Steve asked. Yet, even as the words left his mouth, he realized there was something strangely familiar about the voice on the other end of the line; a voice from the past, but not too far back, one heard more recently.

"You got lucky today, Mr. James, you and that fuckin' stupid cow, Amy Richards. That won't happen again," the gruff voice continued. "Heed my warning."

Steve grew tense. He had heard the same term used by the masked man back at the farmhouse. *Fuckin' stupid cow,* he had screamed and then slapped Amy across the face. But that wasn't the only time Steve had heard the term used. It was said in Rebecca's video, as well. *Stop your moaning you stupid fuckin' cow,* just before the ball gag was slipped into her mouth.

Biting into his lower lip, he tried to contain the rage that wanted to explode out of him. He knew who was on the other end of the line now. Steve was sure of it.

"You're not going to get away with this, Hansen. I'm going to make sure everyone knows what you and your friends did to those girls," Steve said through clenched teeth. "Mark my words, you're going down for this."

"Leave town tonight, or I will kill both of you," Hansen hissed, though he still didn't raise his voice above a whisper.

Steve tasted acid and wanted to spit fire. He was about to tell Hansen that his threats wouldn't scare them away from exposing the truth when the line went dead.

Steve looked at the phone. *How did Hansen get my number?* Then he remembered. He had given his card to Lois Hansen that afternoon. Lois had most likely passed his number to her son at some point, maybe after he and Amy escaped the metal shit box they called a home.

But if Hansen thought his threats would scare him off, he was dead wrong. He was going to get to the bottom of this story, no matter what it took.

Chapter Twenty

The *Sky View Restaurant and Bar* sat in the mountains east of Hanover, with the quaint town tucked into the valley below; lights sparkled for miles in the dusk of the valley floor. Steve wondered how many local couples came to the *Sky View* on their first date, or to celebrate an anniversary while gazing over the expanse as they toasted the years behind and the ones ahead.

He turned away from the breathtaking view and headed for the front door. Sour thoughts of his own failed relationships picked at his brain for some odd reason that he couldn't quite put his finger on.

Inside, Steve walked to the bar and took a seat by the door so Amy would see him when she entered. The restaurant was not busy that evening, and there were plenty of seats available. A few tables were occupied along the row of glass windows that allowed customers an unobstructed view of the town below while they dined. A man, dressed in a nice suit, sat alone across the bar from Steve. He nursed a small glass of clear liquor while chatting on his cell phone. To his right were two women. He did not need to be introduced to know they were a couple – their sensual conversing and playful touches of affection was a sign of their undeniable love for one another.

A petite, blonde waitress came up to the bar.

"What can I get you, hon?" she asked, the words a routine, spoken thousands of times before.

"Bourbon," Steve replied, wanting something different, something stronger than whiskey to help wash the day's events away from his foremost thoughts. *My companion. My only true companion*, he thought. Again, his mind slipped back to former lovers and how his demons had destroyed his relationships.

A moment later, the waitress returned with his drink. Steve paid and brought the glass to his lips. He took a swallow, savored the taste of the fine alcohol as his eyes glassed over, almost tearing up with immense pleasure. It had been a long time since he had anything other than whiskey – which, for Steve, had the potency of water.

The door behind him opened.

Glancing over his shoulder, Steve caught sight of a woman out of the corner of his eye. At first, he thought this woman – this strange woman – was a creature unlike anything he had seen before. Then slowly, like a fog lifting from his eyes, he realized that beauty belonged to Amy. Suddenly, the memories of his failed relationships, all his past lovers and failings as a man, seemed to disappear as if they had never happened. He turned to Amy, smiled, and waved her over to the bar.

Amy's green eyes sparkled with vibrance in the dim light when she saw Steve. Starting across the room to join him, her stride was graceful and elegant. A walk that turned the heads of the few men – and women – in the bar that evening; everyone noticed the thigh-high black dress she had poured herself into, that hugged her toned body in all the right places. A small, matching purse dangled from a thin strap slung across her right forearm. Her red hair fell to her shoulders in fiery exquisiteness.

Steve could not stop himself from envisioning running his hands through her hair as he kissed her and pulled her into him, wrapping her in his embrace. But the image was whisked away when he saw the bruise on the right side of Amy's face as she drew closer. A stark reminder of their day. She had used extra makeup to try to hide the bruising, but the swelling and discoloration remained slightly visible. Yet, the puffiness of her face did not diminish Amy's confidence. And, if she had any reservations about their evening, she wasn't showing them.

"You look..." Steve felt his face redden and warm as she came to the bar beside him. *Is that the bourbon? Surly, surely it's not.* He had never been so attracted to a woman before. What was it about Amy that got his gears misfiring? Could it be because he was working so closely with her on this emotional case? Or was it his need for another human connection, to make him – to make *them* – feel something other than the filthiness of the crimes on their skin. Had it been the stress of their crazy day? Was it Amy's intelligence or her determination to seek the truth? Or was there another, more cosmic reason out of Steve's control? He wished he knew. "...beautiful."

Amy's eyes drifted to the floor, bashfully, away from Steve's gawking, opened-mouthed stare. Her pale skin turned a shade of pink.

"Thank you," she replied timidly.

"Wow! I mean...wow!" Steve said. "Can I buy the lady a drink?"

She returned her gaze to his, smiled. "Please – scotch and water."

Amy slid onto the stool next to him, running her right hand down the back of the dress as she sat. She crossed her long legs, revealing just enough of her thighs to make Steve take notice.

His chest tightened and his palms grew moist. The urge to tell Amy that John Hansen had called and threatened both of their lives gnawed at him. But he decided against bringing it up. *Not now. Later. Don't ruin the evening with that shit,* Steve reminded himself.

When the bartender returned with Amy's drink, Steve suggested they get a table.

"That sounds lovely," Amy agreed.

They were escorted to a table along the windows that overlooked the valley below. Steve pulled Amy's chair out for her and then took his own. But as he sat down, the call from John Hansen returned to his mind.

You need to tell her that Hansen called you. You need to warn her that her life might be in danger. He knew that Amy didn't want to talk shop tonight; she wanted to get to know Steve the man, not Steve the reporter. But if he didn't tell her about Hansen's call, he could be putting her in grave danger.

"Amy, there's something I need–"

"Shhh!" She shook her head and brought her index finger to her lips. "I said no work talk. If you must talk work, let's at least wait until we walk out the front door."

Steve guessed it could wait, at least until after dinner.

When the waiter came, they ordered their meals. Amy had salmon and rice. Steve, a steak and baked potato. The food was exquisitely good. He had not eaten this well for a long time. For Steve, a nice meal consisted of take-out pizza or a burger, Chinese food, Italian, or the occasional gyro from the stand down at the market in the Strip District of Pittsburgh. When he was on an assignment, his meals consisted mostly of cigarettes and booze – a lot of booze.

When he sat back in his chair, he was comfortably full of food and drink. *But one more drink wouldn't hurt - one for the road*, Steve thought, and ordered another when the waiter returned to clear their plates. He watched Amy over the small candle burning in the center of the table; the oily light danced over her soft skin hypnotically, making her look radiant, as if she had been professionally lit by a photographer about to snap her picture.

"So... what really made you become a reporter?" Steve asked, as the waiter sat the second glass of bourbon down.

They had chatted through most of the meal about trivial stuff, but this was the first time the conversation had turned personal. Amy glanced over the flickering candlelight at him; her green eyes held a mysterious glint that intrigued Steve. He liked her inherent ambiguity; it was somehow fitting for such a beautiful woman.

"Honestly?" Amy said, picking up the glass of scotch and water. "It was Rebecca Turner's disappearance that cemented my decision to become a reporter." She took a small sip, lost in the memory; her green eyes shuttled back and forth with the remembrance of days past.

"Back in '99, when Rebecca first disappeared, it was all Hanover could talk about. Rebecca was on everyone's mind. Her face was everywhere back then – posters, TV, the newspaper... on the back of milk cartons even – all in hopes of spreading awareness. It was the single most thrilling, yet truly horrifying event of my young life. I desperately wanted to know what happened to her."

Amy set the glass down. When her eyes rose, there was

a guilted heaviness to them. "I owe my whole life, my career, to Rebecca, I guess you would say. So, when I got the go-ahead from our editor to write a series of cold case stories, Rebecca's case was on top of my list." She smiled woefully. "Sorry, I know I said no work talk, but..."

"I get it. I do," Steve replied.

"What about you?" Amy picked up her glass and took a small sip.

Steve sat upright in his chair. His eyes drifted to the half-empty glass of bourbon sitting there – for Steve, the glass was always half-empty – and then looked back to Amy.

"I kinda fell into this job, actually – it wasn't something I set out to do as a career."

"Really?" Amy placed her elbows on the table and leaned into them, fully invested in hearing Steve's story. "I find that hard to believe, since your writing is fantastic."

"Thanks. But to be honest, I had no interest in becoming a reporter, let alone working the crime beat. I was fresh out of high school in 1996 when I first walked into the Tribune looking for a job, any job. I got hired as a mail boy. Did that for two years. The pay sucked, but it paid the rent and bought food. I met most of the old-school reporters on the staff at the time, became friends with a few of them. One man especially, Harold Adams – he wrote a weekly health column. The funny thing was, Harold smoked like a chimney, drank like a fish, ate any damn thing he wanted, and never touched a weight or treadmill in his life."

Amy giggled. Her laugh was small and sexy; the kind of laugh a man wants to hear come from a woman he's interested in.

"Anyway, Harold would sit at his desk smoking his stogies – this was when you could smoke inside the building

– drinking his coffee – always with Bailey's Irish Cream – and munching on something unhealthy as he wrote articles on how people should be taking care of themselves."

"He sounds like a neat character."

Steve's eyes again drifted back to the half-empty glass of bourbon.

"He was," Steve said sadly, thinking of his old friend. "It was Harold who got me interested in journalism, almost like he knew something about me that I didn't know about myself. And the more I talked to him about the paper and writing articles, the more interested I became in writing my own stories. So, one day after work, I went home and wrote a faux article. The next day I brought it in for Harold to read. I was excited and scared but eager to hear what Harold thought."

He took a sip of bourbon, already wishing for a refill. "So, Harold reads over this article I wrote while chomping on his cigar and sipping at the Irish-creamed coffee. When he was finished, he looked over the paper directly at me and said in this gruff smoker's voice, *'This is horse piss.'*

"'Horse piss?' I said. 'Is it that bad?' I had worked hard on that article the night before and was a little hurt.

"'*Not bad,*' Harold replied, looking back at my paper. '*It would make good nesting for birds.*' He laughed at his own joke.

"'What did I do wrong?' I asked.

"'*You bullshitted.*'

"'Bullshitted?' I had no idea what he meant by *bullshitted,*" Steve said, looking to Amy, whose lips were slightly parted while she listened, captivated by the story. He continued. "'*Yeah. You bullshitted the reader. One thing you must never do is bullshit your reader. They'll see right through it and know you're just another hack writer.*'

"'You bullshit them all the time,' I replied to him. You write about how to get healthy, stay in shape, eat right, but you don't do any of this yourself.'

"Harold smiled at this and said, *'But I don't bullshit them, Steve. What I talk about in my column is real, facts backed-up by scientific research. It isn't bullshit. Just because I don't practice what I preach – which I should – doesn't mean that I'm bullshitting my readers. The first rule of writing any article worth its salt is to check your facts and recheck your facts. Dig in like a tick, and don't let go until you have everything, every small detail, uncovered. Facts, my boy, are what can make or break a reporter's story.'*"

His mind drifted back to that warm day with Harold. He felt Amy's lingering gaze on him, prying past his flesh and bones, searching for something that he knew she would not find.

"So, I took that piece of advice and ran with it," Steve said. "I've used it ever since. Don't bullshit your readers, check and recheck your facts. Dig in like a tick, and don't let go until you have everything, every small detail, uncovered."

"That's what you said to me back at the diner, after we spoke to Wendy the first time," Amy said.

Steve nodded but did not meet Amy's eyes this time. He wanted to avoid their conversation from earlier. Besides, he felt terrible for speaking to her with such a harsh tone.

"Sound advice," Amy added.

Steve said nothing. He was not so sure any advice he gave was sound, especially coming from someone who could not keep *his* demons under control.

"So, the Tribune hired you as a writer after that?" Amy asked.

"No." Steve laughed. "You need a few journalism courses and a college education to become a writer at the

Tribune, which I did not have. But as I became a better journalist and writer, and completed the college courses at night, Harold went to bat for me with the editor at the time. Thanks to Harold, I had a job lined up at the Tribune before I graduated. My first assignment was writing a small column on local restaurants around Pittsburgh. My articles gained a lot of attention and response from the public, so when Charlie bought the paper in 1999, he started putting me onto other assignments, eventually moving into–"

"Crime," Amy said.

Steve nodded.

"And what happened to Harold?"

"He retired about ten years ago, at the age of eighty-five."

"Is he..."

"Alive? Oh, no! He passed about five years after he retired. Not of cancer or anything like that, as you might think. He just went to bed one night and didn't wake up the next morning. The doctors told Harold's wife that he died of old age, nothing more. There were no identifiable illnesses or anything, and he smoked and drank right up until the day he died. Some people are just lucky that way, I guess."

Again, Steve glanced down at the bourbon. He wondered if he would live into his eighties, like Harold, or would death come for him sooner because of his vices and sin, particularly his sin? His body craved a cigarette, and he hated himself for needing the addictive tobacco while thinking about death.

"What about your family?" Amy asked.

Steve met her stare and shook his head. "None. My mother died when I was nineteen. My father... well... we don't talk." Steve picked up his drink and finished it off.

"That's sad," Amy said, her eyes softening.

"What is?"

"That you and your father don't speak. Why is that?"

Steve studied the empty glass and realized there was not enough booze on this earth to get him to speak about his problems with his father. And even though Amy seemed to be a genuinely caring person, someone Steve felt he could confide in, this was one subject he would keep closely guarded.

"Let's just say he and I see things differently," Steve replied.

Amy reached across the table and took his hand. Her hand was warm, soft, comforting in his own. Fitting? Perhaps. Steve met her eyes in the dim light of the room. He sensed that she understood his relationship with his father was complicated. Maybe she had her own complicated relationship with her father as well. He didn't know, and wouldn't ask. Besides, it was not his business.

As Steve held Amy's hands, the candlelight dancing hypnotically on their faces, and soft music playing in the background, an unspoken moment passed between them. It was a connection of two souls that knew they needed to be together, to fill a void of loneliness, to mask the horrors of their day. With their eyes locked, they moved in closer until their lips touched for the first time that night.

They made love in Amy's bed. The passion between them was not of two people who cared for one another deeply, but instead, the lovemaking of two people who had not been with another person in a long time. An animalistic coupling that threw away any sense of decency, reason, or maybe even sanity, in Steve's mind. Their urge to forget, maybe even to protect one another from having to face another night alone, with the heinousness of the crimes playing behind their closed eyes as they tried to sleep, was a welcomed reprieve, even if it was only for a short moment.

In that time, they both let the day float away into the abyss of darkness that enveloped them in Amy's bedroom. Rebecca was forgotten momentarily, the bodies in the root cellar of the farmhouse were put to the side, and the call from Hansen was compartmentalized to the back of Steve's mind. For the moment, they were solely focused on one another, on taking care of each other's physical, and to some extent emotional, needs to disconnect from their investigation.

When they were finished, Steve lay with his arm around Amy in the warm darkness of the room; the musk of sweat and sex lingered in the air. She tucked Steve's arm between her breasts, like holding onto a teddy bear, as though he was her protector and would keep her safe from the monsters in the world. They said nothing to one another as they lay in the quiet black together. Soon, he heard her deep, restful breaths of sleep.

A moment later he drifted off himself. But Steve did not sleep peacefully. His demons would call on him this particular night, and they wanted penance.

Chapter Twenty-One

When Steve awoke from the nightmare, he sat bolt upright in the bed, the scream echoing in his mind. He was covered in beads of sweat, and the sheets were damp. At first, he could not figure out where he was or how he had come to be there. But slowly, the disorientation began to lift, and he realized he was in Amy's bedroom. He had spent the night with her. A stream of bright sunlight shone through the window – it was morning.

But morning or not, the nightmare lingered, turning his mood dour before his feet even hit the floor. Not the way Steve wanted to start his day.

In the nightmare, he was back inside the cave in the Tora Bora Mountains. He was on his knees in front of a camera mounted on a tripod; the camera's light shone into his eyes, burning and blinding him. His hands were bound behind his back, the rope so tight his fingers had gone numb.

Behind him was Lance Corporal Kyle Brenner, his hands also bound behind his back. Brenner was in worse shape than Steve from his injuries; the Taliban had beat him senseless for information, and he was on the verge of death. His face was swollen with bruises, blood spattered his fatigues, his skin was sickly pale and clammy with fever. Time was not on his side if he didn't get proper medical attention – which they would not get inside a fucking Afghani cave.

Taliban fighters stood behind the camera, moving about the stone room, talking, shouting in *Pashto* – their primary language. Steve could only make out their silhouettes through the camera's overbearing light. Then, out of nowhere, one of them was next to him, hollering at him in English, – 'Read! Read!' – a piece of paper thrust into his face. 'Read! Read!' the soldier repeated.

Studying the paper, Steve tried to decipher the cryptic letters. He knew the transcript had been written in English, but for the life of him he could not interpret the words on the page.

Another Taliban soldier – this one could not have been older than twelve – walked around the camera, stepped into the light, and pulled a pistol from his holster – the gun looked huge in his small hand. The child fighter passed by Steve without looking at him, and placed the gun to the side of Brenner's head. He pulled the hammer on the gun and the clicking echoed off the cave walls with a cold, hollow emptiness.

Steve felt his insides loosen with fear, and he thought he might defecate himself – their deaths were surely only moments away. If he did not read the manifesto to the video camera again, to remind American leaders to give in to the Taliban's demands, he and Brenner would be executed.

Steve had tried to explain that American Policy was not to negotiate with terrorists, but they wouldn't listen to reason. In reality, the Taliban didn't care if America followed through with their demands or not. They were making a statement, to show the American public, along with the rest of the world, that they should be feared.

"*Read! Read!*" the man holding the paper said, shaking it in front of Steve's face.

Like before, he couldn't make out the words. They were all jumbled, the letters running together like they were melting into one another.

"I-I can't," Steve said in the dream. "I can't read–"

The butt of a pistol slammed into his back, between his shoulder blades. The blow, delivered by the boy beside Brenner, was enough to knock Steve onto his face in the dirt. He coughed, the wind forced from his lungs from the wallop. He was quickly pulled back onto his knees, and the piece of paper was again shoved in front of him.

"Read, you American dog!" the man shouted into his face, hot spittle speckling Steve's skin.

There was laughter from the fighters behind the camera; it was a big game to them.

"*READ!*" the man screamed.

Steve held his ground. He would not show this man, or any of them, fear. Sure, Steve was afraid of them. Who wouldn't have been? But the Taliban thrived off fear, and he would not give them the satisfaction of his, even if they killed him for his defiance.

"*Read! NOW!*" the man shouted into Steve's face once more.

"I can't!" Steve screamed back. "The words... they're... they're all jumbled-up."

The Taliban fighter's face grew fierce with rage, and he slapped Steve across the back of his head with an open hand. The smack was hard enough to rattle his brain and cause a flash of white light to erupt behind his eyes.

"Read, American scum."

Steve looked at the paper again. This time there were no words on the page. Instead, the video of Rebecca Turner's torture played where the jumbled words and letters had once been.

"Read! Read!"

"I can't! There are no words," Steve tried to explain. "Please, you must–"

Then a crack of gunfire in the cave, so loud in the small confines that Steve felt the sound reverberation in his bones and caused a ringing in his ears. Out of the corner of his eye, he saw the violent snap of Brenner's head as the bullet tore through his skull and brain. A hot mist of blood sprayed across the back of his neck, so hot it was like acid burning his flesh. Lance Corporal Kyle Brenner's body fell away, hit the floor with a *thump* that kicked up a cloud of cave dust.

Steve screamed in terror as Brenner's body began convulsing in the dirt. A thick pool of blood quickly formed around his head and soaked into the sandy cave floor from the large, black hole in his fragmented skull. The blood-pool quickly grew into a large, muddy puddle, and Steve's horrified, screaming reflection was cast back at him. Fragments of white skull and gray brain matter fanned out across the cave floor and speckled the wall; the pieces glinted wetly under the camera's lights.

Brenner then grew still, other than the twitching of his left ring finger; his wedding band tapped against the rock floor. *Tick, tick, tick, tick.*

The dream morphed then, as some dreams do, and Steve found himself no longer in the cave, but bound nude to the farmhouse wall.

But the dreams did share one commonality.

The camera.

Now the camera was mounted on a tripod in the center of the farmhouse floor; the bright light still burned his eyes, blinded him. He felt his eyes begin to water, or was that his tears – tears for Lance Corporal Brenner for not returning home, for himself. Or were they for Rebecca?

He didn't know.

Behind the camera he could make out five strange silhouettes gawking at him. They were not the shadows of Taliban fighters watching intently as they had been earlier in the dream, using him as a tool to spread their hate-filled rhetoric to the rest of the world, but a black mass of hauntingly dark figures that resembled featureless demons.

Then, one of the shapes shuffled forward, its gait restrained as if trapped inside something, and moved into the light; the sound of its movement was like that of a plastic bag being manipulated.

When the dark shape stepped fully into the light, Steve saw it was the first female body he had exposed in the root cellar, still concealed in the black trash bag she had been wrapped in after her death. The hole Steve had torn in the homemade body bag revealed half a skeletal face. One dark eye socket stared at him, appraising him. A clump of black hair had fallen out from the bag and dangled by the closed jaw; red dirt and dead leaves clung to the hair.

The skeleton shuffled forward again; its exposed teeth locked in a perpetual grin. Steve feared it was going to kill him. But instead, the skeleton stopped just inches from him and raised a boney hand holding the empty trash bag – the same one Steve had found on the floor of the root cellar.

Just then, the skeleton's jaw fell open, or rather unhinged, and a scream erupted from the toothy mouth. It was Rebecca Turner's scream, just as Steve had heard it on the video.

Some Kind of Truth

Steve shook the memory – nightmare – away. He looked for his clothes and found them folded on a chair next to the television.

He swung his feet out from the bed and sat there for a moment, trying to get his bearings. The smell of coffee and bacon floated through the house. Amy was making breakfast. It was a pleasing smell, a comforting one, a reminder that he was awake and among the living, not trapped in some hellish dreamworld where the skeletons of the past come to visit.

But, Steve knew, hell was not just in the dreamworld. Hell was out there, in the real world, his world. Hell was a reality that Steve ventured to everyday. He would never get away from it, and like it or not, he was trapped in a hellish world where the skeletons of the past always came to visit, even when his eyes were open.

He stood and crossed the room and pulled on his pants and t-shirt. His blue button-down was not amongst his clothing. Steve looked around the room for his shirt, but he did not see it anywhere. He wanted a cigarette, but more so, he wanted a drink to wash away the nightmare, to help him forget – to quiet those fucking demons— or more accurately, this time, skeletons.

Turning, Steve saw a painting above a decorative fireplace heater in the bedroom. He hadn't seen the painting the night before when he and Amy entered the room; it had been dark, and he was too busy exploring Amy to notice anything other than her.

He was never much for art; he did not see (maybe he did not understand) why anyone would hang paintings around their home. Still, he knew this particular painting - *Fall of the Damned into Hell* – and its creator, Hieronymus Bosch.

There was something about the painting that scared Steve; it was bleak and grim, like he was looking into Bosch's dark heart and seeing the painter's fear of what waited in the afterlife for him. Or was the painting implying more? Was Bosch's painting meant not to elicit the fear of death, but warn about mortal sins and the damnation that would follow if they did not lead a righteous life?

Steve wasn't sure. He had never been gifted with the foresight to see the deeper meanings of art.

When he came into the kitchen, Amy stood by the stove cooking. She wore his blue button-down shirt. The shirt was too big on her and rested just above the seat of her underwear, leaving a small patch of white cotton exposed.

"Good morning," she said, turning from the pan when she heard Steve enter the kitchen.

"Morning." He crossed the kitchen and kissed her. Her lips tasted like salt and grease - a pleasing taste, a taste he could come to love waking up to every morning.

"How did you sleep?" she asked and wrapped her arms around his neck while she searched – probed – his eyes.

But for what?

"Okay," Steve lied. The nightmare crept back into his mind, attempting to spoil the morning with Amy.

"Coffee?" Amy asked.

"Please."

"Have a seat. I'll get you a cup."

Steve took a seat at the island bar while Amy pulled a mug from the cupboard and set it in front of him.

"Cream or sugar?"

He waved her off.

She filled the mug with the hot liquid and placed it in front of him with a smile. He took a sip and found the coffee was surprisingly good – no, not good— great! Robust, dark, full-flavored, just the way he enjoyed a good cup of coffee – well, maybe just a bit of Irish in there too.

"Thank you," Steve said, as the caffeine jolted his body back to life.

"Sure." She smiled again and turned back to the pan of frying bacon.

"Amy?"

She was still smiling when she looked back at him, a happy, content smile. The smile of a woman who was maybe falling in love. Steve wasn't sure. She looked so damn cute wearing his oversized shirt, her hair a tangled mess from sleep and sex. He wanted to wrap her in his arms and take her back to bed and never leave. He wanted to stay in Hanover with her forever, to keep her safe from John Hansen or anyone else that wanted to bring her harm. But the smile slowly faded from Amy's face when she realized something bleak was on his mind.

Steve looked into the mug of black coffee. It reminded him of Lance Corporal Brenner's blood pooling in the sand. The coffee wasn't so good anymore. What he needed now was a stiff drink and a cigarette to get all cylinders firing.

"Hansen called me yesterday," Steve blurted out before he could change his mind. "I wanted to tell you last night at dinner."

"He called you?" Her soft features deepened into a frown, making her look more like the reporter Steve had met a few days ago, than the stunningly beautiful girl he had just spent the night with. "What did he say?"

"That we needed to back off or he was going to kill us."

"Steve, we need to tell Meeker what's going on and have him arrest Hansen, before he–" She stopped. "This guy's a monster, and if he isn't taken down, he's going to harm someone else, maybe us."

Steve did not debate the fact that Hansen was a monster; he clearly was for what he had done. And if left free, he would undoubtedly continue. But they didn't even know where Hansen was or if Meeker was on their side. There were so many unanswered questions in this investigation.

"They also created a monster."

She looked at him crookedly. "What are you saying?"

Steve thought for a moment before speaking; his head was still hazy from the nightmare. Yet, the nightmare – that awful nightmare – was trying to tell him something, wasn't it? Yes, he was sure it was.

"Remember the black trash bag we found on the floor of the root cellar?" Steve said. "The one with Rebecca's necklace inside?"

"Sure."

"What if whoever was in that bag wasn't removed from the root cellar by Hansen or his buddies, but, by someone else?"

"Who else would have removed the body, if it wasn't Hansen, Green, or Hooper – no one knew those bodies were down there?"

"Except for the person who sent me Rebecca's video. Whoever sent it to me knew where the video and her license were being hidden. Maybe they knew about the bodies in the root cellar too. The video was meant to strike a chord, a nerve – an innocent girl tortured in front of a camera was sure to get my full attention."

Amy looked away, unable to meet his hard stare. He did not need to spell out his past; she already knew of his torture and capture, since she was a fan – now a lover. "They wanted to make sure I came here, but why the ruse? There has to be an ulterior motive. What are we missing?"

They were silent for a long while, with only the bacon sizzling in the pan. After a moment, Amy pulled the bacon off the frying pan, and placed it on a plate in front of Steve. He looked at the sizzling pieces of meat but did not touch any; his stomach could not handle food before booze.

"So, what are we going to do now?" Amy asked. "And how do we find this mystery person?"

"Perhaps that's a question best left for John Hansen to answer," Steve said. "When we find him."

"Good luck; the guy's dug-in deeper than a tick."

Steve agreed. He contemplated his thoughts for a moment. His grandmother had a home remedy to remove ticks by putting a match to them, which in theory would cause a tick to pull away from the intense heat. But in actuality, the tick would dig deeper into the flesh to get away from the flame. To remove a tick you need tweezers, something to pry them out of the succulent tissue. Hansen had made sure to bury himself deep so not to be found by the local PD; what they needed now was someone who could act as the tweezers.

There was only one person who had such resources. Someone who could find where Hansen was holing up and get Steve the list of models who had worked for S&M Solutions.

"I'm heading back to Pittsburgh. There's someone I need to talk to."

Chapter Twenty-Two

Steve was brought into a small interview room inside the Pittsburgh Federal Prison Bureau by a guard. A table and chairs were the only pieces of furniture. The walls were bare, except for the two-way mirror along the rear wall by the visitor's entrance. Steve figured the warden was on the other side of the mirror, with hopes that Anthony Palazzo would have a slip of the tongue and say something to incriminate himself further.

There was a loud *buzzing* sound, and the door across from Steve opened. Two guards escorted a shackled Anthony Palazzo into the room. Palazzo wore an orange jumpsuit; he had lost weight, and his luscious silver hair had thinned and turned white. His once tan skin was now the pasty white of a man who rarely saw the sun. His eyes were sunken into his skull with heavy bags of dark flesh under them. His neck and chest looked bare without the gold chain and crucifix Steve had always seen him with. The man had been stripped of everything that had made him who he was, including his dignity.

As the two guards sat Palazzo down and then manacled

him to a ring built into the table, he kept his gaze fixed on Steve, a thin, cocky smirk etched on his face. There was nothing in his black eyes – not fear, not hatred – just a frightening emptiness.

"I was hoping you would come around to my proposal," Palazzo spoke.

His thick Italian accent was hard to understand for most people. But Steve had listened to the man speak for two years, while working on his investigation; he understood every word that came out of Palazzo's mouth with perfect clarity.

"What led you to believe that, Anthony?" Steve asked. "Your goons don't scare me, and neither do you. You're going to trial for what you did."

Palazzo's lips drew over his teeth in a snarl that made Steve think of a dog growling. "What makes you think this is getting to trial? Feds got nothing on me. *You* got nothing on me except a fictionalized story filled with holes! Will not hold up in court, you will see."

"I'm not here about that, Anthony."

Palazzo's face shifted with baffled irritation.

Steve pulled out *La Prostituée Bizarre* from his computer bag and laid it down on the table in front of Palazzo.

"What is this?" Palazzo asked.

"You should know. You publish that magazine."

"It is a clean business. You cannot get me on that one." He smiled wolfishly, more to himself than to Steve.

"Sure it is. But here's the thing, Anthony – this might be hard for you to understand – but not everything is about you." The smile fell from Palazzo's face. "See, you've hurt a lot of people, Anthony – a lot of people. You didn't even know how far your evil had spread. You're like a cancer, a devious cancer eating away the good parts of a human, feeding until there is nothing left but diseased tissue. That's you, Anthony."

"What do you want, James? Get to da fucking point. I have things to do."

"Riiiight." Steve turned the magazine around and flipped to the page with John Hansen and the girl with the runny mascara bound to the wall. He pointed his forefinger at the S&M freak holding the wire. "Where is he?"

"How would I know?"

"Don't fuck with me!" Steve shot back. "Where can I find him?"

"Don't know where he is." Palazzo shrugged, sitting back in the chair smugly.

"S&M Solutions is your publishing company – your clean publishing company, as you say. You hired this prick," Steve tapped the photo. "And these girls."

"So what!" Palazzo chuckled. "They're just people I employ for a photoshoot and some movies. No big deal."

"Until it comes to murder, Anthony."

Palazzo's face twisted confoundedly. Whatever John Hansen and his friends were up to at the farmhouse was news to him, judging by the bewildered look engraved on his face.

"Murder? We did not murder these girls. There was no one harmed on our photoshoots or our films. Everything was just made to look that way." His eyes drifted back to the magazine. "This is all an illusion; makeup, and effects. Nothing more. We did not really hurt these women. I could not have that." Palazzo aimed his index finger at the ceiling. "Never hurt a woman. I take pride in that."

"But someone *did* hurt these women, Anthony – a lot of

women, in fact." Steve pointed at the masked man again, tapping the page. "Him."

"I had nothing to do with that," Palazzo replied. His eyes were sober with fear now, worried that Steve might be able to tie him to the murders somehow. It would be another strike against him going into trial.

"Where is he, Anthony?" Steve pushed.

Palazzo took a long breath, held it, and then let it out slowly. "His name is Hansen. John Hansen. The guy was good-looking, well hung, so we hired him for video and photo shoots."

"How'd you find him?"

"Casting call. Put it out over the internet – the smut sites – and ads in porn mags that we were looking for a muscular, well-hung stud that liked S&M or roleplay. Hansen applied."

"When was this?"

Palazzo lifted his shoulders. "Ten or fifteen years ago?"

After Rebecca had disappeared, Steve thought.

"Did you ever meet Hansen?"

Palazzo nodded.

"Where?"

"Here in Pittsburgh."

"Go on," Steve said.

"So, Hansen comes in for an audition. It was not really an audition, you see, more of a let-me-see-how-big-your-cock-is meet and greet. Like I said, Hansen was well-hung, buff; has this broken front tooth" – Palazzo touched his right incisor – "that makes him look like a goddamned vam-pi-re. He was perfect. So, we hired him."

"What was he like to work with?"

"I never had a problem with him. But some of the girls complained that he was... difficult."

"Difficult? In what way?" Steve asked, sitting up.

"He was too rough on them. Most girls we brought in to work with him did not like him very much."

"Why's that?"

Palazzo shrugged. "He had an intimidating presence, especially toward women."

"He enjoyed his work?"

"Oh, yes! Very much."

"Hansen took his work home with him, did you know about that?" Steve was sure the old man wasn't aware of what Hansen and his pals were doing back in Hanover, but he asked anyway, just to see his reaction.

Palazzo shook his head and his eyes lowered, heavily, to the magazine. "If I had known something else was going on behind my back..." His eyes rose and shifted to the mirror over Steve's left shoulder. He closed his mouth before he spoke too much. Someone could be watching. *Was* watching.

"There's something else," Steve added.

"What?"

"Hansen was making his own videos. I received a flash drive with a video of a sixteen-year-old girl – a child – being tortured and raped, only he wasn't playing make-believe in this one."

The old man's face darkened, and his body grew rigid, as if he had just been told the outcome of an illness that was terminal.

"Are you sure about this?" Palazzo asked in a quiet, yet angry, snarl.

"Yes," Steve said. "What I believe is Hansen picked up a few of these girls while working for you."

Palazzo pursed his lips tight. Steve had investigated the man long enough to know that when his lips tightened, it was time for someone to die. Being on the wrong side of Anthony Palazzo wasn't a good idea.

"Where?" Palazzo asked, in a voice that sent chills up Steve's spine. "Where were they found?"

"About four hours east of Pittsburgh," Steve replied. "After they – oh, there were three men, by the way – were done having their fun with these women, they murdered them, wrapped their bodies up in black trash bags, and stacked them in a root cellar." Anger touched his soul, twisted his heart in an unpleasant way that made him wince. "Help me find this son of a bitch, Anthony. I'll make sure he pays for what he did."

Palazzo's face continued to twitch; the eyes grew sinister and stared off into an evil place that Steve did not want to venture into.

"Why..." Palazzo's voice caught in his throat. "Why was he doing this?"

"I don't know," Steve said. "I haven't put that part together, not yet."

Palazzo was a bad man who had done horrible things to a lot of people, including murdering them to hide his crimes. But as bad as the man was, he did not condone the rape and murder of innocent women. If there was some semblance of goodness in the man, this was it.

"I need to find him, Anthony. I suspect you know someone who can get in contact with him and put me in touch."

Palazzo looked older than he had when he first sat down, as if the anguishes of his life had suddenly overcome his body. The cruel news was hard for even Palazzo to understand, let alone accept.

"I swear to God," Palazzo said, crossing himself. "That we never hurt these girls."

"I didn't think you did," Steve said honestly.

"He got into his work. Sure, we had to reel him back now and then, but never had I thought–"

"You didn't think it was wrong when he went over-board, even in one of your faux S&M photo shoots? You didn't suspect anything was different about this guy?"

"Sure. But why would I care?" Palazzo lifted his hands, palms up. "There was no need to worry. So, some guy got a hard-on for the S&M shit. So what! A lot of guys like him do. Why I made millions off this magazine alone. There are a lot of sick, fucked-up people out there."

"Don't I know it." Steve's mind flashed back to the root cellar, to the girls stacked down there, abandoned, forgotten. "Where is he?"

"If I knew, Steve, I would tell you. Honestly."

Steve realized that this was the only time that Palazzo had ever addressed him by his first name. He was chipping away at Palazzo's tough exterior, but he wasn't through the wall. Not yet.

"Bullshit. A man of your prestige, Anthony, should be able to find anyone at any time."

Palazzo enjoyed his ego being stroked. He sat back in the chair and stared intently at Steve, the corners of his mouth lifting into a smirk. There was something working around in the old man's mind.

"I may know someone who might be able to find out where he is," Palazzo finally said. "And put you two together."

"Call them."

Then, Steve saw what Palazzo had been mulling over in his mind just a moment ago, play across his face. The old man had seen a window of opportunity to get the upper hand, and possibly help save his own ass in the process.

"If I do this for you, what are you going to do for me?"

"Are you asking if I'll retract my story?"

Palazzo smiled but kept his mouth shut; he knew when to speak and when not to.

Steve shook his head. "No." The smile faded quickly from Palazzo's lips. "But what I am going to do is find the man who raped and murdered these girls. And I'm going to see that the truth is exposed, and justice is served. In return for your help, I'm not going to tie you to any of it, and for that alone, you and your goons are going to back off the pressure campaign. You're going to leave me the hell alone, got it?"

Palazzo stared into Steve's eyes for a long time, considering his options. He knew Steve could – and would – fudge the story just enough to connect what Hansen and his buddies were doing at the farmhouse back to him, and be able to make it stick, even if it was a farce.

"Deal."

"I need one more thing from you, Anthony."

Palazzo opened his hands, palms up – a welcoming invitation.

"The names of the women you've hired over the years for photo shoots and movies."

"I don't have access to that kind of information. It's all been confiscated by the Feds."

Steve leveled his gaze on Palazzo and raised a knowing eyebrow. Palazzo was full of shit; he could get the information, he just had to make it happen. But, Steve guessed, he didn't want to incriminate himself in any way with what happened at the farmhouse. Made sense to someone sitting on the inside of a jail cell.

"The information you provide me won't be used against you, Anthony," Steve said. "You have my word on that."

"How can I be sure? I have to protect my best interest and those still in my employ."

"If I wanted more exposed, I would have already released it."

Palazzo grew still, letting Steve's words sink in. He wetted his lips nervously before he spoke.

"You have... more? How much?"

"Doesn't matter, Anthony. What does matter, however, is that you help me with this. And maybe, just maybe, that extra little tidbit I have stashed away for a rainy day, might just find itself among the missing."

Palazzo was not a dumb man. He had built an empire from nothing, so when he saw an opportunity – a deal that was in his best interests - he jumped on it.

"I'll see what I can do," Palazzo finally said.

Chapter Twenty-Three

Steve was to meet with two of Palazzo's guys later that afternoon. Little did he expect that it would be Vinny "Icepick" Rossi and the goon who had been waiting outside his apartment two days ago. They met in a public coffee shop in downtown Pittsburgh. Steve was not about to meet somewhere off the beaten path and end up getting himself whacked, or in this case, an icepick to the jugular.

"We meet again, Mr. James," Rossi said, undoing the button of his black blazer while pulling out a chair to take a seat. His buddy stood behind him with his hands crossed in front of his waist, watching the room like a bodyguard.

"You have information for me," Steve said, cutting to the chase.

Rossi settled into the seat and crossed his legs leisurely, like they were about to start a friendly business meeting. The waitress came up to take his order.

"He's not ordering anything," Steve said to the waitress without taking his eyes off Rossi. "Right?"

"Right," Rossi replied good-naturedly, but anger flashed

behind his dark eyes. The waitress seemed to sense the tension between the two men and hurried off, wanting no part of whatever was going down at the table.

"You have something for me," Steve said.

"I might," Rossi toyed.

"Don't fuck with me. I'm not in the mood. Give me what you have, and you and lug-nut can take a hike. I talked to the old man today; he said you'd cooperate."

A smug smile crossed Rossi's lips and he measured Steve carefully, like a lion sizing up its dinner. He then glanced back over his shoulder to the goon and motioned for him with a flip of his index finger. The big man obediently moved, like a slave called by his master. From inside his jacket, he produced a large manilla envelope and handed it to Rossi.

"What do you want with Hansen anyway?" Rossi asked, tapping the envelope into the palm of his free hand. "He's a nobody. Some dude we hired for the mags and a few video shoots. I don't get your angle, James. Nor why Mr. Palazzo went along with this."

Steve reached across the table and snatched the envelope out of Rossi's hands.

"Goodbye now," he said, looking dead into Rossi's eyes.

Rossi stared at Steve for a long moment. His face twisted, and his eyes fluttered with annoyance and even a bit of confusion. Vinny "The Icepick" Rossi was prone to seeing people he threatened a sniveling mess, begging for their lives at his knees. But not Steve. Not Steve.

Rossi stood and rebuttoned his jacket. He trained his eyes on Steve once more – cold, threatening eyes that were meant to elicit fear. "There's going to come a day when you least expect to see me, Mr. James. But when you do..." Rossi leaned in, right next to Steve's ear, and whispered. "I will be the last person you see."

With that, Rossi and the big goon turned away and headed toward the door of the coffee shop.

Rossi wanted Steve's blood, but he would not do anything without the go-ahead from Palazzo first – he was a good dog that way, obedient to the end.

Steve opened the envelope. Inside was a two-page document with a list of models who worked for S&M Solutions over the years it was in operation. There were no pictures of the girls, nor any contact information, not that Steve suspected there would be. Palazzo would not make this easy. Palazzo provided the names of his models. Steve would have to do the hard work from that point forward. Also in the envelope was a small, folded piece of paper. Pulling out the paper and unfolding it, he found a handwritten phone number scrolled in black ink across the page.

Not too helpful, Anthony, Steve thought. *But I can work with this.*

Chapter Twenty-Four

When Steve got back to the Tribune, his stomach was flip-flopping with excitement, and surging adrenaline twitched his nerve endings, making them feel like they were on fire. He had a phone number, which he assumed would somehow lead him to Hansen's whereabouts, and names of models who worked for S&M Solutions.

He first went to the archives room in the basement of the Tribune and pulled the copies of *La Prostituée Bizarre* that he had collected while working on the Palazzo case, and then headed to his desk.

Since discovering the bodies in the root cellar at the farmhouse, Steve suspected that Hansen, while working for S&M Solutions, had met these girls while working on video and photo shoots. He would entice them back to the farmhouse, with promises of cash, drugs, or both, and then he and his buddies – Green and Hooper – would have their way with them.

But Steve needed to prove this theory before he went

any further, and if he could link these young ladies to Hansen, then he might be able to prove they were the same people wrapped in trash bags in the root cellar at the farmhouse.

From the Ziplock baggies he and Amy had found in Hansen's home, Steve knew the names of the victims in the cellar – Jane, Ann, Lizzy, Sydney, and Willow. Hansen had written their names on the outside to remember who they were, to remind him of their suffering. *He truly is a monster.*

Steve began going through the names provided by Palazzo. There were one hundred and fifty-two names on the list, and it took him over an hour to work his way through all of them. Since he only had what he believed were the first names of the victims, he searched the model list for any matching names to the ones found written on the baggies. Out of the names listed, Steve found five Janes, two Anns, one Lizzy (but three Elizabeths, so he marked them down to vet, Lizzy could have been short for Elizabeth), one Sidney, and one Willow.

He started with the single names first – Sidney Snyder and Willow Grove.

Pulling up NAMUS (National Missing and Unidentified Persons System) on the computer, he began a search on Sidney Snyder and Willow Grove. He got hits almost instantly on both. Sidney Snyder had been reported missing on December 1st, 2005. Willow Grove on March 14th, 2010. Next, he ran the five Janes on the list in NAMUS, but only one came up in the system, a Jane Maxwell who had been missing since June 3, 2012.

He repeated the process with the two Anns and found both of them were missing. Ann Thompson since March 4th of 2000 and Ann Lopez since December 14, 2018.

Since Palazzo had told Steve that he hired Hansen about ten to fifteen years ago, he put Ann Thompson aside and focused on Ann Lopez, because she fit the timeframe when Hansen was employed by S&M Solutions.

Finally, he tackled Lizzy and the three Elizabeths. Of the Elizabeths from Palazzo's list, none were reported missing. But a Lizzy Barlow had been missing since the 12th of May, 2019. Lizzy Barlow would have been the last person Hansen, Hooper, and Green had murdered at the farmhouse.

After completing the task, Steve began to go through each of the victim's backgrounds and found they shared commonalities: they all were young, eighteen to twenty years old, and were from the Pittsburgh area. None of the five girls had an official address and were living with friends, who then reported them missing. All of them were drug addicts with arrest records. And all five had been arrested for prostitution on multiple occasions in and around Pittsburgh.

What bothered Steve more than anything was that these girls were so unwanted, unloved, that not a single one of their parents or relatives ever came forward to report them missing or wondered where they were. Had it not been for the friends these girls were living with reporting them missing, there would be no trace that they ever existed.

Steve pushed his anger aside and continued on. He had to make one final link and he believed it lay in the pages of Palazzo's magazine. Off the NAMUS website, he printed out the pictures of the five girls and laid them out across the top of his desk and then began going through the stack of *La Prostituée Bizarre*.

Paging through the magazines, he looked for the same faces that were laid out across the top of his desk. If one of the magazines did not have anyone he recognized inside its disturbing pages, he dumped it in the trashcan. *Where it belongs.* Steve was so focused on what he was doing, he didn't hear Charlie step up beside him until he spoke.

"I didn't know you were back."

Steve lowered the magazine and blinked his eyes rapidly, refocusing them onto Charlie, trying to rid his mind of the vile images of what was being done to the girls in the magazine.

"This morning," Steve said. "I believe I found the connection, Charlie."

"Oh?"

"Look here. So far, of the five girls I believed were in that root cellar, I found that three of them have appeared in the pages of *La Prostituée Bizarre.* I suspect the other two will appear as well. Not only that, of the ones I found in the magazine, all of them were photographed with this masked guy. See." Steve pointed to the magazines laid out across his desk.

The printouts of the girls from the NAMUS website were laying on top of the issues they appeared in. "That's the third man in Rebecca's video, the one with the broken front tooth, remember?" Charlie nodded. "Anthony Palazzo confirmed that he and John Hansen are the same person when I saw him this morning."

"You spoke to Palazzo? Are you crazy?"

"Yes. But don't worry, we won't have to look over our shoulders any longer. Palazzo and I came to an under-standing after what I discovered. He's going to leave us alone in fear of me tying all of this back to him."

"Does he tie into this?"

"He doesn't... well, not directly. But indirectly, he does. Palazzo hired John Hansen and these five girls. They all went missing after they appeared in the magazine with Hansen. Hansen lured them back to the farmhouse with either money or drugs – since they all were addicts – and he and his buddies did the same thing to them that they did to Rebecca."

"Can you prove that this Hansen guy was indeed the one who took these girls back to the farmhouse?"

"I believe Hansen is the only one who can truly answer that question. I just have to find him first. Once I do, we can take what we have to the police and I'll call the sheriff back in Hanover and let him know what we've uncovered."

"This is dicey, Steve."

"I know. I'm sorry to put you in this situation, Charlie. But I don't see any other way."

"Do you have any clues to where Hansen might be?"

Steve reached over and picked up the small piece of paper with the phone number on it.

"Just this. It was provided by Palazzo."

"A phone number. Did you call it?"

"No. Not yet."

"What are you waiting for?" Charlie's voice boomed with excitement.

Steve picked up the phone and punched in the numbers. The line connected and started to ring.

"Hello," a little boy answered.

"Hello?" Steve said, shocked to hear the small voice on the other end. "Who am I speaking with?"

"Austin."

Austin? Audrey Green said her son's name was Austin.

Strange. Why would Audrey Green's number be given to me? And then it hit Steve. *Holy shit!*

"Hi, Austin. My name is Steve," he continued, trying to keep what he suspected from showing in his voice.

"Hi, Steve."

"Austin, can I ask you a question?"

"Sure?"

"Is your mom's name Audrey by any chance?"

"Yeah."

"Is she around? I'd like to speak to her."

"My mom is at work right now. But my Uncle Jay is here."

"Can you put him on?"

Steve looked at Charlie as the young boy yelled, 'Uncle Jay, phone!' and listened as the telephone was exchanged between Austin and his Uncle Jay.

"Hello," said a gruff male voice on the other end that made Steve instantly grow cold with gooseflesh. He didn't need to see Uncle Jay to know who was speaking on the other end. Because he had heard that voice before, threatening his life.

Hansen.

Steve's eyes shot to Charlie and he felt the color run from his face. He then remembered the emails on Greens computer, the ones sent between he and Hooper. In Hooper's reply he had mentioned someone named Jay. Jay, Steve now realized, was their nickname for John Hansen.

"What?" Charlie whispered.

"Hello?" Hansen said on the other end. "Hello?"

Steve slammed the phone down and shot to his feet. He quickly gathered his things and ran for the elevators.

"What? What's going on?" Charlie asked, hurriedly following Steve across the newsroom to the elevators.

"I know where Hansen's been hiding," Steve said. The elevator doors opened and he stepped in and pushed the first-floor button.

"Where?"

"Martin Green's house," Steve said, as the elevator doors closed.

Chapter Twenty-Five

Steve was already on the Pennsylvania turnpike, heading back to Hanover, when he phoned Amy.

"Hello?"

"I know where Hansen is," Steve almost shouted into the phone.

"You do?" There was a moment of silence on the other end, then: "Steve, I don't understand. How could you..."

"I spoke to Anthony Palazzo. He put me in contact with Hansen. Amy, he's been right under our noses the whole time."

"Where?" Amy asked.

"Martin Green's place."

"Are you sure?" she asked in a voice that didn't sound like hers – it was darker somehow.

"Yes. Palazzo got me a phone number to contact Hansen. But when I called it, a young boy answered. It was Audrey and Martin Green's son, Austin. Hansen's been staying at Green's house all along."

"Was he there when we questioned Audrey?"

"I believe so. Do you remember the floorboards above

our heads creaked while we were questioning her in the living room?"

"Yes."

"She told us it was her son. But what if it wasn't? What if it was Hansen and he overheard everything we discussed with her?"

"And that's how we picked up the tail," Amy said. "He started following us after we left Audrey's house."

Steve thought of something. There *were* three automobiles sitting in the driveway of the Green home the morning they visited. Green's white work truck, a red Mazda3 and...

"The black Dodge Ram," Steve said. "That's where I first saw that truck. It was at Green's home that very morning we questioned Audrey. Hansen was definitely there. Amy, call Meeker and tell him where Hansen is and get this monster off the street."

"I will."

"That's not all. I got my hands on a list of models who worked for S&M Solutions. Other than Rebecca Turner, the names of five models matched the ones we found written on the baggies in Hansen's bedroom."

"He *was* getting his victims from the photo shoots, just like you suspected."

"Sure. These girls were easy prey, and they all had things in common: no families, were addicted to drugs, were prostitutes around Pittsburgh, and had little to no money – most were living with friends."

"Hansen bribes them with drugs or money. Then he takes them back to the farmhouse, and..." Amy trailed off. "But how does Rebecca Turner fit into all of this?"

"I don't believe she does. Rebecca has no connection to S&M Solutions and Hansen didn't start working for them until the mid-two thousands. What they did to Rebecca, I believe, was just for their own sick and twisted gratification. It's why they recorded themselves that night – a fantasy they wanted to live out over and over. But once the video grew tiresome, and repeated viewings no longer fulfilled their violent fantasies, they found new victims.

"They were smart and let Hansen pick the girls from the photoshoots. If a runaway hooker junkie went missing from Pittsburgh, it wouldn't gather much attention, and no one would care enough to look too hard for her. But if more teenage girls disappeared, especially around Hanover, an all-out manhunt would ensue, just like when Rebecca disappeared. They couldn't have the cops snooping around, so they chose these girls from Pittsburgh, ones no one gave a shit about and no one went looking for after they vanished."

Amy was quiet on the line, and Steve wondered if she was still there, trying to digest what he had just explained, or had the call been dropped. He had to admit it was a lot to wrap your head around.

"Amy..."

"Yes."

Still on the line.

"Be careful. If Hansen knows we're this close to him..." Steve didn't want to think of the outcome if Hansen decided to retaliate. "There's no telling what he's willing to do to stay out of a cage."

"Promise," Amy replied, hanging up before Steve could tell her that he was on his way back to Hanover.

When Steve arrived at the police station, he jumped from the car and ran to the front door. Inside, Officer Jonas

Roberts was working at the front desk, writing something on a police ledger.

"I need to speak with Sheriff Meeker right away," Steve said breathlessly.

"Sheriff's out with his daughter," Jonas said.

"Then call him!" Steve snapped, slapping his hand on the desktop. "It's important."

"Sheriff asked not to be disturbed. If you would like to leave whatever information with me, I'll see to it the sheriff gets it when he comes in tomorrow morning."

Fat chance, Steve thought. He didn't need Hansen catching wind that he knew where he was staying.

Steve pulled out his phone and dialed Amy's number. After five rings, and no answer, an automated voicemail picked up and instructed the caller to leave a message.

"Amy, its Steve. I'm here at the Hanover Police Department. I'm trying to get in contact with Meeker and am getting the runaround. Call me as soon as you get this." He ended the call and turned back to Jonas, whose raised eyebrows and tight, befuddled gaze, spooked him. "Would you happen to know if Amy Richards spoke with the sheriff this afternoon? I told her to call him."

"I just said the sheriff was out with her," Jonas replied.

"What are you talking about?" Steve was the dumbfounded one now. "No, Amy Richards, not his daughter."

"Yeah. Amy Richards. She *is* Ben Meeker's daughter. She came in about four hours ago, looking for the sheriff. Whatever it was, something had her agitated. They ran out of here like the devil was chasing them."

"They're... related?" Steve could not fathom what Jonas was saying.

"Yeah." He said this as if Steve should have known. "I don't know if you got some information confused or what, but Amy's father is Ben Meeker." He found this funny and began to snicker.

"But her last name... is... Richards," Steve said, looking to Jonas for clarification. None of this was making any sense.

"Amy uses her mother's maiden name to write for the paper. I guess it separates her from her law enforcement father, and gives her more credibility as a reporter."

Steve was stunned. Why had Amy not told him that Sheriff Meeker was her father? Why the subterfuge? But it made perfect sense when Steve looked back and considered why Sheriff Meeker had been so concerned for Amy's well-being earlier. He turned away from Jonas with a befuddled gaze that made the young officer concerned for his wellbeing.

"Is there anything I can do for you?" Jonas asked.

Steve shook his head slowly. "No. Thank you."

He stumbled out into the cold night on legs that felt numb, weak, his body overcome with guilt and hurt. Why had Amy not been forthright about Ben Meeker being her father? Why had Meeker not said anything about Amy being his daughter?

And then, it all fell perfectly into place.

They used me, Steve thought. *Amy used me. Meeker used me. Neither had known where Hansen was, so they used me to find him so they could...*

Steve felt dirty, as if someone had violated his inner workings. He had been manipulated from the start. The clues had been right in front of his nose the entire time, but he'd been too blind to see them.

But Steve saw them now. He just hoped he wasn't too late to stop what was about to happen next.

313

Pulling the car into the Green driveway behind the black Dodge Ram, Steve killed the engine. *Son of a bitch!* He was positive it was the same Black Dodge Ram that he'd seen outside of the police station and later at the diner. Hansen would have known what they were doing from the moment they left the Green home. He had followed them back to the farmhouse, probably hoping to silence them somewhere he could easily dispose of their bodies.

Steve's thoughts shifted, and his mind played back over the last few days. He was left with little doubt that Amy and Meeker had controlled everything from the very beginning – it also explained how Meeker knew the *hot-shot reporter from Pittsburgh* and was not surprised of his presence in town that morning when they first met.

Steve felt he had discovered nothing that Meeker and Amy had not wanted him to find during the investigation. They had orchestrated most of the clues he uncovered. Given him just enough information so he formed his own opinions and theories to point him in the right directions.

They had exploited his fears, insecurities, and troubled past to get him involved, while at the same time, using his resources as a well-known crime reporter to get to the one person they desperately needed to speak to but couldn't: Anthony Palazzo. Palazzo had the assets to locate John Hansen. *And they needed me to get to Palazzo.*

But why? Who was Rebecca to Amy and Meeker that they were willing to kill two men and hunt down a third in her namesake?

He stepped from the car and hurried up to the house. The lights were on and he could hear a child's laughter coming from inside when he pressed the doorbell. Footsteps soon approached the door.

As Steve waited for the door to open, he wondered how much Audrey Green knew about what her husband and John – Uncle Jay – Hansen were doing at the farmhouse.

The door opened and Audrey stepped out onto the stoop, shocked to see him standing there like a disheveled man looking for shelter.

"Mr. James?"

"Where is he? Where's Hansen?"

"Excuse me?" The question had taken Audrey off guard, Steve saw, from the bewildered look slowly working its way across her face.

"That's John's truck, correct?" Steve asked, pointing to the black Dodge Ram in the driveway.

Her eyes drifted to the Ram and then back to Steve. "No. That's my husband's truck."

"But John's been using it, right?" Steve asked. "Because he's been staying with you."

The muscles in Audrey's face twitched with confusion. "Yes. He's been using the truck while he's been staying with us. I don't under–"

"How long has he been here, Mrs. Green?" Steve asked.

She slowly closed her mouth and eyed Steve up skeptically. Finally, she said, "He came to visit after Martin die... was murdered. He's been helping me with the kids and a few things around the house that Martin wasn't able to finish."

"Was Hansen here that day we came to speak with you?"

"He was. Helping me take care of Austin upstairs as I spoke to you both." She paused and her face pinched with concern. "What's this all about, Mr. James?"

315

"How did your husband know John?" Steve asked.

Audrey took a moment to consider the question before answering. "They were high school friends. They've known one another for years. I still don't understand how John has anything–"

"Is John here? I really need to speak to him."

"No. No, he's not." Audrey seemed to grow irritated suddenly. "When I got home this afternoon from work, Austin was here by himself. That was unusual. John never leaves Austin unattended. But when I asked Austin where Uncle Jay was, he said someone came to the house and that Uncle Jay left with them."

"What time was this?"

"Around six-thirty this evening, just before I got home from work."

"Did your son see who John went with?"

Audrey shook her head. "No. How Austin explained it was that the doorbell rang while he was sitting at the dinner table working on homework. John went to answer it. The next thing Austin knew, John was gone and the front door was hanging open."

Steve felt his heart rate increase and the back of his throat grow taut. He tried to swallow the discomfort away, but it remained locked in place. He turned slowly away from Audrey, knowing damn-well who had come to the Green home earlier that evening, and where they were going next.

The farmhouse.

Chapter Twenty-Six

S teve stood in the farmhouse's kitchen. The lights were on, and the generator's hum vibrated the floors and walls of the old building. It was warm in the kitchen; a fire burned heartily in the fireplace, the crackling of the logs the only sound in the otherwise quiet house.

He turned and looked back outside. Two snowmobiles were parked in front of the old tree Amy had called Sam. One of the two snowmobiles was a double seater with a ski-footed cart attached to the back. To carry John Hansen, Steve presumed.

Steve moved to the doorway that led to the hall and the living room beyond. No one lingered in the dark hall. But human shadows floated across the floor from a light source out of his view in the living room.

"Is the camera's battery charged?" Amy's voice drifted through the house, like a spirit calling out from the grave.

The sound of her calm and collected voice chilled Steve. There was a bitter coldness to it that he hadn't heard before. He had met a disguise, not the real Amy Richards – a woman he would never truly know.

"Yes," Sheriff Meeker replied. "Battery's charged and ready to go. Just cleaning off the lens now."

"Won't be long until he wakes up," Amy said; there was a hint of bittersweet excitement in her voice.

Starting down the hall to the living room doorway, Steve peeked around the corner. There he found Amy standing outside the murder room. Her back was to him. Meeker stood by the old TV on the chair and was wiping a head-mountable Go-Pro camera's lens off with a white rag; it was stained with dried blood when he pulled it away – Martin Green's dried blood.

But there was a third man Steve had not expected to find there that evening.

Dennis Turner – Rebecca's father – sat on the sofa, staring off into nothingness. A blank, expressionless gaze fixed on his despondent face.

"You used me," Steve said, stepping out from behind the corner.

Amy spun around. Meeker did the same; his right hand instantly going to his hip where his service pistol should have been. But Meeker was not wearing his gun belt; he had removed it, most likely for ease of movement, and draped it over the wire holder coffee table, far out of his reach. Dennis Turner slowly rose to his feet, his eyes filled with malice and contempt for Steve's sudden interference for what was about to be done.

"Steve!" Amy said, shocked to see him.

She wore black workman's overalls that were several sizes too big – most likely Ben Meeker's or Dennis Turner's. A heavy leather butcher's apron, spattered with dried blood, stopped above a pair of black, rubber boots. Her beautiful red hair was pulled back and tucked under a black shower cap. Hanging from Amy's neck was a disposable dust mask and a pair of tinted safety glasses. The face gear wasn't being used to keep dirt and grime out of Amy's mouth and eyes, but spraying blood.

Meeker, on the other hand, was still dressed in his sheriff's uniform. He was not the one who would be doing the killing tonight. He was there to help Amy when it was all over, to move the body and dispose of all evidence linking them back to the murders of Green, Hooper, and Hansen.

"You used me to get to Hansen." The words tasted acidic coming from Steve's mouth.

"Steve, I-I needed to find him."

"To kill him."

Her face softened. "Yes." But her bright green eyes remained cold, empty; the sight of Hansen's death was all they wanted to see that night. "We need to do this. For what they did to Rebecca – to all of us, including those girls out in the root cellar."

"Amy..."

"You should just turn around and leave," Meeker said in a low, commanding voice. "Now."

Steve ignored the burly sheriff. "I should have seen it from the beginning. The clues were right in front of me the whole time..."

Harold's voice then floated back into Steve's mind. *"The first rule of writing any article worth its salt is to check your facts and recheck your facts. Dig in like a tick, and don't let go until you have everything, every small detail, uncovered. Facts, my boy, are what can make or break a reporter."*

But Steve hadn't checked and rechecked his facts like he should have. He'd been too consumed with trying to deal with his own demons, trying to quiet them as he navigated his way through this twisted investigation – one reminiscent of his own tragic life – with booze, booze, and more booze, clouding his judgment, blinding him to the facts right in front of his eyes.

That's debatable, Charlie had said about Steve being the best reporter the Tribune had. He hadn't understood what his editor meant then, but he understood now, and it hurt – the truth hurt.

"What was in front of you, Steve?" Amy asked quietly, with an understanding tone; a tone meant to get him on her side, to see that what she was doing – in Rebecca Turner's name – was the only option.

"The clues that it was you the entire time. That you set this all up from the beginning. You were the one who got me involved because you knew me before we met. I thought it was odd that I found my article on your wall that afternoon, but I dismissed it when you told me you were a fan of my writing." Steve shook his head; he had fallen for the flattery of a pretty girl, as so many had done before him. "Did you deliver the box too?"

"No, that was me," Dennis said. His eyes were small, dark slits filled with rage. He, more than anyone, wanted to see Hansen's blood for his part in Rebecca's torture and eventual murder. *Understandable.* "I drove to Pittsburgh, dropped the package off outside your apartment door, and got back out just before you entered the building."

Steve looked back to Amy.

"You needed me because there was one last piece of this strange puzzle you couldn't get your hands on," Steve said. "John Hansen."

Amy nodded. "Hansen went underground after Rebecca's disappearance. He hid himself well. So well, in fact, that no one could find him, except..."

"Except Anthony Palazzo. Who I would have direct access to," Steve said. "You knew about my capture and torture in Afghanistan and used my demons against me – to sucker me in – knowing that once I saw Rebecca's video, I would not – could not – turn a blind eye to what they did to her. Then, once I was involved, you used my connections to Palazzo to help you find Hansen. You put it all together that Hansen was a long-time employee of Anthony Palazzo and S&M Solutions. If there was anyone in this world that would be able to find a monster like John Hansen, it was Anthony Palazzo."

"Use a monster to find a monster," Meeker said, matter-of-factly. "And you didn't disappoint in your participation, Mr. James. You came through, just like Amy said you would."

"Yeah. I'm reliable that way," Steve said.

Meeker grumbled under his breath. He still didn't like Steve, or any reporter – outside of his daughter – for that matter.

Amy looked over her shoulder at John Hansen, bound nude to the wall. His head lolled on his chest, and a long strand of drool leaked from his open mouth. His face was bloody and bruised, but he was alive... for the moment. "He deserves to die – they all did." Her voice was filled with repulsion.

"I know." Steve looked away.

He understood Amy's need to kill. Her need to punish the men who hurt Rebecca. God knew Steve had done the same to the young boy in the cave in Afghanistan to save himself, and to avenge the death of Lance Corporal Brenner.

Shortly after Lance Corporal Brenner was brutally gunned down by the boy, and while Steve was being forced to read from the transcript in front of the camera, with a gun jammed so hard in his temple it left a small round pimple of flesh, a U.S.-led Special Forces team stormed the cave compound.

In the initial minutes of the attack, confusion set in, and Taliban members scrambled to fight off the American onslaught. In this madness, in the chaos of gunfire and explosions, in the insanity of men screaming and dying, Steve was able to free his hands with a dead Taliban fighter's knife.

But as Steve was trying to flee captivity, and traverse the complex cave compound to freedom, he was knocked to the ground, the knife ejected from his hand, and he was attacked by the young boy who had executed Brenner.

Sometimes, when Steve was alone at night, he still heard that boy's cries, could still taste hot blood on his tongue and feel the small, boney fingers clawing at his face while he beat that boy – that child – to death with a blunt rock.

When Steve came out of that cave, escorted by U.S. Soldiers, covered in dirt and the blood of his enemies, he had not felt he had done wrong, but that vengeance had been delivered to atrocious people for their atrocities.

Steve had done what he had to do to survive – his sin to bear and be judged upon for the rest of his life. But what he had not expected were the demons that followed him back home and continued to torment his soul. There were some things in life that a person couldn't come back from; taking a life was one of them, even when that life belonged to a monster.

"You couldn't do this on your own," Steve said, pulling his thoughts from that day. "Hansen, Hooper, and Green were all too big for you to handle, so you asked Meeker – your loving father – to help."

"She didn't ask me," Meeker said, too proudly. "After what they did to my niece, I volunteered."

Steve's eyes shifted to Dennis Turner, questioningly. Turner's gaze did not waver from Steve's, his resolve unflinching.

Meeker continued then.

"I stood idly by as the Abbottstown PD tried to solve this case year after year, with nothing to show for it but dead ends. I saw what Rebecca's disappearance did to my sister, to my daughter, to my brother-in-law - to our family. After Abbottstown closed, it was finally our chance to find those responsible for Rebecca's death. But, as you well know, it was bigger, and more twisted, than any of us ever imagined. That's where you came in, Mr. James."

"How'd you do it?" Steve asked. "How did you put it all together?"

"We did what you would do, Steve. We dug in like a tick and didn't let go until we had every stone uncovered. It took time, but it led us to this very moment," Amy said.

Steve then thought of something. "Back at Wendy Brewer's home, she suspected she knew you. She did, didn't she, Amy? Because you already questioned her. She said to us, 'I already told you people what I know.' I thought by 'you people' Wendy meant the police, but she really was talking about the press."

"I questioned her right after we... dispatched Martin Green. We were looking for Hansen by that point and I needed her to tell me what she knew. I dyed my hair, wore a pair of glasses, dressed down. So, when I returned with you, I'm guessing she suspected something was up, but couldn't put her finger on what it was."

"How much does Wendy know, Amy?" Steve asked.

"Let's just put it this way: she'd be here right now if she knew more than she already told you," Amy said.

Steve felt the air around him grow so cold; ice could have grown off his nose in an instant. Who was this woman he was talking to? He didn't know anymore.

"Did you have Meeker sneak into their homes, beat the shit out of them, and then bring Hooper and Green back here, back to the place where they hurt Rebecca, so the three of you..." Steve looked to Hansen.

"Meeker didn't do any of that," Dennis Turner spoke up. "I did." His gaze was hard, unapologetic. He felt nothing for the lives he helped take, just like those who took Rebecca's felt nothing for her when they tortured his daughter.

Again, understandable. But Steve knew Dennis Turner was not going to disclose the details of how they captured Green and Hooper.

"Steve..." Amy took a step forward.

Steve held up his hand. "Don't. Save it." He felt the betrayal burning a hole in the pit of his stomach. He wanted to say more, but what was there to say? Trying to talk Amy, or any of them, out of killing Hansen was a waste of time.

They were on a collision course and could not be stopped. All three of them needed their retribution for what had been done to Rebecca twenty-five years ago. But they weren't just doing this for Rebecca, Steve realized, they were doing this for those other lost souls in the root cellar, the five victims who did not have anyone fighting to see that justice was served on their behalf.

The Hieronymus Bosch painting on Amy's bedroom wall flooded Steve's brain with its haunting depiction of condemned souls. For the first time, he saw its deeper meaning, and what the painting represented in Amy's broken mind – she had become the sender of the damned to Hell.

An eye for an eye – did Bosch have a painting representing that, too? Steve wondered. He had always felt an eye for an eye righted the wrongs of the world in the end. But now, Steve wasn't so sure. Revenge only took one further into the darkness, from where the soul could never return. Steve's soul was undoubtedly lost to that darkness after he left that cave, and he knew someday penance would come due. Just like it would come one day for Amy, Meeker, and Dennis Turner for the sins they had committed behind these walls.

He turned to leave. There was nothing else to be said.

"Don't you want to know how, Steve?" Amy asked, stepping forward. "Don't you want to know how I put all this together? Don't you want to hear how my Aunt Kathy died a slow, painful death, not knowing whether her daughter was alive or dead?"

A tear slipped from the well of Amy's right eye. She pushed it away with the back of her hand. "Aunt Kathy uttered Rebecca's name just before she passed. Don't you want to know where Rebecca's body is, or who destroyed all the evidence around this place? Don't you want to know why Martin was left in Tully's cornfield? Don't you want to know everything, Steve, so you can go back to Pittsburgh and write about it? Isn't that your code – *the truth must be exposed*?"

Steve shook his head. "It was."

Amy's gaze fell to the floor, and her face twisted despondently; she hadn't expected Steve's shallow reply. She was willing to spill her heart to him, to tell him everything. To purge her soul to the man she had unexpectantly felt more for than she had anticipated when she pulled Steve into this investigation. But those feelings were secondary to her need for vengeance.

But Steve didn't want to hear Amy's confession.

After a moment of silence, she asked, "You're not even going to try and talk me out of this?" Her tone was soft, almost pleading.

"No," Steve said tenderly. "I'm not going to try and talk you out of anything."

A slight smile creased Amy's lips. And for a moment, she looked like the woman Steve had known only days ago, the woman who he might have given up everything for. But their blossoming relationship was over, and there was nothing between them now except a secret.

Steve turned from the room. His heart hurt like someone had reached in and ripped it from his chest while still beating. He wanted to distance himself from Amy, wanted to forget about her, about this place, about everything.

"Steve," Amy called after him.

"I'm sorry." He looked back over his shoulder into Amy's soft and mournful eyes, eyes that begged him to understand why she had to finish what she started. "I really wish we could have met in a different time, a different place."

"Me too."

As he led himself through the snow-crusted field back to his car, with the soft wisps of wind on his face, the shrill screams of John Hansen cut across the crisp moonlit night. Steve did not look back. There was no need. Not now. Not ever. What he needed now was to keep going, for himself, and put the past behind him – all of it.

Some Kind of Truth

Steve had found some kind of truth in all this death and madness. But he would have to live with knowing that what he uncovered had to remain a secret and that the story must stay buried. Sometimes, exposing the truth was a double-edged sword, and it always cut both ways.

THE END

Author's Note

It's been a long road to get here. But I didn't do it by myself. I had a lot of help along the way. First, I'd like to thank my wife, Laurie Smith. Because of your love, unwavering support, and belief in me and my craft, I'm able to do what I love. Thanks to Kristen Weber, my editor, who with her F.B.I-like deep-dive critiques and unapologetic feedback that sometimes stings, but ultimately makes me a better writer. To Patrick Reuman and Wicked House Publishing for seeing the potential of this manuscript. To Heather Daughrity for the final edit. And to Clay Campbell for always being my teacher – both in school and in life.

Made in the USA
Middletown, DE
16 February 2024

49285724R00201